BLOOD WILL TELL

DANA STABENOW

BERKLEY PRIME CRIME, NEW YORK

BLOOD WILL TELL

A Berkley Prime Crime Book / published by arrangement with the author

PRINTING HISTORY
G.P. Putnam's Sons hardcover edition / 1996
Berkley Prime Crime mass-market edition / June 1997

For information address: The Berkley Publishing Group, 200 Madison Avenue, New York, New York 10016.

The Putnam Berkley World Wide Web site address is
http://www.berkley.com

ISBN: 0-425-15798-9

Berkley Prime Crime Books are published
by The Berkley Publishing Group,
200 Madison Avenue, New York, NY 10016.

PRINTED IN THE UNITED STATES OF AMERICA

10 9 8 7 6 5 4

FOR

KATHERINE QUIJANCE GROSDIDIER

WE ARE FAMILY

My love and thanks to Axenia Barnes,
who told all those wonderful stories to
that wide-eyed little girl so long ago,

and my thanks to the Chugach Alaska Corporation
who saw that they were written down, lest we forget,

and my apologies to the Alaska Federation of Natives
for my impertinence in borrowing their convention,
where each year so much truth is spoken
by so many good people.

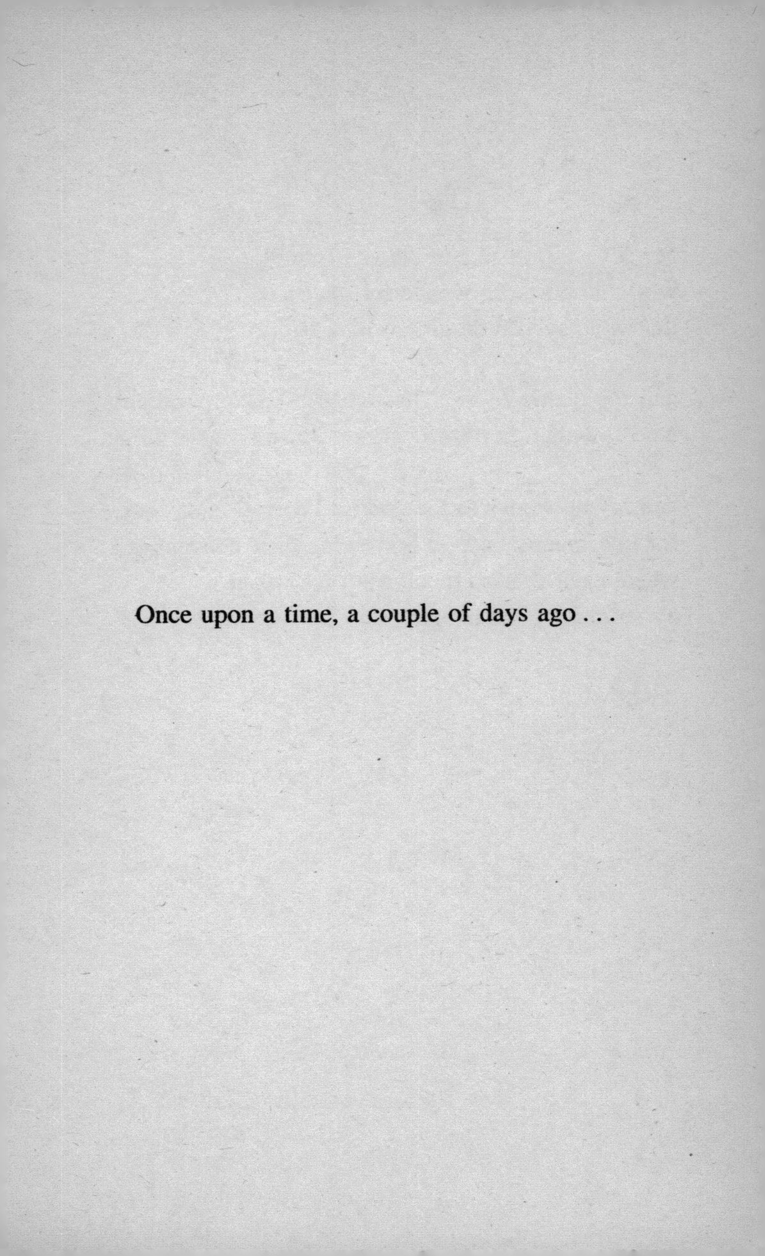

Once upon a time, a couple of days ago . . .

Look at that one, says Calm Water's Daughter.

Which one? says The Woman Who Keeps the Tides.

That One Who Stands Apart, says Calm Water's Daughter.

Ah. That one. She could be a problem, says The Woman Who Keeps the Tides. How long?

Not long now, says Calm Water's Daughter, and she sighs.

What's that you do with the windy mouth, says The Woman Who Keeps the Tides, you've been looking forward to that one coming. She is strong. She is sly. We need her.

So do they, says Calm Water's Daughter.

Excuse me, says Mary, I was looking for the Madonna seminar?

Down the path on the left, says The Woman Who Keeps the Tides.

I'm sorry, says Mary, is that my left or your left?

Ayapu, says The Woman Who Keeps the Tides, go over the stream and turn right, walk ten steps and turn left.

I beg your pardon, says Mary, it's so easy to get lost up here. At least down there we had direction.

Like I said, says The Woman Who Keeps the Tides, we need her more than those ones do.

You could be right, says Calm Water's Daughter.

Is this where the crop goddesses are meeting? says Demeter.

Alaqah, do I look like a road sign, says The Woman Who Keeps the Tides, the next field over.

Thanks, says Demeter, I'm late for the grain ceremony. I just hope I haven't missed the goat sacrifice.

Those Greeks are all alike, says The Woman Who Keeps the Tides, party, party, party.

They're young yet, says Calm Water's Daughter. They'll learn.

BLOOD WILL TELL

ONE

THE BAD NEWS WAS THE BLOOD IN HER HAIR.

The good news was that it wasn't hers.

The day before, the bull moose had walked into the homestead clearing like he owned it, the same day hunting season opened on the first year in six Kate had drawn a permit, on the first year in ten the feds had declared a hunting season in her game management unit. On a potty break from digging potatoes, she was buttoning her jeans in front of the outhouse when the sound of a snapped branch drew her attention. She looked up to find him head and shoulders into a stand of alders whose dark green leaves had just started to turn. For a moment she stood where she was, transfixed, mouth and fly open, unable to believe her luck. One limb stripped of bark, the moose nosed over to a second, ignoring her presence with what could have been regal indifference but given the time of year was probably absolute disdain for any creature not a female of his own species.

He'll run when I move, she thought.

But I have to move; the rifle's in the cabin.

But if I move, he'll head out, and then I'll have to bushwack after him and pack him home in pieces.

But he can't outrun a bullet.

His rack was peeling velvet in long, bloody strips, and as he chewed he rubbed the surface of his antlers against the trunk of a neighboring birch. He looked irritated. Before long, he would be looking frenzied, and not long after that manic, especially when he caught a whiff of the moose cow that had been summering along the headwaters of the creek that ran in back of Kate's cabin. It was late in the year for either of them to be in rut, but then Kate had never known moose to keep to a strict timetable in matters of the heart.

If I don't move soon, she thought, Mutt will get back from breakfast and then he will run and this argument you're having with yourself will be academic.

The bull was a fine, healthy specimen, three, maybe four years old by the spread of his rack, his coat thick and shiny, his flanks full and firm-fleshed. She figured four hundred pounds minimum, dressed out. Her mouth watered. She took a cautious, single step. The ground was hard from the October frost, and her footstep made no sound. Encouraged, she took another, then another.

The .30-06 was racked below the twelve-gauge over the door. She checked to see if there was a round in the chamber. There always was, but she checked anyway. Reassured, she raised the rifle, pulled the stock into her shoulder and sighted down the barrel, her feet planted wide in the open doorway, the left a little in advance of the right, knees slightly bent. She blew out a breath and held it. Blood thudded steadily against her eardrums. The tiny bead at the end of the barrel came to rest on the back of the bull's head, directly between his ears. Lot of bone between her bullet and his brain. Moose have notoriously hard heads. She thought about that for a moment. Well, what was luck for if it was never to be chanced? "Hey," she said.

He took no notice, calmly stripping the bark from another tree limb. "You must lower the average moose IQ by ten points," she said in a louder voice. "I'm doing your entire species a favor by taking you out of the gene pool." He turned his head at that, a strip of bark hanging from one side of his mouth. She exhaled again and the bead at the end of the rifle barrel centered directly on one big brown eye. Gently, firmly, she squeezed the trigger. The butt kicked solidly into her shoulder and the report of the single shot rang in her ear.

He stopped chewing and appeared to think the matter over. Kate waited. He started to lean. He leaned over to his left and he kept on leaning, picked up speed, leaned some more and crashed into the alder, bringing most of it down with him. The carcass settled with a sort of slow dignity, branches popping, twigs snapping, leaves crackling.

As silence returned to the clearing, Kate, not quite ready yet to believe her eyes, walked to the moose and knelt to put a hand on his neck. His hair was rough against her skin, his flesh warm and firm in the palm of her hand, his mighty heart still. She closed her eyes, letting his warmth and strength flow out of him and into her.

A raven croaked nearby, mischievous, mocking, and she opened her eyes and a wide grin split her face. "Yes!" The raven croaked again and she laughed, the scar on her throat making her laughter an echo of his voice. "Hah! Trickster! I see you by the beak you cannot hide!"

He croaked again, annoyed that she had penetrated his disguise so easily, and launched himself with an irritated flap of wings to disappear over the trees into the west.

"All *right!*" She charged into the center of the clearing and broke into an impromptu dance, chanting the few words she remembered of an old hunting song, holding the rifle over her head in both hands, stamping her sneakered feet on the hard ground, not missing the drums or the singers or the other dancers, beating out the rhythm of a celebration all her own. She tossed her head back and saw Mutt standing at the edge of the clearing, a quizzical look in her yellow eyes. Kate dropped the rifle, let out a yell and took the gray half-wolf, half-Husky in a long, diving tackle. Mutt gave a startled yip and went down beneath the assault. They roughhoused all over the clearing in a free-for-all of mock growls from Kate and joyous barks from Mutt that ended only when they rolled up against the side of the garage with a solid thump that robbed them both of breath.

Kate rolled to her back. The sky was a clear and guileless blue, the air crisp on an indrawn breath. A fine sheen of sweat dried rapidly on her skin. It was her favorite time of the year, October, in her favorite place in the world, the homestead she'd inherited from her parents, in the middle of twenty million acres of national park in Alaska, and with one bullet fired from her front doorstep she had just harvested enough meat to last her the winter, with enough left over to share with Mandy and Chick and Bobby and Dinah and maybe even Jack, if he behaved. She laughed up at the sky. Mutt lay panting next to her, jaw grinning wide, long pink tongue lolling out, and seemed to laugh with her, loud whoops of jubilant laughter that rollicked across the clearing to where the old woman stood.

The sound of a low cough cut the laughter like a knife. Mutt lunged to her feet, hackles raised. Kate jerked upright and stared across the clearing.

Her grandmother stood at the edge of the clearing, rooted in place with the trees, a short, solid trunk of a woman dressed in worn Levis and a dark blue down jacket over a plaid flannel shirt, hair only now beginning to go gray pulled back in a severe bun, her brown face seamed with lines in which could be read the last eighty years of Alaskan history. She looked solemn and dignified as always.

"I didn't hear you come," Kate said, looking past the old woman to the trail that led from the road.

"Mandy was in town," her grandmother said. "She gave me a ride."

"Isn't she stopping in to visit?"

Ekaterina shook her head. "She had to get back and feed the dogs. Chick's hunting caribou in Mulchatna."

"Oh." Kate was suddenly aware of the dirt under her fingernails and the birch leaves in her hair. "How nice to see you, emaa," she said insincerely, and stood up, only to rediscover her half-fastened fly when her jeans started to slide down her hips. Ekaterina waited impassively while Kate did up her buttons and tried ineffectually to beat off the dirt caked on the knees and seat of her jeans. Mutt gave herself a vigorous shake, spraying Kate with leaves and twigs and dirt, and sat, panting, her jaw open in a faint grin.

Kate gave her a look that promised retribution and looked back at her grandmother.

It might have been her imagination but she thought she saw the corners of Ekaterina's lips quiver once before that seamed face was brought back under stern control. The old woman nodded at the moose. "There is work to do."

That had been late yesterday morning. Yesterday afternoon they had gutted, skinned and quartered the bull and hung the quarters; that night they'd had fresh liver and onions for dinner. This morning Kate had set up a makeshift trestle table with sawhorses and one-by-twelves and grandmother and granddaughter butchered. There was moose blood up to Kate's eyebrows, her arms ached, her hands felt swollen on the knife as she carved another roast out of the left haunch. Billy Joel romped out of the boom box perched on the tree stump normally used for splitting wood. The cache, a small, cabinlike structure perched on stilts well out of a marauding grizzly's reach, was already half full of meat, and the weather was holding clear and calm and cold.

Kate set the knife aside and wrapped the dozen small, neatly trimmed roasts in two layers of Saran wrap and a single layer of butcher paper. A judicious application of masking tape, quick work with a Marks-A-Lot and the roasts were stowed in the cache. The snow was late this year, but the temperature had dropped to twenty-five degrees the night before. The meat store would be frozen solid before the month was out and it would stay frozen, depending on how early breakup came next year, but at least until April and maybe even May, by which time the first king salmon would be up the river and she could turn back into a fish eater.

She went into the garage and started the generator. The meat grinder was moribund beneath a year's layer of dust. She carried it into the yard, cleaned it off and plugged it into an extension cord. Across the table stood Ekaterina, butcher knife in hand, trimming a slab of ribs. She only had blood up to her chin. Deeply envious, Kate picked up a knife and waded back in.

What couldn't be carved into roast or sliced into steak or

cut into stew meat was ground into mooseburger, packaged in one-and five-pound portions and used to fill in the empty corners of the cache. The hide was trimmed and salted and rolled for Ekaterina to take home to tan. They worked steadily, and by late afternoon of the third day the job was done. Kate plugged in the water pump, put one end of the hose in the creek behind the cabin and washed herself and the table down, and just for meanness, Mutt as well.

That night they had heart for dinner, breaded and fried and served with a heaping portion of mashed potatoes. The laws of physics forced Kate to stop before thirds. "I hate it that my stomach is so small."

Ekaterina smacked her lips and smiled. "He is a tasty one," she admitted. "Strong and fat. Agudar is good to you this year."

Kate glanced out the window, where the slim crescent of a new moon was tangled in the leafless branches of a tall birch tree, the same birch the bull had been rubbing his rack on. "Agudar is good," she agreed. She pushed herself back from the table and indulged in a luxurious stretch, barely stifling a moan of appreciation. Chair legs scraped across the floor and her eyes opened to see her grandmother gathering up the dirty dishes. "Emaa, no," she said, rising to her feet. "You cook, I clean, that's the rule. Go sit on the couch and put your feet up." Kate stacked plates and silverware into the plastic basin in the sink, pumped in cold water and added hot water from the kettle on the stove. She ziplocked the rest of the heart and put it in the boxy wooden cooler mounted on the wall outside the cabin door.

The sound of Michelle Shocked made her turn. Ekaterina was standing in front of the tape player, restored from the tree stump in the yard to its rightful place on the shelf. She had one hand on the volume knob, eyes intent as she listened to the lyrics. Ekaterina had always had a penchant for well-written lyrics. She'd been a Don Henley fan from way back; in fact, one of the first civil conversations Kate could remember having with her grandmother after their long estrangement had been a discussion of "The End of the Innocence." Words were important to Ekaterina, words and the way they were put together. It was probably why she was always so economical with them, even with her granddaughter. Perhaps especially with her granddaughter. She still hadn't told Kate why she'd come out to the homestead. Well, two could play that game. Kate turned back to the dishes.

The table cleared, the top of the oil stove scrubbed with the pumice brick, the dishes dried and put away, she sat down on the other leg of the L-shaped, built-in couch and propped her feet next to Ekaterina's on the Blazo box lying on its side. The couch was little more than a plywood platform with foam cushions covered in blue canvas and might have been a little too firm for some people's tastes. The years had worn a Kate-shaped groove into this particular spot and she leaned back and lapsed into an agreeable coma, too lazy even to read. From a corner came an intermittent, unladylike snore, where Mutt lay on her side because her stomach was too full of scraps and bone to lie directly upon it.

When "Woody's Rag" ended, Kate stirred herself enough to get up and exchange Michelle Shocked for Saffire and surprised a belly laugh out of Ekaterina with "Middle Aged Blues Boogie."

When the song ended Kate turned down the volume and sat down again. "You haven't lost your touch, emaa," she said. "That's about the quickest I've ever dressed out a moose, with help or without it." She smiled at her grandmother, a smile singularly lacking in apprehension or hostility, a measure of how far their relationship had come over the last year. At this rate, by Christmas Ekaterina would forgive Kate for moving to Anchorage when she graduated from college, and by Easter Kate would forgive Ekaterina for her continuous attempts to draft Kate into working for the Niniltna Native Association. They might even become friends one day. Anything looked possible on a belly full of moose. Kate said, "Maybe by the time I'm eighty, I'll be that good with a skinning knife and a meat saw."

Ekaterina gave a gracious nod and was pleased to be complimentary in her turn. "I have not seen better trimming and packing, Katya. When it comes time to cook a roast, there will be nothing to do but unwrap it and put it in the oven.''

They sat there, full of meat and potatoes harvested by their own hands, pleased with themselves and the world and perilously close to a group doze. In fact, Kate did doze, and woke up only as Saffire was explaining why ''Wild Women Don't Have the Blues.'' The tape ran down and stopped. In the wood stove a log cracked and spit resin. The resin hit the side of the stove and it sputtered and hissed, echoing the sound of the gas lamps fixed in wall brackets around the room, the pale golden light reaching into all four corners of the twenty-five-foot square room and as high as the loft bedroom. Kate linked her hands behind her head and blinked drowsily at her domain.

To the right of the door, the kitchen was a counter interrupted by a porcelain sink as deep as it was wide. With the pump handle at rest, the spout dripped water. Cupboards above and below were crammed with cans of stewed tomatoes and refried beans and bags of white flour and jars of yeast and jugs of olive oil, as well as generous supplies of those three staples of Alaskan bush life, Velveeta, Spam and Bisquick. The only thing missing was pilot bread. Kate had never liked the round, flat, dry crackers, not even as a child, not even spread with peanut butter and grape jelly, not even when they were the only things in the house to eat. As far as Kate was concerned, one of the purest joys of reaching the age of consent was not having to eat pilot bread. She refused to keep it in her cabin, even for guests, a defiant rejection of a touchstone of bush hospitality.

The root cellar beneath the garage contained a bumper crop of potatoes, onions and carrots, and at close of business today the cache was full literally to the rafters with moose meat, three dozen quart bags of blueberries Kate had picked two weeks before on a foothill leading up Angqaq Peak, a dozen quart bags of cranberries she had picked next to a swamp a mile up the creek and a dozen quarts of raspberries she had poached from her neighbor's raspberry patch (the remembrance of which made her add another roast to the moose shipment she would be delivering to Mandy later that week).

There were three cords of wood stacked outside the cabin. The dozen fifty-five-gallon drums of fuel oil racked in back had been topped off by the tanker from Ahtna the week before. There was fuel and to spare for the gas lamps and, in a heroic action at which she herself still marveled, she had filled in the old outhouse hole, dug a new one and moved the outhouse onto the new site. She had even gone so far as to sculpt a new wooden seat out of a slice of redwood her father, a well-known whittler, had never gotten around to carving into something else thirty years before. She was sure he would have approved of the use she put it to.

So much for the outer woman. Over the Labor Day weekend Jack had brought the inner woman a box of books from Twice-Told Tales on Arctic Boulevard in Anchorage, seriously depleting Kate's credit with Rachel but nicely filling in the gaps on her bookshelves. There were two histories by Barbara Tuchman, one on Stilwell in China and one on the American Revolution, three paperbacks by a mystery writer named Lindsay Davis starring an imperial informer named Marcus Didius Falco who peeked through Roman keyholes circa A.D. 70—"You will love the story about Titus and the turbot," Jack promised with a grin—and a starter set of John McPhee, beginning with *Coming into the Country*, which Jack swore would not piss her off in spite of its purporting to be written about Alaska by an Outsider. There was a selection of the latest in science fiction, the autobiography of Harpo Marx and a slim volume of poetry by a professor at the University of Alaska, one Tom Sexton, which fell open to a poem entitled "Compass Rose" that held her enthralled from the first line. The care package had been rounded off with a forty-eight-ounce bag of chocolate chips, a two-pound bag of walnuts and four albums by the Chenille Sisters, a girl group previously unknown to Kate but who from the opening verse of "Regretting What I Said" she knew she was going to love.

All in all, Kate was rather pleased with Jack. She might

even give him some of the backstrap, that small strip of most tender and most flavorful meat along the moose's backbone which she usually hoarded for herself. She dwelled on her own generosity for a pleasurable moment.

In fact, the only fault Kate could find with her current physical and mental well-being was the fact that the scar on her throat itched. To relieve the itch she would have to move. She considered the matter, and came to the inescapable conclusion that she had to move sometime in the next five minutes anyway or she'd be settled in on the couch for the night. She hoisted herself into a more or less vertical position and went first to the tape player. Saffire was succeeded by "The Unforgettable Glenn Miller," an album she knew her grandmother would like and one she didn't find hard to take herself. The wood stove cracked and spit again, moving her all the way across the floor to the wood box. The heat from the coals struck her face like a blow and she jammed wood in as quickly as she could and adjusted the damper down. She opened the door to check the thermometer mounted on the cabin wall next to the cooler. The needle pointed to nineteen, and the sky was clear. It was only going to get colder. She stood a moment, savoring the crisp, cold, clean air on her face, the warmth of the room at her back and the pale glitter of stars far overhead.

The couch creaked and she came back inside, the door thumping solidly and snugly into its frame behind her. "Want some tea, emaa?"

Ekaterina nodded, yawning, and Kate moved the kettle from the back of the wood stove, which heated the cabin, to the oil stove, what she cooked on. She adjusted the fuel knob to high, removed the stove lid and pushed the kettle over the open flame. Waiting for it to boil, she rummaged in the cupboard over the counter for a jar of Vitamin E cream and rubbed it on the white, roped scar that interrupted the smooth brown skin of her throat almost literally from ear to ear. With fall came drier air, and her scar was better than a barometer at calling the change of the seasons.

The kettle whistled and she spooned samovar tea from the Kobuk Coffee Company into the teapot. The spicy orange odor brought back memories of the neat cabin on the bank of the Kanuyaq, habitation of the hippie ex-cop with the ponytail and the philandering grin. Her smile was involuntary and Ekaterina, who had come to the same conclusion Kate had and moved to the table while she still could, said, "What's with that smile?"

Kate poured water over the tea leaves. The teapot and two thick white mugs went on the table along with a plate of Dare short-bread cookies. Still smiling, she slid into the seat across from Ekaterina. "I was remembering the last time I smelled this tea, emaa."

"When?" For politeness, Ekaterina took one of the cookies and nibbled around the edges.

Kate stirred the leaves in the teapot and replaced the lid. "Last summer. A man with a cabin on the Kanuyaq." She poured tea into the mugs through a strainer.

Ekaterina clicked her tongue reprovingly. "How am I supposed to read the leaves if you won't let any get into the mugs?"

"Oh. Sorry, emaa, I forgot," Kate said, who hadn't but who disliked straining tea leaves through her teeth while she drank. "Next time."

"This summer," Ekaterina said, stirring in three teaspoons of sugar. "At Chistona?"

Kate nodded, smile fading. The dark events that had followed easily overshadowed the lighthearted encounter with Brad Burns.

The spoon stilled. Ekaterina fixed stern brown eyes on Kate's face. Her voice was equally stern. "You did what you could."

"It wasn't enough."

"You were a year too late." Kate said nothing, and Ekaterina's brows drew together. "You worry me," she said.

This was unexpected. "I worry you?" Kate said.

Unsmiling, Ekaterina nodded.

Knowing she shouldn't, Kate said, "Why?"

Ekaterina put the spoon to one side and contemplated her tea. "You care too much."

When Kate found her tongue again she said, "*I* care too

much.'' When Ekaterina nodded a second time, she said wryly, ''Emaa, you've got that backwards, haven't you? You're the one who cares too much.''

''No.'' Ekaterina shook her head.

''No?'' Kate said, half smiling.

''No,'' Ekaterina said firmly. ''I care *enough*.'' The old woman blew across the top of the steaming mug and took a delicate sip. She set the mug down on the table again and looked at her granddaughter, her face set in lines that were firm, yet dispassionate. Ekaterina was delivering a verdict, not passing judgment. ''You care too much. You always have. You cared too much about your mother and father, so much so that now you can barely speak of either. You cared too much for the old—'' Ekaterina paused almost imperceptibly and continued ''—for Abel, so much so that it blinded you to what you should have seen from the beginning. You cared too much for the children you worked with in Anchorage, whose lives you only made better, so much that you allowed it to cloud your judgment, and got you that.'' One bony, slightly cramped forefinger pointed at Kate's scar. ''You care so much for your family and your people that you have to hide out here on the homestead where you don't have to look at them, at what their life is like, at what life is doing to them.''

Kate stiffened, the rosy glow of self-sufficient satisfaction that had permeated the last three days vanishing with her grandmother's words. ''Emaa.'' She took a deep breath and swallowed an angry rejoinder with a sip of tea. When she could calmly, she said, voice tight, ''Please don't start that again, emaa. I can't and I won't live in the village.''

''No,'' Ekaterina agreed, ''I see that.''

Kate's head jerked up and she examined her grandmother with suspicious eyes, searching for the catch.

''I see that, Katya,'' Ekaterina repeated. ''I see you happy with the land. Agudar blesses you with food. You walk with the anua. The land makes you strong. I am not blind. I see.''

Kate stared hard at her grandmother, waiting for the other shoe to drop. Ekaterina met the blatant skepticism placidly, what might have been a twinkle lurking deep at the back of the steady brown eyes. For a moment Kate wondered if perhaps Ekaterina's body had been snatched by aliens who had replaced her with a pod. It was as likely a theory as Ekaterina deciding to stop harassing her granddaughter into taking what Ekaterina considered to be Kate's rightful place in the tribe.

Glenn Miller gave out his phone number to whoever happened to be listening and Ekaterina freshened their mugs from the teapot, without the strainer this time. Kate watched her, wary, waiting, still suspicious. Ekaterina caught sight of her expression and laughed out loud. It was the same belly laugh she'd given earlier, a solid, hearty sound, a laugh that sounded like she looked, a laugh Kate remembered hearing often during her childhood, one she had heard less often since. "You look at me like Fox looks at Raven," Ekaterina said, still laughing.

Her laughter was infectious and Kate had to grin. "I remember what happened to Fox," she retorted.

Ekaterina choked over her tea and this time they laughed together. It felt good, good enough to put her back into charity with Ekaterina, so good that when she realized it Kate felt suspicious all over again. Old habits die hard.

"Ay." Ekaterina sighed and drank tea. Her brown eyes were old and wise and never failed to make Kate feel much younger than her thirty-three years. The room was silent except for a saxophone and a clarinet an octave apart, the crackle of the fire in the wood stove and the hissing of the lamps on the walls. Kate studied her grandmother's face over the rim of her mug. By some trick of the light the lines in it had deepened. For the moment, authority had given way to sorrow. She stretched out a hand, touching her fingertips to the brown, wrinkled back of Ekaterina's in an involuntary gesture of comfort that one of them recognized as an unprecedented event. "What's wrong, emaa?"

Ekaterina shifted in her chair and raised her right hand to rub her left elbow, gnarled fingers digging deep into the aching joint. Her rheumatism was acting up, Kate thought. "You know the Alaska Federation of Natives convention is next week."

Kate stiffened. Ekaterina had been trying to get Kate to go to the annual AFN convention for the last three years. Kate's refusal stemmed from three things: one, it was in Anchorage, two, it was in Anchorage at the time of year Kate most loved to be home, and three, it was in Anchorage.

"The Niniltna board also will meet at that time."

Kate gave a wary nod.

"There are matters before the board," Ekaterina said.

Kate's smile was sour. Ekaterina was notoriously close-mouthed on Association affairs, even to the granddaughter she hoped would succeed to her position. "Come on, emaa. If you're going to tell me any of it, you've got to tell me all of it."

Ekaterina appeared to see the sense of this. "There is a logging contract under consideration. With Pacific Northwest Paper Products."

"Another one?" Kate shrugged. "I thought the corporation had three or four deals with PNP."

"We do."

"Their checks aren't bouncing, are they?"

Ekaterina shook her head. "Those ones are even talking about putting in a new mill in southcentral Alaska, so that we can build our new Association offices with lumber processed from timber harvested from our own land."

" 'Those ones.' " Ekaterina was talking like an old one, an elder. Kate looked across the table at the worn, lined face and with a tiny shock of recognition realized that Ekaterina was in fact an elder. She gave herself a mental shake. Of course she was an elder, she was eighty years old, maybe more. "Sounds like a good idea," she said. "The Association has always encouraged the development of local industry and local hire. What's the problem?" Ekaterina's face was wooden, and Kate paused with her mug halfway to her mouth. "Emaa," she said. "Where for this time? What part do they want to log?"

"Iqaluk."

Kate's mug thudded down on the table.

Iqaluk was fifty thousand acres of land that fronted the eastern shore of the Kanuyaq River and the Prince William

Sound coast, with dozens of creeks draining into the Kanuyaq. It had some of the richest salmon spawning grounds in the Sound, hence the name, iqaluk, the Aleut word for salmon. It was part of the coastal rain forest extending from Cook Inlet to the Canadian border south of Ketchikan, and included commercial stands of western hemlock, Sitka spruce and Alaska cedar.

Iqaluk was one of the last unexploited old-growth forests in the state, and the subject of hot debate between the Niniltna Native Association, Raven Corporation, the state of Alaska and the federal government in the guises of the Forest Service and the Department of the Interior. Ekaterina and the Niniltna Native Association wanted the land deeded to them as part of the tribal entity's compensation under the Alaska Native Claims Settlement Act. Passed by the U.S. Congress in 1971, signed into law by President Nixon, the settlement and in particular certain land allocations included in the settlement were still under negotiation at state and federal levels, with all concerned fighting over who got the best parts. Raven, the parent corporation for Niniltna's region, wanted the land deeded to them so they could lease it out for logging and have the profits accrue to the corporation and its shareholders. The state wanted title for the same reason and for the corporate taxes it would generate for the state, which would not be forthcoming if the land was deeded to Raven. The timber companies didn't care who got title to Iqaluk so long as it wasn't the Department of the Interior, which would turn it over to the National Park Service, whose stated intention was to declare the area a wildlife refuge, which would exclude exploitation of any kind. Declaring it a refuge would also put limits on hunting and fishing, and Iqaluk had been a subsistence hunting and fishing area for Park Natives for the last five thousand years, which brought the controversy full circle back to Ekaterina and the Niniltna Native Association, who wanted to reserve the right of the People to continue to feed their families.

Problems of land ownership in Alaska were further compounded by the suit filed against the state by mental health advocates. Prior to statehood, Alaska had been granted a million acres of federal land with the proviso that some portion of revenues generated by the land be used to fund mental health programs in the state. Naturally the state reneged on the deal, and of course the mental health advocates sued, and at present the case languished in the courts. It was a complex, convoluted issue made more complex and infinitely more convoluted by the approximately 3,946 lawyers involved, all of whom billed by the hour, and it made Kate's head hurt just to think about it. "What about Iqaluk?" she said. "I thought title to the area was still being contested by everyone involved."

"It is."

"But?" Kate said.

"But that lawyer tells the board that it looks as if the court is making a decision soon. That lawyer says he thinks the federal government will get it."

"Could be worse," Kate said. "Could be the state government."

Ekaterina nodded. "Whatever is decided, the board needs to make some decisions. If we get the land, we need to be ready."

"Decisions? What are you talking about, what decisions? I thought the board supported leaving Iqaluk alone, keeping it for traditional purposes, hunting and fishing and like that."

"I support that," Ekaterina said.

"You support it?" Kate frowned. Ekaterina Moonin Shugak was the board of the Niniltna Native Association, its oldest member, chair and conscience. "What about what the board supports? What's going on?"

"There are five members on the Niniltna board."

A feeling of apprehension grew in Kate's breast. "You, Billy Mike, Enakenty Barnes, Sarah Kompkoff and Harvey Meganack. You've got a four-to-one majority. Don't you?"

There was a dirge-like quality to Ekaterina's answer. "Sarah Kompkoff is dead."

"What? Sarah? Emaa, are you sure?"

Ekaterina's nod was heavy.

Sarah Kompkoff was Kate's second cousin, or third

cousin by marriage, or maybe both, she couldn't remember at the moment. They hadn't been close but Kate remembered her vividly, a short, compact woman with a quick lip and a quicker laugh, a first-rate cook and the first villager to sign on with the rural sobriety movement. She'd trained in and then taught substance abuse workshops at the school, and she had been the community health representative for the tribal association. "She couldn't have been more than fifty."

"Fifty-two," Ekaterina said.

"What happened?" Kate asked, afraid of the answer. Sarah had been sober for six years. The last thing Kate wanted to hear was that she'd fallen off the wagon. "Was there an accident?"

"No."

"What then?"

"They said she died of botulism."

"Oh, no," Kate said, surprised and appalled and, yes, a little relieved. "From her salmon?"

"Yes."

"Oh no. Did she make up her usual warehouse full of cases this year?"

"Yes."

"Damn," Kate said. "If she made a bad batch, we'd better track it down. You know how she gives it out to the whole town of Ahtna, not to mention anybody else who happens to be driving by her house."

"Dawn and Terra and Rose are already asking around."

"Good." Sarah's three daughters were reliable people. "Emaa. Even with Sarah dead, you still have a majority on the board." Enakenty Barnes was a first cousin, and unlike Kate, where Ekaterina led Enakenty followed. Billy Mike was Ekaterina's hand-picked successor as tribal chief, and had been in Ekaterina's pocket since before ANCSA. Harvey Meganack, on the other hand, wasn't a cousin that she knew of. He was a commercial fisherman and a professional hunting guide who sat on the state board of Fish and Game, and was so pro-development he was almost gubernatorial material. He openly supported developing Iqaluk, and a significant number of shareholders backed his stand, in particular some of the fishermen still suffering the effects of the *RPetCo Anchorage* spill. Ekaterina had backed Harvey's election to the Niniltna board as a sop to the pro-development forces within the Association, and because she thought she had him boxed in by the four traditional board votes. "It's still three to one," Kate said, relaxing.

"Perhaps," Ekaterina said.

Something in her voice made Kate sit up again. "Enakenty? It sure as hell can't be Billy, emaa." Ekaterina had the knack of saying more without saying a word elevated to a fine art, and Kate, openly incredulous, said, "But I thought Billy Mike held more for the old ways."

"So did I."

"You mean he's changed?"

Her grandmother made no move except to lower her eyes. "I don't know."

"But you are worried." Kate waited. Ekaterina didn't answer. "Emaa. I won't run for Sarah's seat." Ekaterina was silent some more. Kate set her teeth and groped around for her self-control, which seemed almost always to scuttle under the bed when Ekaterina walked in the door. "What reason do you have to suspect that Billy has changed his mind about Iqaluk?"

Ekaterina practiced looking impassive.

Kate took a deep breath and counted to ten. In Aleut, whose harsh gutturals were more satisfying. "So. The Niniltna board meets next week, at the same time as the AFN convention. The subject of Iqaluk is bound to come up. One, maybe two members of the board want Iqaluk opened for development, two don't. The fifth is dead. That about cover it?" Ekaterina hesitated a moment too long. "Emaa?"

The old woman said firmly, "That's all."

The two words were the same two words used to end every story and legend Ekaterina recited daily to an ever-increasing horde of grand-and great-grandchildren jostling for position in her lap. Kate remembered Olga Shapsnikoff using the same words in Unalaska, and she wondered if the elders in Toksook Bay and Arctic Village ended their stories the same way.

She also wondered what Ekaterina knew that she wasn't telling her. She went to bed wondering.

The ladder squeaked beneath her feet the next morning as she slipped from the loft and went outside to the outhouse. The coals in the wood stove were buried in gray ash and still red hot beneath. Kate fed it bits of kindling until it reached out hungrily for a real meal of logs. She turned up the oil stove and put the kettle on for coffee. Her grandmother was a still lump of blankets on the couch. Kate brushed her teeth and sluiced her face with water from the kitchen pump, skin tingling from its icy touch. She pumped up more to drink and it burned clean and cold all the way down. When she leaned over to place the glass in the drainer, she caught sight of her reflection in the tiny, rectangular mirror hanging crookedly on the wall next to the window. The sun wouldn't be up for another hour and her slanting image was shadowed in the somber half-light of the single lantern she had lit and turned down low.

Her skin was dark from a month of picking mushrooms at Chistona, and another month of gillnetting reds on the flats at the mouth of the Kanuyaq, and still another month of picking blueberries and cranberries and raspberries in the Teglliqs. It had been a long, hot summer with record high temperatures; every hour of every day was burned into her skin, turning its natural light golden cast a deep and abiding amber. The black of her hair was unchanged, a shining fall straight to her waist. She bound it back in a loose French braid, fingers moving quickly, mechanically. Hazel eyes stared out at her from beneath straight black brows, the expression in them reserved, restrained, waiting.

For what?

Giving her head an impatient shake, she took the down jacket from the caribou rack hanging on the wall next to the door and slipped noiselessly from the cabin into the stillness of the morning. Mutt padded forward to thrust a cold nose into her hand and she knotted her fingers in the thick, comfortingly familiar gray ruff.

Twenty feet behind the cabin was the bank of the creek, in which water ran clear and cold and deep. Beyond the far bank the land fell away to the east in a long, wide valley, to rise again in the distant foothills and peaks of the Quilak Mountains. Angqaq loomed largest of all, rearing up against the dawn like a wild horse with a stiff white mane, the biggest and strongest and most headstrong of the herd. Kate grinned a little at the thought. More than one impertinent climber had been bucked off the Big Bump. She raised a hand in salute. As usual, Angqaq ignored her with aloof indifference, but she had stood once on his summit and they both remembered the occasion, whether he would admit to it or not.

There was a large boulder on the near bank, the top worn smooth from years of use by Shugak backsides. Kate sat down. Mutt sat next to her and leaned up against her legs, a warm, heavy presence. They watched the horizon, waiting.

At first it was no more than a luminous outlining of the distant peaks, a deceptively soft suggestion of what was to come. For a while it remained so, the light snared in the spurs and crags of rock and ice as it gathered in strength and presence. When the peaks could no longer contain the flood the light welled up and spilled through the gaps, glimmering trickles that swelled into gleaming streams and gleaming streams into bright rivers, the sun in spate. The bowl of the valley was filled to its ragged brim with a torrent of light that splashed down the Kanuyaq and up every feeder creek and spill stream. Engulfed in the backwash, the shallow canyon at Kate's feet was too narrow to contain it all and it splashed off the banks and fountained up to catch at the tips of an eagle's wings, soaring high overhead.

Her heart ached with the beauty of it. She didn't want to leave, the Park, the homestead, her home, her place in the universe. Her grandmother had said she would not take Kate from the place that gave her strength, in truth had not asked her to come. She didn't have to. Implicit in her acceptance of Kate's right to remain was an expectancy of self-sacrifice upon the altar of Ekaterina Moonin Shugak's almighty tribe, and an equally implicit assumption of Kate's presence among the host of the all-volunteer army to preserve and protect it. Kate resented it, resented her grandmother's appropriation of her time. The garage walls needed insulating and she had planned to wire it for electricity so she could plug in a space heater and have a warm place to putter during the cold winter months. The snow machine needed a tuneup to make it fit for the round trip to Niniltna, so she could pick up her mail each month. There were traps in need of repair, plans for a new bookcase, and long walks to take with Mutt before the first snow fell. She had books to read, and bread to bake, and wood to split. Her place was here, on the homestead, not two hundred miles away in a city she disliked as much as she distrusted.

Mutt nosed her arm and Kate looked down. Mutt's eyes were wide and wise, as wise as Ekaterina's. She stood three feet at the shoulder and weighed in at 140 pounds, all of it muscle. There was Husky in her solid torso; her long legs and her smarts were all wolf. Proving it, she nosed Kate under the arm again. "All right, all right, don't get pushy." Kate rose on stiff legs and led the way back inside.

A neat pile of folded sheets and blankets rested on one end of the couch. Ekaterina was at the stove. She turned at Kate's entrance to hand her a plate full of eggs over easy, moose steak fried crisp on the outside and rare on the inside and toast made from homemade bread dripping with butter. Kate sat and began to eat. Ekaterina served herself and sat down across from her.

When her plate was cleared, Kate poured coffee and carried both mugs back to the table. Ekaterina started to clear the breakfast dishes and Kate said, "No, emaa, sit. I'll do it in a minute." She sugared and creamed her coffee, blew across the steaming surface and sipped. "After, I'll take the truck into Niniltna and get Bobby to call Jack, see if he'll come out and pick us up tomorrow. If not, we can always fly George. If the Skywagon's running, which isn't likely. How much does he charge for a one-way into Anchorage these days?"

"You are coming to town with me?"

As if you didn't know, Kate thought, and gave a curt nod. "I can sniff around the convention, maybe talk to Billy, see how he feels so you'll know what to expect when it comes time to speak out on Iqaluk. Maybe talk to Enakenty, too, just to make sure he's still on our side. The board doesn't meet until a week from today, next Saturday, right?"

"You are coming with me?" Ekaterina repeated.

It could have been the hint of disbelief in Ekaterina's voice that did it. It might have been the slight, incredulous lift of her left eyebrow. Or maybe it was the way one corner of her mouth quirked in an expression that wasn't quite a smile.

Whatever it was, it caused Kate to add, "My fee is four hundred a day. Plus expenses." She drank coffee, and said with elaborate nonchalance, "I'll throw in the expenses." She looked Ekaterina straight in the eye and added, "Family rate."

Ekaterina's eyebrow stayed where it was as one hand delved into a pocket of her jeans and produced a folded white envelope. Inside the envelope were ten one-hundred dollar bills, creased from residing in Ekaterina's pocket for the last three days. "You call that one a retainer, I think."

On the face of another, less dignified woman, Ekaterina's expression might have been called smug. Ten years ago, even one year ago, Kate would have said so. Today, she closed the envelope, folded it twice and stuck it into the back pocket of her jeans.

TWO

IN NINILTNA, THE VILLAGE TWENTY-FIVE MILES DOWN THE old Kanuyaq River & Northern Railroad roadbed from Kate's homestead, the airport consisted of a single dirt strip forty-eight hundred feet long with a wind sock stuck on a pole at one end. There were half a dozen planes tied down next to the hangar on one side of the strip and a log cabin post office on the other side, the U.S. flag flying next to it. On a busy day in the summer during the salmon season or in the fall during moose season there were maybe forty planes in and out every day, but that would have to be on a weekend and a CAVU weekend at that, ceiling and visibility unlimited. The Niniltna strip was just about Kate's speed, maybe even a little over it more often than she would like.

In Anchorage, two air hours away southwest, Merrill Field handled up to a thousand operations per day, a traffic load generated by air taxies hauling passengers from Tyonek to McGrath, air freight outfits hauling cases of pilot bread to Nabesna and castellated wing nuts to Nome, and eight flight schools, whose students kept the dozen aircraft parts stores in business. The airfield was surrounded on four sides by the city of Anchorage, which included four other airports: Anchorage International Airport, these days a subcontractor for Federal Express; Elmendorf Air Force Base, which since the Cold War ended was doing more AirSea Rescue operations than they were scrambling to intercept Soviet Backfire bombers; Lake Hood, which boasted the largest per capita population of float plane owners in the world; and Campbell Airstrip, a dirt strip cozied up to the Chugach Mountains, which made for interesting crosswinds.

All of which meant that at any given moment on any given day of the year there were more people in the air over Anchorage than there were on the ground in Niniltna, including the student pilot who tried to land on Merrill's Runway 1533 at the same time they did. Jack's hands were steady on the yoke and his face was calm but Kate, holding the Cessna 172 up in the air by the edge of her seat, noticed that the line of his jaw was very tight, never a good sign. Once they were safely on the ground, Kate could even find it in her heart to feel sorry for the student pilot.

They taxied to Jack's tiedown and he left Ekaterina and Kate to unload while he went over to discuss the little matter of the straying student pilot and his inattentive instructor with Merrill Tower. When he came back, his almost-ugly face was as serene as before. Kate looked for blood on his hands, didn't find any, and deduced that the tower had promised to handle the situation, though probably with less blood spilled than Jack had demanded. She tested the line on the right wing, judged it tight enough to hold the Cessna steady against any wind, stowed her duffel in Jack's Blazer and climbed into the back seat. Jack got in behind the wheel, next to Ekaterina. "Where am I driving you ladies?" he inquired, looking into the rear view at Kate.

"The Sheraton," Ekaterina said.

"Your place," Kate said at the same time.

Jack's blue eyes held Kate's.

"I'll be staying at Jack's, emaa," Kate said to her grandmother's bun.

Ekaterina didn't turn or speak. "Next stop, the Sheraton," Jack said brightly, and started the Blazer.

The Sheraton was ten blocks from the airport and the trip was accomplished in silence. Kate carried Ekaterina's bags up to her room and set them on the bed. There was a pad and pencil next to the phone; she scribbled down Jack's number. Ekaterina watched her, impassive. "So. I'll be going."

Ekaterina said nothing.

Grandmothers are better at guilt than anyone, even mothers. With subtle guile, Kate said, "Maybe we should make Jack buy us dinner. How about Mama Nicco's?"

Ekaterina's face didn't move a muscle. She wasn't going to be easy or cheap. "Lasagna?"

Kate hid a smile. Everyone had their weak spot, and her grandmother was a closet Italian. "And garlic bread, and maybe even tiramisù."

"Tiramisù? What's that?"

"Something Jack introduced me to last time I was in town. You'll love it. So. We'll pick you up downstairs at six?"

The phone rang before Ekaterina could answer. "Aha," Kate said, "you can run, but you can't hide. How much you want to bet that's Billy Mike?"

Ekaterina answered the phone. "Hello. Yes. Hello, Billy. Yes, we just got in. Kate. Yes, she is here, too. No. No, not yet." She covered the mouthpiece and looked at Kate.

Kate understood. "See you at seven. Downstairs, at the front door?"

Ekaterina nodded and Kate let herself out of the room.

In the elevator, she wondered what Ekaterina was now discussing with Billy Mike that she did not want her granddaughter to overhear.

Jack's townhouse stood on the edge of Westchester Lagoon, facing south. The garage was in the basement, the kitchen, living room, dining room, den and half bath on the second floor, and three bedrooms and two full bathrooms on the third floor. Upon arrival on previous visits to Anchorage, Kate rarely caught more than a passing glimpse of the first two floors before it was instantly and invariably replaced by a view of the ceiling in the master bedroom on the third. Contrary to standard operating procedure, this afternoon Jack seemed to be loitering with intent over the hang of her jacket from the hook by the door. "What's wrong?'' she said, truth to tell a little disappointed. She had been looking forward to rewarding Jack for his care package since she'd made the decision to come to Anchorage. They'd been in the house five whole minutes without him making a move, and she was starting to feel like a woman scorned.

He turned. ''Why should anything be wrong?''

She folded her arms, one eyebrow raised in polite incredulity, looking, did she but know it, the spitting image of her grandmother in that moment.

He sighed. ''Want a Diet 7-Up?''

The eyebrow went down and the corners of the mouth curved up. ''Why, Jack. You shopped for me. This must be love.''

Embarrassed to be caught out in a display of sentiment, Jack said, ''Yeah, yeah, you want one or not?''

He got her the 7-Up, himself a beer and Mutt a bowl of water and they adjourned the discussion to the living room. She sat on the couch, he on a chair. She gave a pointed look at the acre of empty couch surrounding her, he refused to be baited. She pouted a little. Not proof against a pout of that wattage, he told her to cut it out. They compromised on him moving to the couch and her promising to keep her hands to herself. He palliated the severity of the sentence by draping an arm around her shoulders and pulling her closer. When she slid over, she felt the tension in the line of his body. She tipped her head back to study his face. ''What's going on, Jack? You're wound up tighter than a clock spring.''

He tilted the bottle of Full Sail Golden Ale and drank deep. ''We go to court tomorrow.''

It was such a non of a sequitur that she was confused. ''Who do? You mean the office? You're testifying? What, a case?''

The rigidity she'd attributed to the near miss with the student pilot was back in his jawline. Come to think of it, he hadn't said much more than hello since Niniltna. ''I'm testifying, yes, but it's not in a case for the office.'' He looked at her and she recoiled inwardly from what she saw there. "Jane's coming after Johnny."

"What?"

"She wants full custody."

Kate sat up. "Wait a minute. You told me last month she'd agreed to an interim settlement. You told me Johnny told Judge Reese he wanted to live with you, and that Jane had agreed, and so had the judge."

"She changed her mind."

He was angry, a steady, bone-deep rage. It radiated off him in waves, like heat. "I see," Kate said.

"No," he said, very precisely, "you do not see."

"You're right, I don't," she said at once.

"Don't be so goddam soothing," he barked.

"Sorry."

"And don't be so goddam apologetic when I yell at you."

"Okay."

"And don't be so goddam agreeable when I'm correcting your behavior!"

Mutt sent them an annoyed look, rose to her feet and turned three circles, laying down again with her back to them.

Into the silence Kate said in a soft voice, "I won't let you pick a fight with me, Jack." She added, "Not over this, anyway."

Half his remaining beer disappeared in a single gulp. He closed his eyes and ran his free hand through a thatch of brown curls that hadn't been very tidy to begin with. When he spoke again, this time she heard the fear underlying the anger. "There's nothing I can do, Kate, except show up tomorrow and pray there's at least one human bone in Reese's body."

"He won't like it that she backed out of the interim agreement," Kate said. "Judges never do like that."

"Makes more work for them," Jack agreed. He opened his eyes and looked at Kate. "Will you testify?"

She was startled. "To what? Everything I know is hearsay."

"You picked him up at the 7-Eleven last March, when

she took his shoes away to keep him from walking over here.''

She was silent, frowning down at the can she held between both hands. ''For a devout and practicing Catholic, old Jane sure doesn't go in for Christian charity in a big way, does she?''

''Nope.''

''She still think I'm the whore of Babylon?''

Jack nodded. ''Everybody needs somebody to hate.''

''Glad to be of service,'' Kate said, an edge to the words.

''Don't make this about you. It isn't.''

Kate, ashamed of her flare of temper, said, ''No, it's not. I'm sorry.''

Jack went for another beer. ''Will you? Testify?''

''To that one incident? Yes.'' She drained the can. ''How'd Jane get a court date this soon?''

''Somebody canceled, the archdiocese pulled strings, her lawyer flew the clerk into Theodore River for some silver fishing, take your pick. You know how it works.''

''Yes.'' She went to the kitchen to toss the can in the trash and returned to the living room to stand in front of the window, staring out across the lagoon, a thin, fragile sheet of ice slowly creeping across it, as yet no snow. Like the homestead. She wished with all her heart that she was there instead of here.

Then again, there was one thing available to her in Anchorage she didn't get much of in the Park.

Jack caught the quirk of her mouth. ''What's so awful goddam funny, Shugak?''

She grinned at the frozen expanse of water. ''You are.'' Turning, she clasped her hands and cast down her eyes, trying for demure. ''You didn't want to seduce me under false pretenses.''

''Oh.'' The anger dissipated, and the scowl eased into a slow smile. ''No.''

''I appreciate your honesty,'' she said gravely.

''Thank you.''

She strolled over and began unbuttoning his shirt. ''Now, when was it you said Johnny gets home?''

• • •

They were still upstairs when the kitchen door slammed. Kate shot out of bed and into the bathroom. Jack pulled on jeans and a sweatshirt and went downstairs to find his son and heir juggling a loaf of bread, a package of cheese slices and a jar of mayonnaise under Mutt's interested eye. There was a can of Coke tucked between chin and chest and a package of shrink-wrapped bologna in his teeth. ''Hi, Dad,'' he mumbled around the bologna. ''Kate here yet?'' Can and sandwich makings tumbled into a heap on the kitchen counter and he caught the Coke just before it hit the floor. He ripped open the package of bologna to toss Mutt a slice.

''Yeah, she's upstairs, taking a shower. Don't open that Coke!''

Of course he did, and of course it sprayed all over Jack and the kitchen, and of course mostly Jack since Johnny was holding the can. Clearly the only thing to do was retaliate, and Kate arrived on the scene to find Jack blasting Johnny with the sink sprayer, the cold water on full bore and puddles gathering all over the floor. Mutt stalked from the carnage, the expression of disgust on her face somewhat marred by the water dripping from her muzzle. Johnny tried cowering behind the refrigerator door, and when that didn't work charged his father with a chair, legs extended at shoulder arms. The sprayer changed hands, there was a half-suppressed yelp of laughter from Jack, an exuberant whoop from Johnny, and the battle raged around the stove, up the trash compactor and down the dishwasher. Kate stood in the doorway, safely out of range, until the battle was fought to a draw and a truce was declared.

Johnny mopped his face and saw her. He grinned, his softer, smoother face a youthful echo of the craggier one opposite. He had his father's blue eyes and his mother's tow-colored hair. ''Hi, Kate.''

''Hi, Johnny.''

He hooked a thumb at his father. ''You still hanging with this guy?''

She shrugged. ''Looks like.''

He shook his head. ''I guess love really is blind.''

Kate laughed, and Jack cleared his throat and changed the subject before things got any more out of hand. ''How's your mother?''

''Still nutty as a fruitcake, how do you think?'' Johnny's reply was cheerful and not ridden with any angst that Kate could detect. By the expression in Jack's eyes, he couldn't either, and the tense set of the big shoulders relaxed. ''How was basketball practice?''

''Good,'' Johnny said. He finished mopping up a puddle and tossed the dishtowel into the sink where it fell with a sodden splat. He got another Coke out of the refrigerator, drank half of it down in a single gulp and burped. ''Excuse me. Coach says I need to work on my free throw.''

''Free throws win ball games,'' Kate said.

''That's what Coach Stewman says. How'd you know?''

''All coaches say that.''

''Oh.'' Johnny assembled bread, mayonnaise, bologna and cheese slices and paused, giving the result a critical frown. He went back to the refrigerator and found an onion. A thick slab went into the sandwich, followed by a sliced dill pickle, half a tomato, most of a head of lettuce and the remainder of a round of caribou sausage he dug out of the meat drawer. At that point the refrigerator ran out of ingredients, and he picked up the sandwich and actually managed to squeeze one corner of it into his mouth. ''Um.'' It was a grunt of pure ecstasy. He opened his eyes and saw the two of them watching. ''What?'' he said thickly.

''Oh, nothing,'' Jack said.

''Nothing at all,'' Kate said. ''Don't fill up, we're going out for dinner.''

Johnny brightened. ''Just a snack,'' he assured her.

Mama Nicco's was a restaurant in Huffman Business Park, a collection of flat-roofed buildings at the intersection of Huffman and the New Seward Highway that were much of a muchness in architecture, and if they had been connected would have been called a mall. The restaurant was a long, rectangular room filled with tables, presided over by a tall, strong-featured man with a full head of iron-gray hair and a rare, charming smile. Tall-hatted chefs cooked on an open grill behind a counter, their waitress was friendly and efficient, and after his first sip of the house Chianti Jack pronounced dinner an unqualified success.

"We haven't even ordered yet, Dad," Johnny said, hunched over the menu. "What's cioppino?"

"Garlic with seafood," Jack said.

"Oh. What's pasta alla panna?"

"Garlic with pasta."

When the waitress returned Johnny ordered both or tried to, Jack ordered veal scallopini, Kate ordered pasta al pesto, and Ekaterina ordered lasagna. The waitress brought out two more bowls of bread, setting one in front of Johnny, who had accounted for most of the first bowl, another glass of Chianti for Jack and one for Ekaterina, a Coke for Johnny, and a Perrier with a twist of lemon for Kate. Johnny looked at her from the corner of one eye and said softly, "Yubbie."

Kate looked at him and said, just as softly, "Yubbie."

Suspicious but unable to refrain from asking, he said, "Yubbie? What's that?"

"The real thing. A young urban brat."

Jack laughed. Even Ekaterina smiled, which made Johnny, who was a little afraid of her, relax. The old woman unbent even further, enough to say, "Jack, the Raven Corporation is having a party Wednesday night at the Captain Cook. Will you come?"

"A party?" Kate said. "What party?"

Ekaterina smiled down upon her, very benign, and every self-protective hair on the back of Kate's neck stood straight up in alarm. "Just a little get-together for the friends of Raven. All the Niniltna and other tribal corporation shareholders will be there. It'll be fun."

Kate opened her mouth to decline with thanks but Jack kicked her under the table. She gave him an indignant glare, which slid right off him, and he said to Ekaterina, smooth as silk in spite of the fact that he was a little afraid of her, too, "It sounds like fun, Ekaterina. What time?"

"Seven o'clock." Ekaterina smiled, this time a real one. "There will be food."

He grinned. "I'll be there."

Ekaterina looked at Kate, who knew there was something else going on here, she just hadn't figured out what. The food arrived and she left the problem for another time. Ekaterina exclaimed over the lasagna, Jack went into raptures over the veal, Johnny was up to his eyebrows in fettucine and the lure of basil and pine nuts proved irresistible for Kate. Everyone was on their best behavior, there was much talk and more laughter and the evening looked as if it were going to be a social occasion of the first water.

Until the arrival of the people who had reserved the table next to them. One of them was John King. The other two men made Ekaterina stiffen in her chair and Kate swear beneath her breath. Jack observed both reactions with a sense of impending doom and began cutting his remaining veal into very large pieces. "Dad," Johnny said, shocked, "slow down, you're being a pig."

Jack said around a mouthful of veal, "Eat fast, kid, or you might not get to eat at all."

Harvey Meganack saw Ekaterina at the same time she saw him and paused in the act of pulling out a chair for the trophy blonde who was definitely not his wife. A sheepish smile spread across his broad, brown face, a look not to be confused with the fierce expressions on the two solid gold rams' heads on either side of the gold nugget watch weighing down his wrist. "Ekaterina. Hello."

Ekaterina inclined her head in a frigid, infinitesimal bow. "Harvey."

The third man looked up and said ebulliently, "Ekaterina!" He was thin and fiftyish, with sparse fair hair standing straight up from the crown of his head. He bustled around the table and grabbed Ekaterina's reluctant hand in both of his, pumping it up and down with enthusiasm. "How the hell are you! Ha HAH!" His laugh was automatic, like a spasm or a tic, used to punctuate. He sounded like Woody Woodpecker.

Kate held her breath but Ekaterina only recovered her hand and nodded again, twice as frostily this time. "Mr.—" She hesitated for so long that he rushed to supply the rest.

"Mathisen, Lew Mathisen," he said, "ha HAH!"

A third thin smile, as frosty as the first two. "Of course. Mr. Samithen."

It was a Force 10 Arctic gale, impossible to mistake. Johnny's eyes widened. Jack ate faster. Kate waited, fatalistic, for Mathisen to dig himself in even deeper.

He was smart enough not to correct Ekaterina. Instead, he assumed an expression of deep concern, and said, "Say, it's a damn shame about Sarah, isn't it? Harvey just told me, and I can't say how sorry I am. I know how much you're going to miss her." He smiled again, showing off six thousand dollars' worth of dental work in the upper incisors alone, and managed to restrain the laugh this time.

At that Kate thought Ekaterina would say something and she braced for it, but just then John King looked over and saw Jack. "Morgan," he growled. His eyes traveled past Jack to Kate. "Shugak." He was square-headed, thickset and blond, wearing the same mustard-yellow, silver-toed cowboy boots Kate had seen in March. He looked exactly what he was, a roughneck who had started out throwing the chain on a rig floor in Louisiana and ended up, to his own and everyone else's bewilderment, not to say consternation, at the head of the board room of Royal Petroleum Company, throwing his weight around.

"Hello, King," Kate said, leaping into Ekaterina's frozen silence with foolhardy abandon. "You get that wellhead off Tode Point yet?"

Johnny looked puzzled. Jack choked on his veal and had recourse to his Chianti. Ekaterina looked on Kate with what might actually have been approval.

King's scowl deepened. Without answering he seated his date, a brunette with a face so artificially smooth you could skate on it and eyes so opaque it was hard to tell their color. There was a wide gold band on her left hand, the only thing about her that surprised Kate. The oil man sat down next to the brunette without introducing her, folded thick arms across his chest and glowered at Lew Mathisen beneath lowered brows.

"And Kate, too, by God," Lew Mathisen said, "how'd

we get so lucky, ha HAH!'' He reached out and Kate gave him a bright smile across a full fork, thereby occupying both hand and mouth so she would have to neither shake his hand nor reply.

''Hello, emaa,'' Axenia said from behind him, her smile containing only a trifle less wattage. ''Sorry we're late. Hi, Kate.''

''Axenia,'' Kate said, ''hi. I didn't know you were coming.''

''I called her this afternoon,'' Ekaterina said.

''Hey, babe,'' Lew said, and gave Axenia an exuberant kiss. ''What are you doing here?''

''I'm meeting my grandmother for dinner.'' She put her arm around his neck and kissed him back with interest, when she was done looking a clear challenge first at her grandmother, then at her cousin. Kate thought if Ekaterina stiffened any more she might snap in half where she sat.

A short, stout man with a moon face and shiny black hair beamed over Axenia's shoulder. ''It's my fault, Ekaterina. Axenia said I'd get a free meal if I tagged along, so I made her wait for me. Hi, Kate.''

''Hello, Billy.'' Billy Mike had succeeded Ekaterina in the position of tribal chief of the Niniltna Native Association only because Ekaterina had refused to run for a fourth five-year term. He was also one of the four surviving Niniltna board members. Ekaterina, then Harvey, now Billy. Kate wondered when Enakenty was going to show up.

''And Billy, too, great to see you again!'' Mathisen smacked his hands together. ''Well, isn't this great, ha HAH! Can we buy you nice folks a drink? Honey, bring my good friends here a bottle of whatever they're drinking. And another one for us while you're at it.'' As if the idea had just occurred to him, he said, ''Say, why don't we push our tables together? Make a party of it, ha HAH!''

''No, thank you,'' Ekaterina said clearly.

Johnny, who had inherited his brains from his father, began shovelling in pasta in a manner reminiscent of a steam shovel excavating a gravel pit.

''Oh, hey, Lew,'' Jack said, ''ah, we're already halfway

through our dinners here, let's save it for another time, okay?''

''Well, hell, you can drink, can't you, ha HAH? Honey, can we slide these tables together, what do you think? Ha HAH!''

Kate leaned over to whisper in Ekaterina's ear. ''Would you like to leave?''

Ekaterina, straight-backed in her chair, looking neither to the left nor to the right, conveyed a healthy portion of lasagna to her mouth without replying.

''Since they're almost done,'' Axenia said, ''maybe Billy and I should join you instead.''

''Well, if you're sure,'' Mathisen said, disappointed. ''Honey? Honey? Could we have a couple more chairs and place settings here? Fine! Well, great to see you, Ekaterina, we'll be seeing you all at the convention, ha HAH!'' He waved a hand at Ekaterina's table and went back to his own. Billy, smarter than Axenia, or perhaps just less in need of proving a point, declined the invitation to join Mathisen's party and pulled up a chair between Ekaterina and Kate.

The waitress arrived with two bottles of Chianti. Behind her came the couple who would be taking the table on the other side of Jack's party. ''Oh fuck,'' said Jack under his breath.

''Oh fuck,'' said Johnny, way under his.

''Hello, Jane,'' said Kate, and wondered why very thin people always looked so peevish. Probably hunger.

The tall towhead's skin matched the color of her hair. The lids of her blue eyes were weighed down beneath thick layers of shadow, liner and mascara, only emphasizing the malevolent expression in them. She responded to Kate's greeting by snapping at Jack, ''Is she staying with you?''

Jack, more relaxed now that the attack was directed his way, gave an equable nod, his face displaying nothing more than a polite disinterest in Jane's next words. Next to Kate, Johnny was strung as tight as a wire, and she couldn't resist a brief touch of his shoulder. ''Relax,'' she mouthed. ''Everything's okay.''

Jane's eyes narrowed. ''Get your hands off my son!''

"Jane." Jack's voice was deep and hard. "Back off."

Kate gave Jane her sweetest and most dangerous smile.

The line of Jane's mouth tightened, and then relaxed. Her eyes snapped with malicious triumph. "I guess I'll have something to say to the judge about the degenerate home life you're providing for my son," she told Jack. "I'll wind up with full custody for sure this time. You should pick your whores more carefully, Jack."

"Jane." Jack's voice lashed out. "I said, back off."

Conversation in the restaurant slowed and heads turned in their direction. From the next table, Axenia smiled at Kate. It wasn't a friendly smile. Jack looked angry. Johnny shrank down into a miserable huddle. Into the growing silence Ekaterina leaned over to whisper in Kate's ear. "Would you like to leave?"

Their eyes met for a long, pregnant moment. Somewhere deep down Kate felt a bubble of frantic laughter rise to match the hilarity she could see in Ekaterina's eyes, and together they burst out laughing.

Jane's colorless skin flushed a dark, congested red right up to the roots of her colorless hair and her eyes narrowed to slits. Her date, a plump, uneasy man hiding behind a pair of glasses with thick tortoiseshell rims, tugged at her elbow. "Jane. Come on."

Jane glared at him. "Yes, let's. The food's much better at Sorrento's anyway." She turned on her heel. Over her shoulder she said to Jack, the sneer back, "See you in court."

The remark was largely wasted since Jack could barely hear her over Kate and Ekaterina, who were still laughing as Jane stalked out the door.

When the laughter had died down to the occasional hysterical hiccup, Jack judged it time to produce his pièce de résistance, tickets to that evening's performance of the Whale Fat Follies. They adjourned forthwith to Spenard and the Fly By Night Club, where for the next three hours they were accosted by nothing more serious than woolly mammoths, tap-dancing outhouses and humpies from hell.

• • •

It wasn't until after Jack was asleep that night that Kate had time to wonder why the president and chief executive officer of Royal Petroleum Company was dining with a member of the Niniltna Native Association board, in company with Mathisen, one of the most notoriously corrupt lobbyists in the history of Alaskan politics.

The board member's motivations were unambiguous, as best exemplified by the watch Harvey had been wearing. She wondered who had given it to him, and decided it had probably been Mathisen, but she was willing to bet the funds for it could be traced back to John King by way of a lobbyist's fee.

She hadn't had a lot to do with Lew Mathisen, but she knew of him by reputation. Everyone did; he was on retainer for half the Outside corporations doing business in the state. RPetCo was one of them.

The previous spring, Kate had worked for John King in Prudhoe Bay, tracking down a cocaine dealer who had been putting his half of the oil field into substance abuse orbit for months, a dealer his in-house security forces had been unable to apprehend. Kate had apprehended the dealer and the dealer's organization, as well as putting a halt to a sideline in the illegal obtaining and selling of Alaska Native artifacts from an archaeological site on the Arctic coastline. The job had resulted in satisfaction for John King and a more than satisfactory financial gain for herself. Oil companies might be immoral monoliths concerned only with making money, but they sure paid well. In fact, Kate had left RPetCo with everyone except for the security chief in a more or less happy frame of mind, and she wondered why King had been so unhappy to see her at the restaurant this evening. She wondered if it had something to do with the wellhead on Tode Point, the remains of an unlawfully drilled test hole on the archaeological site. Maybe it was still there, in spite of King's agreement to move it. Maybe he had a guilty conscience over it, and that accounted for his surly behavior.

Somehow, Kate didn't think so.

It was evident that Axenia was on terms of intimacy with

the lobbyist, who had to be at least thirty years older and infinitely wiser than her cousin in the ways of the world. Terms intimate enough that she would abandon her grandmother's company for his, in a public display of tacit disrespect that commanded not only Kate's dismay, but a small, secret, sneaking sense of awed admiration as well.

Two years before Axenia had begged Kate to get her out of the Park, away from Niniltna and a love affair gone bad and a lifestyle she loathed. Unlike Kate, Axenia yearned for the bright lights of the big city. Against Ekaterina's wishes, Kate had found her cousin a job with Kate's old employer, the Anchorage District Attorney's office. They had met twice the previous spring when Kate had been working for RPetCo. Axenia hadn't talked much about herself then, and Kate had left it alone, old enough to know that when pushed, the first instinct of the young is to push back, hard.

It might be time to change tactics.

She thought again of Axenia and Mathisen's embrace over the dinner table. Beauty and the Beast.

It might be more than time.

THREE

EARLY THE NEXT MORNING KATE AND MUTT WENT FOR A walk down the Coastal Trail. Johnny went with them.

The bike path ran between Jack's townhouse and Westchester Lagoon, splitting at the western edge of the lagoon. The right fork led uptown to Second Avenue. They took the left fork, past the KENI radio tower and through the tunnel beneath the Alaska Railroad tracks to emerge on Knik Arm. There wasn't a cloud in the sky and the sun wasn't high enough yet to give it any color. Cook Inlet lay like a sheet of gray glass, stretching south to where sight ended and imagination began.

"I can't believe I'm saying this, but I wish I was in school."

Kate grinned. "Thanks a lot."

Johnny flushed in the awkward way of an adolescent caught in a social faux pas. "I didn't mean it like that."

"I know you didn't."

They walked in silence for a few moments. "You've been to court," Johnny said.

Kate nodded. "Many times."

"What's it like?"

Kate told him the truth. "Scary."

His stride broke. "Scary?"

"Sure."

He didn't believe it. "You were scared?"

She didn't smile. "The law's a serious business, Johnny. In a criminal case, the kind I testified in when I was working for your dad, what you say under oath can change someone's life forever. You have to be right. You bet it's scary."

They reached the bridge over Fish Creek and paused to watch the incoming tide sweep slowly and inexorably up the muddy channel. Mutt left the trail to investigate the trees lining the creek bed. Mallard ducks pecked up the goose grass growing on the mud flats. A container ship slowed almost to a halt off Point MacKenzie, waiting for a berth at the Port of Anchorage. Behind MacKenzie, a hundred and thirty miles to the north, Denali, attended by the lesser peaks of Foraker and Hunter, rose clear and cold and white against the horizon. A hundred miles closer, Susitna lay peaceful and calm beneath a soft blanket of snow.

"Susitna means 'sleeping lady,' doesn't it?" Johnny said.

Kate nodded.

"Does a story go with it?"

Kate smiled. "In Alaska, a story always goes with it, Johnny."

"Tell me," he said.

A bird appeared from behind the tops of a stand of scrub spruce, wings fixed in a graceful glide, fierce eyes searching the tide line for breakfast. The brown wings stretched seven feet wingtip to wingtip, and the white head gleamed in the first, tentative rays of the morning sun. Kate touched Johnny's arm and pointed. As she did, a second eagle slipped from behind the trees. The flocks of mallards became silent and very still, their fat bodies trying to blend in with the muddy bank. The first eagle slipped by, the second, both without striking.

"Must not be that hungry," Johnny said.

"Why work for it?" Kate said. "They're probably looking for dead salmon."

"Kind of late for silvers," Johnny said, eyes squinting after the eagles as they banked to follow the gravel bed of the Alaska Railroad.

"Kind of."

"What then?"

"Anything they can find." She grinned, remembering. "I saw one take off with a poodle, once."

"Ick!"

Kate shrugged. "Protein is protein."

The eagles were lost around the bend of Bootlegger's Cove. An enormous spiral of Canadian geese massed over Knik Arm already at a thousand feet and ascending higher into the sky between Carin Point and Point MacKenzie. "Listen," Kate said. In the still, early morning air, the plaintive honks came clearly to where they were standing.

Johnny's voice was soft. "Where are they going?"

"British Columbia, Washington, Oregon. Some of them as far as northern California."

"Thousands and thousands of miles. How do they know how to get there? How do they know?"

Kate had no answer for him, and they watched in silence as the flock ended their upward spiral in a disciplined vee formation. The vee moved south, down the western side of Cook Inlet, by the long, still form of Susitna. A 737 roared off the runway at Anchorage International and the geese were heard no more. Johnny gave a long, drawn-out sigh. "So. Tell me."

"Tell you what?"

"The story that goes with Susitna."

"Oh. Well, let me see. It's been a long time since I've heard it myself." Kate leaned on the bridge railing, looking for inspiration at the long, sweeping outline of the woman slumbering peacefully beneath a white coverlet. Her right profile faced them, her hands were clasped at her waist. If you looked closely enough you could almost see her breast rise and fall. "Once upon a time, a couple of days ago," Kate began, and without knowing it slipped into a faint echo of the rhythmic chant of the storyteller.

"Once upon a time

"A couple of days ago

"A young woman goes walking in those woods

"She has long black hair

"She has big brown eyes

''She fills out a kuspuk pretty good, too
''In those woods she meets a young man
''That young man he loves her right away
''He is tall and handsome
''He is a good hunter and the fish they jump into his trap
''But that young woman she is afraid
''She runs
''He says stop but she is afraid
''She runs very fast
''He chases her
''She runs to the mountains
''He chases her
''She runs to the forest
''He chases her
''She runs to the water and jumps in, all over wet
''She can't swim as fast as she runs
''She starts to drown
''He sees this
''He jumps in after her.''

Kate paused. ''What happens?'' Johnny demanded. ''Did they both drown? What, Kate?''

Kate stared at Susitna. Just beyond the sleeping lady's feet, she thought she caught a glimpse of another mountain.

''Then a bunch of belugas comes in the water
''They talks to that young man
''They says, What you do in that water?
''They says, You not salmon
''They says, You not otter
''They says, You not whale
''They says, You drown
''Young man cries out
''He says, Help me to swim
''The beluga they looks at him
''They sees he is strong and good
''They says, We help this one
''They gives him gills to breathe
''They gives him fins to swim
''They gives him blubber to be warm
''He is beluga then

"He swims back to Susitna
"But them whales they takes too long to make up their minds
"Susitna she is dead
"That young man who is beluga now he takes her upon his back
"He carries her to that mountain
"He lays her down on top of that mountain
"He covers her with a blanket of snow
"He lays down beside her
"They sleep together now
"They sleep together now always
"That's all."

There was a long silence.

"Geez, Kate," Johnny said at last. "That's great. That's just—great. And her name was Susitna?"

Kate nodded, sober as a judge. "The Sleeping Lady."

"What was the guy's name?"

"Beluga, of course."

"Beluga! Wow! There's another mountain behind Susitna called Beluga, did you know that?"

Kate looked again beyond Susitna's feet. "Yes."

"That's great," he repeated. "And belugas are the white whales that chase the salmon up the Knik every summer, right?"

"The very same."

"I never heard that story before."

Possibly because I just made it up, she thought but didn't say.

"How come I never heard that story before?" Without waiting for her to answer he said, a touch wistful, "We don't have anything like that. No stories or legends like that." He added, "White people, I mean."

She looked at him. "What do you call all those legends about Zeus and Athena and Hercules and the rest of them?"

"You mean like in the Ilyat and the Oddsea? Those are just baloney," he said, disparaging. "One-eyed monsters and singing rocks. No whales—" he pointed at Beluga "—or bears or eagles or—" he looked at Mutt, nose down, trotting along the creek "—wolves. Huh. They don't mean anything to me."

"Just stories," she said. Clearly, Johnny stood in eminent danger of rejecting his tribal myths. This must be rectified. "Come with me."

"Where?" She didn't answer. Puzzled but willing, he followed her off the bridge and past the three benches tucked into the curve of the trail.

Between the thin layer of topsoil holding up the scrub spruce and the birch trees and the flat expanse of mud flats made of centuries of glacial silt washed down the Knik and Matanuska Rivers, there was a narrow strip of dark-grained sand, as much as ten feet wide in places, almost wide enough to merit the designation of "beach." Kate jumped the two-foot embankment.

"What are you doing?" Johnny said. He jumped down next to her, and scuffed at the sand with a doubtful foot.

She found a stick of driftwood and drew a long line in the sand. At the right end of the line she wrote the current year. Working backward, she broke the line into equal sections. Mutt, looking down at them from the bank, decided that this was going to take a while and trotted off to find something more interesting to occupy her time, like breakfast, in the form of a nice, plump, juicy rabbit.

"Each one of these is ten years," Kate said, pointing with the stick. "One decade. What year were you born?" He told her. "Okay, so this is you," she said, making a mark just behind the first decade mark from the left. "When was your dad born?" He looked uncertain. "He's, what, forty-six?"

"I think so."

"So he would have been born, let's see, about here." Kate marked it on the time line, with the notation, "Jack born" beneath it. "Okay. When was your mom born?"

His face closed down.

"Come on," Kate said impatiently, "she's still your mom and part of your family history. How old is she?" He mumbled something. "What?"

"Thirty-nine," he said, raising his voice. "She turned thirty-nine this year."

His eyes slid away from Kate's. Amused, she said, tongue in cheek, "I take it it wasn't the happiest day of her life." A snort was his reply, and with real nobility she forbore from pressing for more information. "Okay, forty, that means she was born about here. When did she come to Alaska?"

He brightened. "She flew up with my grandfather."

Elbows resting on her knees, she looked at him. "Now that sounds like a story comes with it. Tell me."

Uncertain, he said, "I don't know. A story?"

"Tell me," she repeated. "What time of the year was it? When they flew up?"

"May. 1955, I think."

"May, 1955. Alaska was still a territory. So your grandfather was a pilot?"

"Yeah. Um, he was the copilot, and my grandmother and my mom and my aunt and my uncle were all on board. The plane they flew in on was a DC-3 Starliner, and it took eight hours to get from Seattle to Anchorage, and Uncle Jim got to go up front with the pilots and Auntie Margaret drank so much pop she barfed all over Yakutat." The words came out by rote, as if he had heard just those words said in just that order many times.

Kate grinned. "And your mom?"

"She was just a baby. But Auntie Margaret had a kitten. They took her picture when the plane landed and it was on the front page of the paper."

"What happened to your grandfather?"

"He died before I was born."

"Too bad. Pilots are like fishermen. They tell all the best stories." Kate made a mark before the one indicating Johnny's birth. "What happened to your grandmother?"

"She's retired. She lives in Tucson, Arizona. We go down to see her every year."

"What did she do before she was retired?"

He straightened up and preened himself a little. "She lived in Charlotte Amalie."

He looked at her, expectant, and she didn't disappoint him. "Charlotte Amalie? Never heard of it. Where is it?"

"On St. Thomas."

Again he waited. Again she played straight man. "Where's St. Thomas?"

"In the Virgin Islands," he said, triumphant.

"The Virgin Islands," she said. "In the Caribbean?" He nodded. "Wow. How did your grandmother get from Alaska to the Caribbean?"

He shrugged. "I don't know. She went there after my grandfather died, I guess. She had a job with the government. She used to send me the greatest presents. One time I got a voodoo doll."

"The kind you stick pins in?" He nodded proudly, and Kate gave an elaborate shudder. "Eek." She gave him a stern look. "Did it work?"

He grinned. "I'll never tell."

She put her hand to the side of his head and shoved. He toppled over into the sand, laughing.

"So," she said, contemplating the time line, "your grandparents, your mother, your aunt and your uncle flew up to Alaska in the fifties. How about your dad? When did he come north?"

"Nineteen-seventy," he said at once.

"Oho." Kate made a mark on the time line. "Right after the Prudhoe Bay nine-hundred-million-dollar lease sale. Okay."

"Okay what?"

"Okay, what we got here is a family legend. Look." She pointed at the mark indicating his family's arrival. "Your mother's side of the family came up before Alaska was even a state. In fact, they came up the year of the constitutional convention. The territorial governor, Ernest Gruening, gave the keynote address to the constitutional convention in Fairbanks." She looked at Johnny with a twinkle in her eyes. "In which he compared the territory of Alaska to revolutionary America and the federal government to King George III."

Johnny brightened. "We've been studying King George III in school. Isn't he the guy that on the day they issued the Declaration of Independence wrote in his diary, 'Nothing of importance happened today'?"

"That's the guy. You know what Ernest Gruening said at the convention?"

"No, what?"

Kate pulled in her chin and deepened her voice. " 'Inherent in colonialism is an inferior political status!' " she thundered. " 'Inherent in colonialism is an inferior economic status!' "

"Wow," he said, awed. He didn't understand all the words but he caught the drift.

"Makes you want to run right down and throw tea in the harbor, doesn't it?" Kate agreed.

"Isn't that, like, you know, treason?"

"That's why we've got a First Amendment, so you can say what you think without getting thrown in jail for it." She returned to the time line. "So your family was in Alaska almost five years before it's even a state. They might even have landed at Merrill Field, which at that time was still out of town." Kate made a mark for statehood. "In 1964 is the Big One."

"The earthquake?" he said quickly. "Were you born then?"

"I was three. I don't remember it. Of course, we didn't get it as bad in the interior as they did on the coast, anyway. They got the tidal wave. Whole villages were wiped out on the coast. An entire suburb went in Anchorage." She nodded at the houses on the rise of ground behind the trail. "The next big one, they slide right into Knik Arm."

"Really?"

"Really. Your father's a moron. Promise me you'll never buy a house anywhere on the Coastal Trail. The view won't be worth it, trust me."

Johnny was agreeable. "Okay. What's next?"

"Let me see. After statehood, Fish and Game outlawed all the fish traps at the mouths of the rivers and in the late sixties the salmon started coming back. About that same time we started to fish for king crab commercially. Then in 1968, they discovered a super-giant oil field in Prudhoe Bay, the largest one in North America. In 1969, they had a lease sale, and—"

"—in 1970, my dad came up!"

"Right. When did your mom and dad get married? What year? Do you know?"

"Ten years before I was born."

And you were born the same year as the divorce, Kate remembered. She made a mark. "Right here, construction began on the Pipeline. Oil in was 1977."

"Oil in where?"

"Into the pipeline. That's how they call it. Oil in."

"That's right, you went up there this year, didn't you? Did you catch the bad guys?"

"Ah-yup," Kate drawled in her best Dodge City sheriff imitation. "We run thim varmints right outta town." She tapped the sand in front of the time line, drawing his attention back to it. "So what do we have here?"

He contemplated the scratches in the sand.

"What we have here," she said, "are stories. Just stories."

He looked up, uncertain. "Stories?"

"Sure. Just stories about people. Without any one-eyed monsters or guys with magic cloaks in them. Or guys that chase girls into the water and get turned into whales. Still, just stories."

She pointed at him with the stick. "But wait a thousand years. By then, your grandfather will have become the god of travelers himself." He looked blank, and she said, "Mercury."

"The guy with wings on his shoes?"

"That's the guy."

He thought about that for a moment. "Draw your time line."

She smiled. "That would take up the whole day and most of the beach." She tossed the stick to one side and thought how to say it. She'd probably only get one chance, and she wanted it to come out right. "When you go to court, Johnny, and you have to get up on the witness stand and speak your piece." She could see him stiffening, and kept her voice neutral and her eyes on the time line. ''When you get up there, and your mom's lawyer is asking you questions, and maybe you hear some things you don't want to hear and maybe she makes you say some things you don't want to say, and you're maybe getting a little mad at your mom, and maybe even your dad, too?'' Kate pointed at the timeline. ''Remember this. It's just another story, just another part of the family history. Some stories are good. Some are bad. Some are both.'' She pointed at Susitna. ''Like that one.''

''Is that what a legend is?'' She nodded. ''So,'' he said slowly, ''so *she* could be like Medusa, and I could be like Perseus.''

Remembering what had happened to Medusa and who did it to her, Kate was a little alarmed. ''Yes. Well. I suppose you could—remember, Johnny, the Gorgons had the heads and arms of women. They may have been monsters, but they were partly human, too.''

He looked unconvinced, and she decided it was time to leave before she waded any further into that particular mire. They started walking again, staying down on the sand instead of climbing back up onto the trail. There was a soft swish of wings and they looked up to see the two eagles returning, flying low and slow, the tips of their wings almost brushing the tops of the trees. Across the water the white peak of Mount Spurr reared up against the pale blue of the sky.

They paused to admire it, and a gray streak cannoned into Johnny from behind, knocking his feet out from under him. He landed on his back in the sand. ''Whoof.'' He blinked up at the sky for a moment before elbowing himself up and looking around.

Kate was standing next to him, shaking with laughter. A few feet away Mutt crouched down, tail wagging furiously, eyes begging for fun. Johnny caught his breath and said, ''So you wanna play rough, do you? You asked for it!''

Mutt gave a joyous yip and raced off, he tore down the beach in hot pursuit, Kate close behind, and for the rest of the walk Johnny was just a boy playing tag with a dog and a friend.

They arrived back at the townhouse at ten-thirty, red-faced and breathless. Jack greeted them at the door with a scowl. "We're going to be late. Get upstairs and into the shower. I've got a clean shirt and your good jacket laid out on your bed. Hop to it."

Johnny disappeared up the stairs and Jack transferred his scowl to Kate. "Where the hell were you?"

"I told you we were going for a walk," she said mildly, shrugging out of her coat. "Relax, Jack. Court's not in session until one o'clock, and didn't your attorney tell you the trial might be delayed a few days anyway, if the one the judge was trying on Friday dragged over?"

He shook his head. "Ganepole just called, she says today's the day." He went into the living room. Kate went into the kitchen to pour herself a cup of coffee before following.

He was pacing back and forth in front of the picture window, hands alternately fussing with his unnaturally slicked-down hair and the knot of his tie. Kate found a seat out of the way and drank coffee. "Do you need me in court today?"

He shook his head without looking at her. "Ganepole says the testimony of the current girlfriend is too easily discredited."

"So you won't need me at all?" Kate said, relieved.

"I don't know. I don't think so. Not unless things really get ugly and we have to throw everything we've got at her. Jane, I mean."

"She wants sole custody, right?"

He nodded, pacing.

"She won't get it, Jack. She can't stop you seeing him. You're his father, and you haven't done anything wrong."

He paused long enough to shoot Kate an impatient, angry look. Again, she saw through to the fear beneath. "Jane is vicious, malicious and entirely without scruple."

Kate couldn't have put it better herself.

"Who knows what she's going to say once she gets on

the witness stand? She's a good liar, Kate, the best.''

''Not the best,'' Kate said. ''Johnny has never believed anything she said about you.''

His brow lightened. ''That's true.'' He stopped pacing. ''That is true.'' He sat down next to her and rubbed his palms over the creases in his pant legs.

In ten years Kate had never seen him in anything other than blue jeans. The suit had stretched out of shape at the shoulders from hanging so long unused in the closet. Probably where the horizontal creases in the legs came from as well. The tie, a nauseous shade of lime green, she recognized from his court appearances. The judge undoubtedly would, too. She put a hand over his. ''Jack. Relax. You're not going to do Johnny any good if you get yourself all worked up. Jane is at her best on the attack. Don't let her make you scared. And don't let her make you mad. Tell the truth, and keep telling it. Wear her down with it.''

She found herself caught in a rough embrace, his face buried between her shoulder and her neck. ''I'm scared, Kate. I'm scared to death. She says she wants to move to Tucson, be near her mother. I'll never see him then.''

Kate pressed her cheek to his and stroked his head, one eye on the mug of coffee she still held in her left hand, trying to keep it from spilling down his back. His hands gripped her, hard, once, before he let her go. His laugh was a little shaky around the edges. ''Sorry. I must really be shook.''

''Don't be.''

''Which one?'' he said with an attempt at a smile. ''Sorry, or shook?''

She cupped his cheek in a brief caress. ''Either.''

He leaned forward as if to kiss her and the phone rang. He swore and got up to answer. ''If it's Ganepole with a delay, I'll—hello? Oh, hello, Ekaterina. Yes, she's right here. Hang on.'' He handed the telephone to Kate.

''Hello, emaa,'' Kate said. ''No, I've been up for hours. Johnny and Mutt and I just came back from a walk. I'm sorry, what were you saying?'' A pause. ''What?''

At the window, Jack became aware of a change in Kate's

silence and turned to look at her. She stood with the telephone to her ear, coffee mug forgotten in her left hand, all expression wiped from her face. "All right," she said at last. "Give me the address." She scribbled it down. "No, emaa. No. Just stay there. As soon as I know anything, I'll come tell you. Emaa. You hired me for this. Well okay, maybe not this, but you've got me on retainer, right? So let me handle it." A long pause. "Good. All right. Yes." She hung up.

"What's wrong?" Jack said.

She looked at him and through him, intent eyes focused on some distant object. "Enakenty Barnes is dead."

Kate took Minnesota to International Airport Road and turned right. She didn't run more than three red lights and the journey was accomplished in eight minutes flat. She turned right off the frontage road, bumped over a set of railroad tracks, passed through a gate and started looking for apartment numbers.

The condominium complex was arranged in six buildings, a smaller horseshoe inside a larger one with detached garages in front of each building. Parked in the fire lane between the two buildings on the right was a blue-and-white. Behind the blue-and-white was an ambulance. Kate went past them, found a parking space and walked back down, arriving at the ambulance at the same time as the paramedics and the stretcher. On the stretcher was a covered body.

Neither of the medics was known to Kate. She took a deep breath. "Excuse me."

The medic at the head of the stretcher looked up. "Yeah?"

Kate nodded at the stretcher. "Enakenty Barnes?"

The medic at the foot of the stretcher nodded. "That's what his driver's license says."

"How'd he die?"

"Broken neck," said the first medic.

"Wasn't that far a fall, but he landed wrong." The second medic demonstrated with his hands. "Spine snapped like a piece of dry wood."

"I'm a cousin," Kate said, her voice even. "I can I.D. him for you."

They exchanged a glance. The first medic shrugged and dropped the stretcher legs. The second folded back the blanket.

Enakenty's eyes were closed but he didn't look as if he were sleeping; he looked, in fact, a little puzzled, as if not quite sure how he came to be there, in that place, at that moment. That made two of them, Kate thought.

Up to this point, she had not been angry. Since she had come of age she had shunned anything to do with Association business, avoiding Native politics like the plague, so that when Ekaterina asked her to look into the board's current machinations she was able to acquiesce while remaining detached, if a little annoyed at being maneuvered into it. But as she stood there, looking down into Enakenty's lifeless face, something deep down began to stir, something very like anger.

There wasn't any blood or obvious contusion on the square face with the heavy jaw. His skin was darker than Kate remembered it, and his dark hair lighter, but that might have been the gray forming at the temples. The last time she'd seen Enakenty Barnes was at the Class C state basketball championship in Niniltna, in March the year before. He had one kid each on the boys' and girls' teams and never missed a game. On the surface he and Martha had had one of the better marriages in the Park, although Kate thought she remembered some rumors of Enakenty playing around. It could have been true. It could just as easily not have been true, given the fact that rumor, gossip and innuendo were the only things that kept the Park going between Halloween and breakup. Enakenty had been a good fisherman, delivering fish on his father's permit when his father's back went out, making the payments and the insurance premiums on the boat every year, taking his kids out with him, paying them a crew share. He was a responsible if unimaginative board member, never missing a meeting, fulfilling his duties and representing the shareholders without complaint.

Enakenty Barnes had been an ordinary man, a regular

guy, maybe even a good old boy. He wasn't anything special or extraordinary, neither a hero nor a villain. He got along with his wife, he loved his kids, he made his boat payments, he worked for his community, and now he lay dead in front of Kate, forty years before his time. There was something obscene in the very sight. Her anger grew.

Sarah Kompkoff's death, alone, she might have accepted as accident. But a second board member so soon afterward, and so conveniently before one of the most important board meetings in the Association's history? Kate hated coincidences.

Iqaluk meant money for some, subsistence and a centuries-old culture for some, politically correct kudos for others. If it had meant death for Enakenty Barnes, cousin, husband, father, fisherman, tribal leader, Kate Shugak was going to know the reason why. For just a moment she let the anger flare up and beat hot and hard within her breast. She didn't let it take over, but she tasted it, got used to the flavor, felt its strength. Anger, properly contained and channeled, was a good motivator and a useful tool.

Doors slammed and the ambulance pulled away. Kate put the anger in storage somewhere down deep inside and looked around with a cool, steady, detached gaze, a cop's eye that gathered in and stored information for later retrieval and evaluation. The blue-and-white was empty. Over its roof she saw a flash of yellow, and followed it between the garages and the condos to a back yard fenced with chain link and festooned with crime scene tape. The building had three floors. The second and third floor apartments had railed balconies; the first floor had unfenced patios. The roof was steeply pitched and shingled with cedar shakes.

A police officer stood in the center of the taped-off area, next to a spray-painted outline of a body, frowning over a notepad. He looked up at the crunch of Kate's feet on dead grass. "Ma'am, you can't come—" His eyes focused on her face and his voice changed. "Shugak? Is that you?"

"Sayles?"

He was tall and solid and looked bulkier than he was in his uniform. His face was a wedge of flesh and bone, his eyes were deepsunk beneath bushy brows and he had a smile like a piranha, all teeth and appetite. He strolled over to the tape and raised the pencil to push her collar to one side. He tsked over the scar. ''What's the matter, Shugak, you piss off somebody with a bad aim?''

She didn't move. APD Officer Steven Sayles knew the story as well as she did; he'd been first on the scene and had called in for the ambulance. He was probably responsible for saving Kate's life. She hadn't thanked him then. She didn't now. She nodded toward the outline. ''What happened?''

He looked faintly disappointed not to get a rise out of her. ''You related?''

''A cousin. What happened?''

''You got here pretty fast. How'd you hear about it?''

''You called the landlord to find out who he was. He called Enakenty's wife. She called my grandmother. My grandmother called me. What happened?''

He used the pencil to point to the top balcony on the end. ''A perfect ten in the Alaska Landings Swan Dive Invitational.''

''Jump or pushed?'' Sayles shrugged. ''Any witnesses?'' O'Leary shook his head. ''The apartment open?'' He nodded. ''Mind if I take a look?'' He raised a weary eyebrow and one hand, palm up, which she took for official authorization. He went back to his notepad while she went around to the front of the building. The front door was locked. There was a keypad next to the door and she pushed buttons until she got an answer. Kate identified herself as an investigator and a woman with a shaky voice buzzed her in. Two and a half flights up on the left, the door was open. Something crunched beneath her foot as she stepped inside.

The living room had a cathedral ceiling that stretched all the way up to the inside peak of the roof. The kitchen was small, the dining room smaller. There were two good-sized bedrooms and two full bathrooms. The living room had a sliding glass door, open. Kate crossed the living room and went out onto the balcony.

The overhanging eave of the roof was festooned with five

different sets of wind chimes made of glass, brass and wood. They hung motionless and mute in the still air. Sayles, busy with his notepad, didn't bother to look up. The railing came to Kate's breast. She was five feet tall. Enakenty hadn't been much more than five-three. The rough wood of the railing was spotless in a coat of smoke-gray paint. No blood stains, no broken slats, not even a footprint on the top rail. There was a barbecue filled with ash and a yellow-and-white plastic deck chair folded up in one corner. A door on the right opened into a storage closet, filled with empty boxes, firewood, a bag of charcoal, a box of Sterno logs, a bag of kitty litter and a bag of cat food.

Kate went back inside. The kitchen was completely furnished. All the cups matched the plates, the Revereware pots all had lids that fit and the white plastic utensils looked fresh out of Costco. The refrigerator contained a loaf of white bread, a package of English muffins, a half gallon of two-percent milk, a carton of eggs, a two-pound block of Tillamook Extra Sharp, a pound of bacon, a pound of pork sausage, a pound of butter and a jar of strawberry preserves. There were two whole pineapples. The date on the milk said it was good for ten more days. The jar of preserves hadn't been cracked. Neither had any of the eggs. There was a pound of unopened Kona Macadamia Nut coffee from the Lion Coffee Company in Honolulu in the freezer.

The guest bedroom was empty but for a full-size bed, a nightstand and a lamp. A copy of Donald Trump's autobiography was on the nightstand. A copy of Lee Iacocca's was on the shelf beneath. The closets were empty. The adjacent bathroom was immaculate.

Down the hall in the master bedroom, one half of the closet was given over to what Kate presumed were Enakenty's clothes. There weren't many of them, half a dozen plaid shirts, two pairs of Levis, three T-shirts with Crazy Shirts Hawaiian logos and a pair of bermuda shorts with neon fish swimming across them. The other half of the closet was so empty it echoed. The bed was made. Kate stripped back the covers and sniffed the sheets. They smelled like soap, and from the creases looked just put on that day. She looked for and couldn't find the used sheets.

The master bathroom was bare but for a single toothbrush, a tube of toothpaste, a bar of soap and a set of plush towels that matched the set in the guest bathroom.

Kate had stayed in Holiday Inns with more warmth and charm.

She came out of the bathroom and a spot of color behind the bedroom door caught her eye. She swung the door wide. On the floor behind it was a tiny puddle of red silk, which when Kate held it up seemed even less substantial than it had on the floor. It looked like a delicate lace bra with a pair of panties attached, of a size to fit a skinny thirteen-year-old. The last time she looked, Enakenty's wife Martha had been a robust thirty-seven.

Kate's hands felt large and clumsy holding the scrap of silk and lace, and she dropped it back down on the floor for Sayles to find and inventory.

Something crunched underfoot in the entryway off the front door again, and this time she stooped to look at it. Tiny grains of some white, rocklike substance, like they put in aquariums, only smaller and lighter. She wet a forefinger and picked up a couple and took them out to the balcony. The grains inside the bag of kitty litter matched those on the floor of the entryway. She bent over to sniff at the floor, and caught a faint whiff of old urine.

She went downstairs. There was a slender blonde just going out the front door. "Excuse me, ma'am?" Kate called from the landing. "Could you hold up a minute?"

The blonde was slender and pale with big blue eyes that looked on the verge of bursting into tears. She couldn't have been more than nineteen. She had moved into the bottom right condo the previous week, she was renting from the owner, she had just finished her training at Reeve Aleutian Airways, she was beginning a new job as a flight attendant the next day, this was her first very own apartment and she didn't know why this had to happen to her. Kate refrained from pointing out that it hadn't happened to her, it had happened to Enakenty, and said, "Did you see anything, Ms. Coffey?"

"No, I didn't, I got home from Carr's just after. There was an ambulance and everything. It was awful." She sniffled. "Why is this happening to me? Everything was so perfect! Why did this have to happen to me?"

"Did you know the people who lived in A304?"

The blonde shook her head and hunted through her purse for a square of Kleenex with which to dab at her eyes. "I just moved in. I'll have to get a new apartment now, I couldn't possibly stay here with dead bodies all over the place, and this one is so convenient to the airport, I'll never find anything—"

"Did you ever hear a cat upstairs?"

The blonde blinked. "A cat?"

"Yes. As in meow?"

Ms. Coffey blinked back tears. "Why, yes, now that I think of it."

"Lately? As in last night?"

"I don't know." The smooth brow creased with effort. "I got home late last night—we were celebrating our new jobs, you know—I don't—"

"Think about it for a minute," Kate urged.

The blue eyes widened. "Is it important?"

"It could be."

The smooth brow creased with thought. "I came in about one o'clock. I remember because I dropped my keys—" she held up a large bunch of keys "—and on this floor they make a lot of noise." The floor was of ceramic tile. "When I bent over for the keys I dropped my bag."

Kate waited.

The blonde brightened. "You know, there was a cat meowing from somewhere upstairs. I remember, I apologized for waking it up."

Kate was beginning to get the picture. It must have been a good party.

"Of course," Ms. Coffey added, "there are five other apartments that open onto this entrance, including mine. The cat could have been in any one of them."

Kate nodded. "Thank you very much, Ms. Coffey."

"You're welcome, I'm sure. I'm just glad I was able to

help.'' The blonde paused on the sidewalk outside the door, looking up at the kitchen window of A304. ''It must be nice living on the top floor.''

''I suppose,'' Kate said.

''Nobody walking on your roof all the time. And that one's on the end, too, so you'd only be sharing one wall with somebody else.''

''Yes,'' Kate said, edging away.

''Would you happen to know—''

''No,'' Kate said, and ran for it. She went back up the stairs, pausing on all three landings to knock at the doors of the other four condos. There was no answer at three, and no sounds of animal movement behind them. The fourth door was opened by a disheveled A and P mechanic who had just come off the night shift with Alaska Airlines, and he was neither a cat owner nor happy at being woken up. Kate went back out to the yard.

Sayles had just risen to his feet next to the spray-painted outline and was dusting the knees of his uniform pants. ''Hey,'' she said.

He looked up. ''Hey yourself.''

She nodded up at the condo. ''You know who owned it?''

''Some property management outfit.'' He pulled out his notebook and flipped through the pages. ''Arctic Investors.''

''You talked to them?''

Sayles nodded. ''They have an office downtown. According to them, Enakenty Barnes rented it nearly a year ago. Hasn't missed any rent or been late paying it. Other than that, they haven't heard a peep out of him.''

''Nobody was in the apartment when you got here?'' He shook his head and tucked his notebook back into his hip pocket.

''What are you calling it?''

He shrugged. ''It'd make my life a lot easier if I called it an accident.''

Kate thought of the chest-high railing. ''Is that how you're calling it?''

He shrugged again, and Kate knew from the flat expression in his eyes that he'd reached the limits of his generosity. Indeed, he'd been positively helpful, for Sayles, and she was grateful. "You about done here?" He nodded. "Want a burger?"

They went to Gwennie's on Spenard Road, where Kate drank coffee and watched the burly police officer down two cheeseburgers, a double order of fries, and a large wedge of apple pie, à la mode. It was a small price to pay for a little professional courtesy.

"It looks like he just got there. There are groceries in the refrigerator but nothing's been eaten."

"He just got back."

"He's been gone? Where was he?"

"Hawaii."

"Hawaii," Kate said. That explained the tan and the streaked hair. And the pineapples and the coffee, and, she remembered, the shorts and the T-shirts in the closet. "In October? In October it's not been cold enough long enough to go to Hawaii." And then she said, "Since when does Enakenty Barnes have enough money to go to Hawaii? The Prince William Sound fishing seasons have been in the toilet ever since the *RPetCo Anchorage* spill." Ekaterina said nothing, and Kate said, "Okay, emaa, what's going on? What does Martha say?"

"Martha," Ekaterina said, her face empty of expression, "wasn't with him. She's still in Niniltna. She is flying in this evening on George."

"Oh." Kate thought. "Enakenty went to Hawaii without his wife?" Ekaterina nodded. "The kids stay home, too?"

"Martha said Enakenty said it was a business trip. For the North Pacific Fisherman's League's annual convention. He said they were paying his way, and he told her he couldn't afford to take the family along, and that they'd probably all be bored stiff anyway."

"Uh-huh." Kate would like the chance to be bored in Hawaii. She walked over to the window, which looked out on a cemetery. If she pressed her face up against the glass, she could see the Chugach Mountains off to the left. "Emaa. When did Sarah die?"

"Sarah died on September 12."

They both thought about this in silence. ''Two board members dead,'' Kate said finally, ''days before the AFN convention and the board meeting. Where the decision on Iqaluk will be made.'' Ekaterina nodded. Kate didn't like it, not at all. She framed her next words with care. ''Emaa. I hope you are in good health?''

There was a brief silence, followed by the unexpected and incongruous sound of one of Ekaterina's larger, louder belly laughs. ''Yes, Katya, I am very well.''

''Good,'' Kate said, disconcerted. ''Let's make sure you stay that way.

Ekaterina said, ''Katya, it is all too silly. I cannot think of someone wanting to kill me.'' She sobered. ''I cannot think of someone pushing Enakenty off a balcony. I cannot think of how someone could make Sarah's salmon go bad.''

''I can,'' Kate said. ''As many people as are—or were—in and out of Sarah's house? All somebody would have to do is drop by while she was cooking it, wait around for a free moment in the kitchen and pull one of the jars out before it was done. Or crack open one of the jars in the cupboard. I'd have to check with an expert to be sure, but I think it would only take a second, and then they could just sit back and wait for her to use that jar.'' She thought and added, ''Of course, they'd be taking an awful chance she didn't stir up some salmon salad out of the tainted jar for a guest or two. Or give it away to someone else.''

''Katya,'' Ekaterina repeated firmly, ''it is too silly.''

''Maybe.'' Kate was equally firm. ''But it is also convenient as hell.''

The old woman was silent, the momentary flash of humor gone, the flesh seeming to sink back into her skull. The skin of her face seemed weighted down with lines of care and fatigue. She rubbed her left arm absently, as if there were pain there but it would have to wait its turn.

''How about I run down to the drugstore,'' Kate said, ''and pick up some Heet or some Absorbine, Jr.? I'll rub it in for you.''

Ekaterina blinked at her, and Kate pointed at the old

woman's elbow. "Your rheumatism's acting up again, isn't it?"

Ekaterina looked down, seeming to realize what she was doing for the first time. She dropped her hand. "It is nothing. A small ache. It will go soon."

"Still," Kate said. "It won't take but a minute."

She paused at the door to look back at her grandmother, a short, sturdy figure standing all alone at the window, hand rubbing her arm now, wrist to elbow and above and back again, a slow, steady movement of which she was unaware. Her old brown eyes were staring blindly south, and, for just a moment, for the first time in her life Kate saw her grandmother as vulnerable, susceptible to distress, something less than sovereign and supreme.

The old woman shifted, as if she had felt the weight of her granddaughter's gaze, and looked around. Her eyes held their usual steady, self-possessed expression, and the moment vanished as if it had never been.

But Kate knew what she had seen. Emaa, she thought, shaken, what do you know? What aren't you telling me?

What, heaven help us, are you afraid of?

When they walked in the door that afternoon, Jack's face was grim and Johnny's eyes were red. The boy went straight up to his room without speaking, and Jack headed for the bottle of Glenlivet in the kitchen cupboard. He poured two inches into a glass and drank it down. He poured out two more without pausing.

"That bad, huh?" Kate said.

He tossed back the whiskey. "She told the judge I hit her."

"What?"

He looked around at her, and Kate very nearly recoiled from the barely restrained fury she saw in his face. "She says I hit him, too."

Kate closed her eyes for a moment. "Oh, Jack."

"Yeah." He poured out a third drink. "Johnny told the judge it was a lie. He told him he wanted to live with me. Jane said I was exerting undue influence. 'Undue influence,' that's a good one, she must have practiced for a week to get it to come out right.'' He drank and stood still, one hand gripping the glass, the other the edge of the sink, eyes shut tight. His face looked gray. ''The thing is, she sounds so goddam plausible.'' His eyes opened. ''Remember that baby raper we caught that time out in Eagle River? Remember how he almost talked us out of arresting him, until his neighbor's wife came forward and said he'd raped her kid, too?'' He shook his head and drained the glass. ''He had nothing on Jane.''

''The judge must not have believed her.'' Kate gestured upstairs. ''He let Johnny come home with you.''

''How long will that last? How long before Jane has him snowed, too?'' He would have poured out another drink if Kate hadn't reached around and taken the bottle from him. ''You're not my mother, Kate,'' he said through his teeth.

''You're right,'' she said, replacing the cap on the bottle, ''I'm your friend. If you want to get drunk, I'll be happy to pour them out for you, one at a time.'' She put the bottle back in the cupboard and closed the door. ''After the trial.''

Both hands gripped the edge of the sink now, and Kate watched his knuckles whiten. With a muffled curse he spun around and left the room, yanking at his tie. She stood where she was, listening to the sound of his angry footsteps going up the stairs. The footsteps paused. ''Johnny?'' There was no answer, and after a moment the footsteps continued on into the master bedroom. A door slammed.

Kate let out a breath she hadn't realized she'd been holding. With a hand that was less than steady, she rinsed out the glass and put it in the drainer to dry.

Dinner was a quiet meal. Nobody was very hungry. Afterward, Johnny went back upstairs. Kate and Jack sat in the living room, watching the news. Enakenty's death was mentioned, with the police listing the cause as a possible suicide.

Jack switched off the television. ''What's it look like?''

''Sayles wants it to be accidental.''

''Sayles? Was he there?''

''The responding officer.''

Jack rolled his eyes, the first sign of real animation Kate

had seen since he walked into the house that afternoon. "Bet it was fun meeting up with him again. He's never forgiven us for clearing up that armed robbery when he and his partner dropped the ball that time."

"Actually, he was okay," Kate said.

"How okay? Did he let you look at the apartment?" She nodded, and told him what she'd found. His brow creased. "Like a furnished hotel room."

"Except for the kitty litter and the cat food," Kate said. "Emaa says Enakenty just got back from Hawaii, and that he didn't take his wife with him." She paused.

"So?"

"So, I'm thinking maybe Enakenty didn't go to Hawaii alone."

"The cat?"

Kate nodded. "Enakenty lives—lived in the Park. He wouldn't keep a cat in Anchorage. Hell, this is the first I heard about him renting a condo here."

"So you think he had a friend who brought her cat with her when she visited." Kate nodded. Jack made a skeptical face. "Not what I'd bring along to an assignation with my lover, but oh well. Any witnesses?"

Kate shook her head. "I only talked to two of the five people who live there. One just moved in and hasn't had time to get to know anyone. The other works nights. They're both airline people, and I'd bet the other tenants will be, too. It's five minutes from Anchorage International."

"So, a lot of coming and going and probably not much getting to know your neighbors."

"No."

"Too bad."

"Yes," she echoed him, "too bad." The anger was still there, a solid presence in the pit of her stomach. She probed at it, the way a tongue would a sore tooth, and welcomed the sharp flare of response.

"How much?"

She understood immediately what he was asking. "Two cheeseburgers, a double order of fries and a piece of apple pie. À la mode."

Jack snorted. "Sayles went easy on you."

"Cheap at twice the price," she agreed.

That night in bed, she said, breathless, "Hey. Jack. Take it easy."

He muttered something. His shoulders were slick with sweat against the palms of her hands, his knees hard against the insides of her thighs. "I mean it, Jack." She pushed. "That's enough. It's starting to hurt."

He went still, his weight heavy on her. She pushed harder. He gave a sound that was half curse, half groan, and rolled to one side. She drew her legs together, muscles protesting.

They lay on their backs without touching, staring up at the ceiling. "I'm sorry," he said.

"I'm not Jane," she said.

His voice hardened. "I know who you are."

She rolled over to face away from him. He got up and went downstairs. A moment later she heard a cupboard door open in the kitchen and a clink of glass on glass.

When at last Kate slept the dream was back, the one with the children, bleeding children, crying children, abandoned, abused, forsaken children, their families lost to them, themselves lost in an impersonal system that all too often harmed as many as it helped. One child with dark, matted hair and a terrifyingly blank stare looked at her and through her, gone to a place where no one he loved and trusted could ever hurt him again.

She came awake with a start, her face wet with sweat and tears. Next to her Jack was still, too still to be asleep. Together in their separate hells, they waited out the night.

FOUR

WHEN KATE GOT DOWNSTAIRS THE NEXT MORNING IT WAS still dark outside. October was the darkest month of the year in Anchorage, worse even than November. November had less daylight but by then there was snow on the ground, a layer of white that reflected every source of light tenfold, porch lights, street lamps, the Budweiser signs in bar windows. This year the snow had kept itself to itself, high above the tree line. Termination dust, the Alaska name for that first light layer of snow on the mountains in late August, signified the termination of summer and the first accumulation of winter's dust, a dust that would remain there until spring roared in to clean house with a chinook wind in one hand and twenty hours of daylight in the other.

Kate stood at the living room window with her first cup of coffee, wondering if the snow had yet to fall even up on Hillside, south Anchorage's four-wheel-drive suburb.

There was a pressure against her knee and a furry snout pushed against her palm. Mutt looked up at her with wise yellow eyes that told her to relax, that winter was not so far away. ''You're right,'' Kate told her, ''but then you usually are.'' Mutt gave a deprecating sneeze. Kate ran a bowl of fresh water and found her a bone in the freezer.

An hour later Jack came down, his eyes bloodshot, what she could see of them because he wouldn't look at her. He poured himself a cup of coffee, the spout of the carafe rattling against the rim of the mug, and sat down at the kitchen table. She brought him a plate of sausage and eggs. He sat still, looking down at the plate, the eggs over easy, the sausage perfectly browned, the toast whole-wheat and dripping with butter. He almost gagged, but there was something more important he had to tend to than his hangover. She reached for a mug and he snagged her wrist. "Kate. I'm sorry."

She tugged against his grip and he released her at once. Johnny wasn't up yet so she turned off the burner beneath the frying pan and brought her mug to the table. "Can I drop you off at court today, take the Blazer?"

"We're not going to court today."

"What?" She looked at him. "Why?"

He looked at the toast and closed his eyes against the sight. "I don't know, the judge has to rule on a motion or sentence somebody or something. We're continued until tomorrow at eleven."

"So you're going to work?"

He nodded, and winced, one hand going to his head. Well, now, Kate thought. If Jack had to go to work, Jane probably did, too. A possibility presented itself, neatly wrapped and shining with potential. "So I'll drive you to work instead."

He nodded, more gingerly this time, eyes on his mug. She reached across for his chin and pulled his face up by main force. "Cut it out, Jack. You said you were sorry. I accept your apology. Let's leave it at that."

"I'm ashamed of myself," he muttered. "I lost my temper, and I lost it with you, the last person in the world I want to hurt."

"And I'm mad at you for doing it," she agreed, "but it's over now. Let it go." He opened his mouth as if to say more and she repeated, "Let it go."

She sat back and reached for the cream and sugar, her face serene. He watched her for a moment before transferring his gaze to his plate. The eggs didn't look quite as revolting as they had sixty seconds before. His head didn't hurt as bad, either. He reached for his fork.

Ten minutes later he sat back and patted his belly and burped. "Good stuff." He looked across the table at her. "Aren't you eating?"

She shook her head, a ghost of a twinkle in the back of her eyes.

"You made this huge breakfast all for me, knowing I would probably be too hung over to eat it?" he said, just to be sure.

She smiled.

He leaned over and grabbed a handful of hair. "Bitch," he said, and kissed her.

"Prick," she said, when he turned her loose.

"I resemble that remark." He put his dishes in the dishwasher and went back upstairs to shower and shave. Johnny still wasn't down, so with a mental shrug Kate put the carton of eggs back in the refrigerator. He would eat cold cereal and like it if he couldn't be bothered to get up on time.

She slipped up the stairs. Jack was still in the shower and the door to Johnny's room was closed. She tiptoed past it into the third bedroom, Jack's office at home, and tossed the desk for Jane's address. She found it on an old bill. She paused a moment, reading through it and then going through the pile she had found it in. Not only had Jack let Jane stay, rent-free, in their side of the duplex after the divorce, he had evidently been paying the utilities as well. She sighed and shook her head. Magnanimity hadn't worked. Poor Jack. There was something in bitches that just naturally zeroed in on the nice guys of the world and took them to the cleaners, every time. Of course the sons-of-bitches took more than their share of prisoners, too. It probably all evened out on the cosmic scale, but in Kate's view it was time for someone to shift the weights a little more in Johnny's favor.

She returned the desk to its previous condition and slipped downstairs again. Jack kept all his more expensive toys, the ones he bought, used once and forgot, in a closet next to the front door. In a very short time she found what was needed. A trip to the garage and she was ready. She might even be armed and dangerous. She hoped so.

Jack came briskly down the stairs, buttoning one of his favorite Pendleton shirts.

''Ready to go?'' she said.

''You'll have to take Johnny to school, too. He's missed the bus.''

''I'm not going,'' Johnny said from behind him.

Jack looked around. ''Yes, you are. Get dressed and get your books.''

Something in the tone of his father's voice told Johnny not to push his luck. He stamped back up the stairs and wreaked his disapproval on the bathroom door. Kate smiled to herself, glad and, she admitted, a little relieved. But then, no son of Jack Morgan was about to have his spirit broken by a little matter of parental malice.

Jack looked at her, a smile in his eyes. ''Convention starts today?'' She nodded. ''So you'll be downtown. Lunch?''

''Where and what time?''

''Let's make it late. One o'clock? Downtown Deli?''

''Sounds good.''

Kate dropped Jack at work and Johnny at school and drove to the Sheraton. Ekaterina was waiting for her in a booth at the cafe, a mug of coffee steaming unnoticed in front of her. The lines of her face seemed even more deeply carved this morning, the frown of her brow more strongly marked, as if she had not slept well the night before.

''Emaa,'' Kate said.

Ekaterina looked up quickly, and if Kate hadn't been watching for it she would have missed the expression of relief that came and went so rapidly in her grandmother's eyes. ''Katya. Sit down.''

She signaled the waiter and he brought a mug of coffee for Kate. ''You take cream?''

''Whenever I can get it,'' Kate said, and he brought some.

''You ready to order or you need a few?''

''I'll just stick with coffee,'' Kate said.

Ekaterina ordered a cheese omelet with white toast, and

the waiter collected the menus and went away. "Have you talked to Martha?"

"No." Ekaterina's wrinkled hands wrapped around the mug. She sipped, more for comfort than for taste. Her eyes strayed to the door. "She got in late last night. I called her room and told her we'd be—here she comes now."

Kate turned to see Martha Barnes threading her way through the tables. She didn't look quite natural since she had no children attached to her. A short woman, thick through the torso, she had beautiful skin the color of old gold and dark eyes dull with grief. Kate's memory had not failed her; that red silk scrap of nothing behind the door of the condo's bedroom would have fit snugly around one of Martha's solid thighs.

She came to the booth and sat down heavily next to Ekaterina, who put an arm around her. For a brief moment her head rested against the old woman's shoulder, drawing strength from the embrace, before she straightened and managed a smile with so much pain in it that Kate had to look away. "Hello, Kate."

"Hi, Martha. I'm so sorry about Enakenty."

The smile again. Kate hoped her flinch didn't show. "I am, too. He was a good provider. A good father. I don't know what we're going to do without him. The home mortgage, the boat payment, insurance—" She gave a helpless shrug.

"Was he insured?"

Martha nodded. "Yes, but not for much. And not enough to support us for long."

Kate thought of Martha's three children, and the anger that had never been very far away since she saw Enakenty's body licked up again. Someone would pay for this. She would see to it personally.

"I'll have to see if I can get a job in the cannery," Martha said, "but what with the bad seasons since the spill—"

Ekaterina's voice was deep and certain, no age or fatigue detectable now. "You'll manage."

"Of course." Martha's chin came up a fraction of an inch. "Of course we will."

Emaa will make sure of it, Kate thought, and looked across the table at her grandmother. Your children won't go hungry and you won't go homeless. Trust Ekaterina Moonin Shugak to take care of her own. Pride welled up in her. Kate didn't recognize it at first, but that's what it was, pride in her grandmother and in her grandmother's determination to make things right. She was a solid presence in a world that crumbled around the edges a little more every day, like a rock on the beach, something to hold on to when The Woman Who Keeps the Tides tried to pull you out to sea, something to hold on to while you waited for Calm Water's Daughter to succeed the storm.

The waiter came with a third cup for Martha. "No, just coffee," she said. "Thank you." She added two spoons of sugar to the mug, set the spoon down carefully on her napkin, and said without looking up, "He wasn't alone in Hawaii. He had a woman with him." A tear slid down her cheek and she ducked her head and swiped at her face. "Sorry," she said, trying to laugh. "Didn't mean to get all sloppy on you." Ekaterina squeezed her shoulder and Martha sent her a grateful smile. "I'm okay. Really. I knew he had a girlfriend. When he told me he was going to Hawaii for this North Pacific Fisherman's conference and I wanted me and the kids to come, he said the board was paying his way—" Ekaterina's brows drew together in a frown "—and that we couldn't afford me and the kids to go, too." She sipped some coffee. "So I wondered."

"How did you find out for sure?"

"Harvey Meganack's wife Betty called me this morning. Harvey was at the same conference." Martha's lips twisted. "Betty was with him. She saw them together all over the place."

Bitch, Kate thought. Not only did Betty call Martha to commiserate over her husband's death, she had to make sure Martha knew he was screwing around on her at the time. Betty was such a miserable person she had to make everyone around her miserable, too. She reminded Kate of Jane. "Martha, I know this is tough," she said, "but did Betty tell you what the girlfriend looked like?"

Martha shrugged. "White, brown hair down to her butt, perfect figure for a bikini, was all Betty said. Enakenty never introduced her, and she didn't talk much."

Kate nodded. There was a brief pause. "I identified Enakenty," she said. "You don't have to go down to the morgue."

"Thanks, Kate," Martha said. "I want to see him. I have to." She stirred more sugar into her coffee. "I don't think I'll really believe he's dead until I do."

The waiter brought Ekaterina's breakfast. She jellied a piece of toast and handed it to Martha. "You have to eat something."

Nobody said no to Ekaterina Moonin Shugak when she spoke in that tone of voice. Martha accepted the toast. Every bite took an obviously concentrated effort. She washed down the last of it with coffee and said, "There is the one thing I can't figure out."

"What?"

"What he was doing out on that balcony in the first place."

"Why?"

"Enakenty was afraid of heights." At Kate's look she nodded. "Yeah. He got dizzy looking over the edge of the dock in Cordova during fishing season. He could barely make himself go down the ladder to the boat at low tide." She shook her head and rose to her feet. "You couldn't have forced him out on a balcony at gunpoint."

But he might have been led there, Kate thought. It all depended on the incentive, and to what part of his anatomy it had been offered.

Martha refused a ride to the Egan Convention Center—"I just can't face all of those people yet"—and Kate and Ekaterina joined Mutt in the Blazer.

"The board didn't pay Enakenty's way to Hawaii," her grandmother said.

Kate waited for a break in the traffic to pull out onto Fifth Avenue. The light at Cordova was red and she stopped in the right-hand lane. "Are you sure, emaa? I've heard how the board gets with the discretionary fund sometimes. And as a board member Enakenty would have had access.''

''I am sure.'' Ekaterina was definite. ''He would have needed a second signature on the check, and Quinto Boone would have had to make it out.''

Quinto Boone was the Association accountant. ''He would have told you?''

Ekaterina nodded.

''You're keeping a pretty close eye on Association finances,'' Kate observed. If she'd been hoping for a reply she was doomed to disappointment. The light changed to green and they drove in silence, slowed by a city bus with a black and white paint job that made it look like a diesel-powered Black Angus. The title ''THE MOOOOVER'' was painted on the side, surprising an involuntary smile out of Ekaterina.

''You ought to see the one with Bart Simpson on it,'' Kate told her.

''Who?''

''Never mind. It's better you should not know.'' The bus stopped between E and F, at the Egan Convention Center. Kate pulled up behind it. ''I'll drop you off. I've got to run an errand.''

Ekaterina looked at her. Not a muscle moved in her face.

Kate sighed. ''It won't take long, emaa. An hour at most. I promise I'll come right back.''

Ekaterina kept her gaze fixed on her granddaughter's face for a full minute before putting her hand on the door.

''Emaa,'' Kate said.

Ekaterina looked over her shoulder.

''It might be interesting to find out just who did pay for Enakenty's trip to Hawaii.'' And for the condo in Anchorage, she thought.

There was a brief silence. ''Yes,'' Ekaterina said, and opened the door. Her legs too short to reach the ground, she slid off the seat and landed on the sidewalk with a solid thump. ''It would be very interesting.''

Kate's brows snapped together. ''Emaa? Do you know? Emaa! Talk to me, dammit!''

Ekaterina's broad back disappeared into the convention center. Kate sat back in her seat and fumed in silence for a moment, before slamming the Blazer into gear and peeling out into the traffic.

The side-by-side duplex was a single-story dwelling with a peaked roof and two carports. The lot was large which meant that it was an old one. There weren't that many large lots in Anchorage.

At one time a habitat fit only for moose and mosquitoes, the Anchorage Bowl was squeezed between Elmendorf Air Force Base on the north, Chugach State Park on the east, Cook Inlet on the west and Turnagain Arm on the south. It was a land-poor community and new housing developments fought Costco, K-Mart, Walmart and a few home-grown strip mall kings for rights to develop what little land remained. The eight-member municipal zoning board, seven of whom were real estate agents and all of whom were nominated by the mayor, himself an insurance salesman, zoned city tracts with gay abandon and no forethought. This resulted in abortions like Arctic Boulevard, where at one point a welding business dispensed acetylene, argon and CO_2 in happy proximity to an elementary school, a residential subdivision and several churches, not to mention a pair of busy railroad tracks on which vehicles were regularly hit by trains at four in the morning. But it made for a solid tax base, and that was all that mattered to the zoning board and the mayor.

The Dickson Street neighborhood had fared better. Dickson was lined with older houses on large yards filled with birch and mountain ash and honeysuckle and lilacs. In Jane's yard there was a chokecherry tree some twenty-five feet high, a veritable giant among Anchorage trees. It was neatly trimmed and the grass, still green in mid-October, had been recently mowed. The coat of paint, she knew from her sneak peek at the bills, had been applied only last fall. She kept going, down the street and around the corner, pulling into a driveway and turning around to drive back again. She stopped the Blazer a half a block away, killed the engine and reached over the back seat for the camera bag she had stowed there that morning. It was an old Canon, an AT-1, with an assortment of lenses. She loaded it with the roll of Tri-X she'd picked up on the way and after a few fumbling attempts managed to attach the telephoto lens. As expected the battery was dead, and she replaced it with the one she'd gotten when she bought the film. She shot a few frames, getting the feel of the camera. It had been a long time since she'd looked through a lens at anything. She hoped she hadn't forgotten how.

Both carports in front of the duplex were empty. Most of the driveways on the street were vacant as well, all the two-income families at work. Kate adjusted the lens and got a couple of shots of the duplex, the numbers of the address outlined clearly in large wooden letters next to the door. When ten minutes passed with no traffic coming down the street in either direction and no curtains moving in the windows of the houses facing the street, Kate started the Blazer, drove around the block once just to be sure and returned to Dickson to pull into the right-hand carport. She switched off the engine and got out of the car, the camera in one hand, closing the door behind Mutt. She didn't hesitate and she didn't look around to see if anyone was watching, having discovered early in her career that as long as you didn't look actively furtive, people tended to ignore you. Most of the time they were so preoccupied with their own cheating husbands, delinquent children and overdrawn checking accounts that they didn't see you at all.

She mounted the step to the porch and tried the handle. Locked. Without pause she turned and went around the house. The chain-link fence had a gate, unlocked. In the back, the fence divided the yard in half. Each unit had a sliding glass door leading onto a small, shared deck. She climbed the steps to the deck and tried the right-hand door. It slid open smoothly. Mutt stuck her nose in and curled her lip. "Stay," Kate told Mutt, who looked relieved.

The sliding door opened into the living room and it was immediately obvious that Jane was not a dedicated housekeeper. The coffee table was lost beneath a pile of magazines and catalogues that spilled onto the floor. A plastic basket of unfolded clothes sat on one end of the couch. A television with a VCR on top of it and a cable box on top of the VCR dominated the room. Facing it was a recliner. On the floor next to the recliner was a plate with a gnawed pork chop bone on it. It went with the dust balls in every corner, the cigarette butts heaped in several ashtrays and the stained and matted carpet. The smell pretty much matched the look of the place.

Kate, who gave the word "neatnik" a whole new meaning, wondered if the squalor was due to Jane's natural talent or if she lived this way to spite Jack, making his property as unattractive as possible to prospective buyers. It had been Jack's home originally; he had moved out when they split up and had let her stay in the duplex rent-free so that Johnny would have a decent home with a yard to grow up in. Jane had repaid his generosity by contesting the title to the duplex when he had finally tried to put it up for sale. That case was on hold while the custody battle was being fought. Kate wondered how Jane was paying her lawyers. The litigation habit was an expensive one to maintain, and although Jane had a good job with the federal government, Kate was pretty sure it didn't pay that well. No job did.

She picked a fastidious path through the detritus to the door that led into the kitchen. The sink was stacked with dirty dishes. The table looked promising, piled high with mail, some opened, some not. Kate went past it and into the hallway that ended in the front door. She unlocked and opened the door for a look at the street. Silent still, silent all.

The bathroom was on the left of the hallway, Johnny's bedroom next to it. There was a single bed shoved into one corner, a nightstand next to it and a couple of cardboard boxes shoved under it with what Kate identified as Johnny's clothes dumped inside. A University of Alaska Anchorage Seawolves banner was tacked over the head of the bed. Two books sat on the nightstand, *Between Planets* and *Star Rebel*, but the nightstand was missing that essential of life, a reading lamp. Johnny must have read in bed by the overhead light, controlled by the switch just inside the door.

When he wanted to go to sleep, he'd have to get up and cross a cold floor on bare feet to turn it off. Kate was appalled. In her opinion, a reading lamp next to the bed was the absolute minimum required to qualify for a civilized lifestyle. An ironing board, a rickety rocking chair piled high with old *National Geographics* and *Catholic Youth* magazines and a copy machine filled up the rest of the room.

A copy machine. Jane's use of Johnny's room as a laundry and storage area while he wasn't there Kate found understandable, if tacky, but a copy machine made her ask herself what was wrong with this picture. She walked over to it and found the on/off button. It took a couple of minutes to warm up, but it made a perfect copy of Kate's hand when it did. She pursed her lips. What did Jane need a copier for? Kate would have thought the federal building would have all the copy machines Jane could wish for, and she wouldn't have to pay for supplies. There were three reams of paper on the floor next to the copier, one open and half the paper used, and a cartridge of ink. Kate stooped to look at them. Government issue, all right. There was no wastebasket, and no scrap of wastepaper lying around, in itself odd, considering the condition of the rest of the house.

The second bedroom, Jane's, was across the hall. The bed wasn't made. The nightstand next to it yielded a well-thumbed Bible and a tube of K-Y jelly squeezed almost all the way to the end. One drawer of the dresser contained an assortment of lingerie that gave Kate one possible answer to a question that had always puzzled her: why Jack had stayed married to Jane for as long as he had. There were several of those bra-panty things she'd found in Enakenty's love nest, all very skimpy, one of them with no crotch. Convenient. Maybe Jane was Enakenty's missing lover. Kate liked that idea, a lot, so much so that she wasted an entire minute speculating on ways and means of tying Jane into Enakenty's death. It might be an idea whose time had come.

In contrast to the rest of the house, Jane's closet was a symphony of carefully hung two-and three-piece wool suits in discreet hues of gray and blue and black in summer and winter weights. Among the suits hung shirts in white and beige. Half of them had floppy ties at the neckline, the remainder buttoned up to the top. All were made of silk, and all but one were still in plastic bags from the dry cleaners. All the shirts had Nordstrom's labels, which was what every label in each of the suits read.

Kate shuddered. She bought her jeans and jackets from the Eddie Bauer catalogue and her T-shirts, socks and underwear from the Hanes discount catalogue. The only time she ever went in a store was to buy shoes, having found out the hard way that you can't order shoes by mail and expect them to fit worth a damn. Nordstrom's was beyond her ken and she wanted to keep it that way. She went back through to the living room and opened the sliding glass door. Mutt looked around, expectant. "Give me fifteen more minutes," Kate told her. Mutt sat down with a disgruntled thump.

Kate spent the fifteen minutes sorting through the mail heaped on the kitchen table, uncovering an adding machine, a couple of well-gnawed pens and an Oreo cookie along the way. She ate the cookie while she used one of the pens to write down account numbers and card limits and anything else she felt might be useful on the back of an empty envelope. The bank statement was at the bottom of the pile and the balance in the checkbook opened her eyes. Ten thousand and change. Maybe she'd been wrong about the bureaucratic pay scale. Maybe she should hit Dan O'Brian up for a ranger job.

There was no evidence of a savings account, or investments of any kind other than the amount deducted from Jane's paycheck for retirement. There was a slip of paper taped to the bottom of the adding machine, where Jane could not fail to find it. Neither could Kate. On it was a word, printed in block letters:

WARDWELL

Wardwell was Jane's maiden name. A smile tugged at the corners of Kate's mouth. In the last envelope in the pile, another missive from the bank included a plastic card and a four-digit number, 9148. The smile widened and Kate shook her head and clicked her tongue. "Leaving the back door open, leaving your credit card bills and your password and your brand new cash card and PIN number lying around where anyone could find them? Jane, Jane, Jane. Somebody ought to teach you a sense of security."

Somebody was about to. She took pictures out of every window in the house and finished up the roll on the back yard, paying special attention to how the neighbors' windows overlooked the property. She was pretty sure she wouldn't need them but at this point everything was possible ammunition and Kate was arming for a long siege.

On the way out she paused at the pile of catalogues next to the easy chair in the living room. Considering the size of the pile, the risk was small that Jane might notice the absence of a few. Kate selected half a dozen, all with their very own 800 numbers.

Thirty minutes after she went into the duplex she was sliding the glass door shut behind her. Mutt trotted ahead to take the fence in one lope and was waiting at the Blazer when Kate opened the door. Mutt jumped up, Kate climbed in next to her, the engine turned over on the first try and thirty seconds later they were around the corner and out of sight, the street quiet and still behind them.

Kate looked over at Mutt. "It's a good thing for the law-abiding citizens of this state that we didn't go in for a life of crime."

Mutt panted at her, tongue lolling out of a wide, wolfish grin.

They stopped at a gas station, where Kate squeezed a gallon into the mostly full gas tank and used up a handful of the station's paper towels to scrub off the dirt she'd daubed on Jack's tags.

The first floor of the Egan Convention Center reminded Kate of nothing so much as the livestock barn of the Alaska State Fair in August, sans cows and with folding chairs instead of stalls. Enormous banners hung from the ceiling, decorated with beads and feathers and elaborate embroidery and appliques, each representing a Native region or subsidiary or tribe. She craned her neck to admire the Southcentral Foundation banner, beautiful in blue suede, white beads and eagle feathers. The Raven banner hung next to it, made of some black material with a dull sheen, lavishly embroidered in silver beads.

The chairs fanned out from a rectangular stage set up against the far wall and were divided into sections for each corporation. Signs on six-foot poles indicated what region; NANA from the Kobuk, Bering Straits from the Seward Peninsula, Calista from the Yukon-Kuskokwim Delta, Aleut from the Aleutian Peninsula and the Chain, Bristol Bay from Bristol Bay, CIRI from Cook Inlet, Sealaska from the Panhandle, Ahtna and Doyon from the interior, Raven from interior-southcentral-southeastern, and the Arctic Slope. It was a largely wasted ordering as no one stuck to their assigned seating, preferring to circulate and visit with friends and family they hadn't seen since last year's convention. There were at least a thousand people in the cavernous room, all talking at once and laughing out loud and, truth to tell, not paying much attention to who was addressing them from the podium on the stage.

Of course, there hadn't been much to listen to. The mayor didn't show, and the convention chairman asked him in absentia for forgiveness for all our parking tickets. The governor did show but considering the condition of relations between the state government and the bush villages shouldn't have. He made his usual pitch for the development of Alaska's natural resources and everyone immediately thought of the *RPetCo Anchorage* spill. He condemned the federal wetland policy and everyone immediately thought of the Copper River Highway debacle. He touted the jobs created by the Bering Sea fish processors and everyone immediately thought of the State Department of Fish and Game's closure of the Yukon River to subsistence fishing two months before, thereby eliminating the river villages' main food staple. He asked the audience if they really thought the government Outside knew better than their very own state government how to manage Alaskan resources, and several voices yelled "Yes!" He carried on, oblivious, and departed to very little applause, all of it polite and from elders.

One senator didn't show, the other did, and Alaska's lone congressman phoned in his regrets from a duck hunt in Oregon. The convention chairman recaptured the podium to introduce the assistant secretary for Indian affairs with a funny story about the last secretary's Alaskan visit, when they all stood around the runway waiting for "the great white father" to land, and compared him to the present secretary, a Native American woman, whom he referred to as "the big brown mama." She didn't stamp offstage in a huff, which Kate thought diplomatic of her, and spoke for fifteen minutes on vital issues like tribal sovereignty and subsistence, which was probably why people actually stopped talking long enough to listen.

But then speakers who agreed to address the convention were usually well aware in advance of their competition, which wasn't only shareholder conversation. When the proceedings broke for lunch at noon, the shareholders would stream outside for hamburgers at Burger King and then combat shop through the Fifth Avenue Mall on the way back to the convention.

And today was only the beginning. Throughout the rest of the week there would be pre-dawn raids on Carr's and afternoon assaults on Costco and evening attacks on Fred Meyer. They'd held the convention in Fairbanks one year, Kate remembered, resulting in a near revolt of the membership. What was the point of coming all the way in from the bush, on foot and by boat and snow machine and airplane and even a few diehard throwbacks by dog team, if you had no place to shop once you got there? It was not to be borne, and the next year the convention returned to Anchorage to stay, to the delight of local merchants and bush shoppers alike. It didn't hurt that the permanent fund dividend check came out at the same time. This year the PFD had been nine hundred and change, and Kate estimated that of the $475,000,000 cash money (representing one half of the yearly interest on the state's legislature-created, Prudhoe Bay-tax endowed Permanent Fund) distributed this year by the state of Alaska equally among its citizens, approximately half of it would be spent before the convention reconvened at one-thirty that afternoon.

If a disinterested onlooker didn't know better, they might think the annual Alaska Federation of Natives annual convention served no greater purpose than to provide a forum for long-lost friends and relatives to catch up on the news, and as an excuse to come to Anchorage and shop. To talk and to shop, Kate thought with a mental grin, that's our motto and we're sticking to it. On that note she waited until the dais was between speakers and took herself downstairs, where a crafts fair took up the entire basement of the convention center. There were tables jammed up against every wall and in lines down the center of the room, leaving very little space left over for customers, who jammed themselves in anyway. The room was redolent of the smoky, slightly acrid aroma of cured animal skins. There were seal mukluks, beaver hats, pelts of bear and strips of baleen, jewelry made of wood and antler and bone and ivory and beads and silver, kuspuks made of corduroy and trimmed with gold braid and edged with wolf and marten and mink, ivory carvings of whales and bears and seals and—oh. Kate halted, not moving even when three or four people bumped into her. She let them walk around.

There were a dozen ivory carvings on the table in front of her, no more. Some were walrus tusk, white and smooth and creamy. Others were of fossil ivory, yellow and cracked with age. There was a gray whale not five inches long, a solid presence with graceful flukes. There was a seal, skin stretched taut over round belly, sleeping in the sun on the ice next to his hole. There was a polar bear stalking another seal, smooth cunning in the set of his head, blunt menace in every line of his muscular body. And there was a kayak, paddle at rest across the thwarts, a tiny seal anua fixed to the bow, a hunter in a visor and gut tunic sitting amidships, spear upraised in one taut and steady arm. It was a study in patient vigilance, a portrait of cultural history, and the finest example of the carver's art Kate had ever seen.

She raised her eyes. The man seated behind the table was

thin to the point of emaciation and had bright, brown eyes surrounded by a mass of wrinkles that shifted with every change of expression. His blue plaid shirt was buttoned up to the collar and down to the cuffs and the flannel material folded in around his bones. He had a full head of hair, some of it still black, combed flat against his skull, making his cheekbones seem pointed and more prominent than they actually were, giving him a sculpted look that resembled his work. A boy with the same cheekbones and plaid shirt stood next to him. The old man said something, Kate thought in Yupik. She shook her head. "I'm sorry, uncle, I have no Yupik."

He seemed to sigh. "You like?" he said, with a nod at the table.

She nodded in return. "I like." She touched the kayak gently, as much to see if it was real as anything else. She pulled out the tiny bag that never left her pocket and produced a three-inch ivory otter, standing on his hind legs, balanced on the thick curve of his tail, head cocked, fur sleek with water, black eyes bright, whiskers quivering with curiosity. He held his front paws just so at his breast, ready to drop down on all fours to scamper to the water's edge and plunge in. She set him on the table.

The old man took one look and said, "Wilson Oozeva."

She nodded, unsurprised. Carvers often recognized work by others. They admired the otter together, the hum of conversation swirling around them. Other shoppers paused to look and passed on. She shifted her gaze to the kayak and the hunter, touching the visor with a reverent finger.

He watched her, bright eyes curious. "What does this one have, that pleases you so much?"

She was silent for a moment. "Anua," she said. "It has anua, spirit." She raised her eyes from the carving and said gently, "You shouldn't sell it, uncle."

He gave an almost imperceptible shrug. That shrug could mean he needed the money to eat. It could mean that he needed the money to drink. It could mean that he needed the money to buy more ivory to make more carvings, or to send his grandson to school.

"I'll tell you what, uncle," she said. "I will buy it from you. But you keep it for me." She saw the instinctive rejection in his expression and improvised. "You keep this one, and make me another one."

He was silent. "You keep this one, uncle," she repeated, "and you make me another one and send it to me. Later, sometime, you could give this one to—maybe to a granddaughter?" She smiled at the boy. "Or perhaps your grandson's wife? Someone who sees in it what you see." She stretched out a hand and nudged the kayak a little closer to him, a little farther away from her. "Put it away, uncle. Please?"

His eyes lowered from her face to the kayak. "What kind of carving you want?" he said finally.

She picked up her otter and looked at it, her thumb rubbing over his water-soaked fur. "Whatever the ivory shows you," she said, and put the otter back in its bag and the bag back in her pocket. She waited while the boy removed the kayak from the table and put it in a box before going in search of a cash machine. Jane's cash card and PIN number worked right the first time. The machine spit out cash, card and receipt. Modern technology was a wonderful thing. Kate couldn't understand why some people were so afraid of it.

She left the receipt in hopes a larcenous technophile would find it and use it to further deplete Jane's bank account, and walked over to the pay phone she had passed on the way to the cash machine. She pulled the rolled-up catalogue from her hip pocket. The 800 number rang once before picking up. "Hello, Eddie Bauer? I'd like to order a few items from your latest catalogue. Sorry? Which credit card would I like to use?" She smiled. "American Express. Ready for the number?" She gave it to them, along with the expiration date, and confirmed the Dickson address they already had on file from previous orders. Thumbing through the pages of the catalogue, she proceeded to order a pair of velvet dress pants for $108, a down jacket for $250, good to twenty below, three dresses between $75 and $150 each, a pair of black suede flats and a pair of Rockport brogues.

To instruct Jane in the art of authentic malice, Kate gave

Jane's dress size as sixteen and her shoe size at four and a half, and was pleased to hear that all items were in stock and would be shipped in seven to ten days. She thought about requesting FedEx next-day air instead, and came to the reluctant decision that tomorrow was too soon for packages to be arriving on Jane's doorstep, thereby alerting her to the shopping spree being undertaken on her unknowing behalf. Kate had other purchases to make.

She hung up and went back downstairs to complete her transaction with the old man. When she gave her name and address to the boy to ship the new carving to, the old man gave her a sharp look. ''Ekaterina Shugak is your grandmother?'' She nodded. The pen paused, the boy looking from the old man to Kate and back again. After a moment the old man grunted, giving Kate no clue as to whether he saw the relationship as good or bad, and the boy finished writing down the address. ''Thank you, uncle,'' she said, inclining her head in his direction.

Ten steps from his table, a voice at her elbow said, ''What makes you so sure he won't put the kayak back out the minute you leave the room?''

The speaker was a woman almost as old and almost as wrinkled as the old man but not nearly as frail and who barely came up to Kate's shoulder in height. A grin broke out across Kate's face. ''Olga!''

The two women embraced. ''Hello, Kate.''

''It's so good to see you,'' Kate said. She stepped back and looked around. ''Okay. Where is it?''

Olga played it cool. ''Where is what?''

''Where is your table? Baskets, right? Attu baskets? Where are they? I want to see.''

''You're awful pushy for such a young one,'' Olga grumbled, but she led Kate through the throng, growing in size and volume with every passing moment as the crafts fair drew in customers from all over Anchorage and the state, Native and non-Native alike. With every convention the reputation of the quality of the goods available for sale grew. By the afternoon, when most of the bush folks had arrived in Anchorage and with all the local hardcore crafts shoppers out in force, you'd be lucky to get across the room in under an hour.

This morning they made it in ten minutes, Kate getting momentarily sidetracked by a pair of fur-lined moccasins and a beaded hair band that would be perfect for fastening off her braid. Olga's table was presided over by three young girls sitting in a row, perched on chairs like little birds on a branch, hands clasped in their laps, round faces solemn. "Hello, Becky," Kate said.

The girl in the middle was very much on her dignity with the responsibility of her position. "Hello, Kate Shugak," she said, very composed, and spoiled the effect by elbowing her friends. "You guys remember I told you about Kate Shugak? This is her. Kate, this is Jeannie, and this is Norma."

"Hello," Kate said. The two girls smiled shyly and ducked their heads and said hello back in voices so soft she could barely hear them. "Where's Sasha?" she asked Olga.

"She stayed home." Olga smiled. "So many stories to tell here, she might go right out of her head."

Kate smiled, thinking of the squat little figure hunched over her knifestories in the sand of the beach at Unalaska. "You can tell her all the stories you hear when you get back."

"Those are my orders," Olga said. "What are you doing here? I've never seen you at an AFN convention before, I thought this time of year you were holed up on the homestead, dug in for the winter."

"I wish," Kate said beneath her breath. "I came with my grandmother."

"Oh?" Olga raised her eyebrows and gave Kate a long, speculative look.

"She asked me to," Kate said, and even in her own ears the words sounded touchy and defensive.

"Umm," Olga replied, which ambiguous sound could have stood for anything from approval to amusement. Kate was relieved when all Olga said was, "I haven't seen Ekaterina yet."

Kate's mouth twisted up at one corner. "She's probably still upstairs working the room."

Olga shouted with laughter. "Ay, that woman, she never stops. Well, what do you think?" She waved her hand at the table. "How did we do?"

The baskets were many and tiny, some no more than an inch high and an inch in circumference. All were exquisite, woven of tiny strands of grass, each with a painstaking design worked out in the same grass dyed blue and red and yellow and green, each with a tight-fitting lid with a tiny knob. "Rye grass?" Kate inquired, one eyebrow up.

Olga shook her head. "Raffia. Cheaper, and the tourists don't know the difference." She rummaged behind the table and produced a drum and a stick. "And we're making these now, too." She tapped out a brisk tattoo, grinning, and Kate stretched out a hand. It was a round of translucent skin eighteen inches across, stretched tautly on a circular wooden frame two inches wide. "Go ahead," Olga said, extending the beating stick. "Try it."

Before she could there was a tap on her shoulder. She turned. "Cindy," she said, surprised and pleased. The older woman, short and solid without an ounce of fat on her, gave her a hard hug, pleasure at the meeting sitting easily on her broad, flat face. "Olga, this is Cindy Sovalik from Ichelik, I met her on the North Slope this spring. Cindy, this is Olga—"

"Hello, Cindy," Olga said coolly.

"Olga," Cindy said, just as coolly.

"Oh," Kate said. "You two already know each other."

"Are you on the sovereignty panel this afternoon?" Olga said, not to Kate, but not quite looking Cindy straight in the face, either.

Cindy gave a curt nod. "Of course."

"I will see you there, then," Olga said.

It wasn't quite a clang of broadswords coming together but it was close enough for Kate. "Maybe we could visit later, Olga?" she said with a big, all-inclusive smile. "Where are you staying?"

"At the Sheraton," Olga said, still curt.

"Good, so is emaa, I'll call you there, see you later." Kate turned and shepherded Cindy off in another direction, any direction. "What are you doing here, Cindy?" she said brightly. "Are you selling your kuspuks?"

Cindy led her back through the crowd, so jammed in now that it was a slow, steady process of "excuse me, pardon me, excuse me, pardon me" all the way across the room. Eventually they arrived at a table presided over by a grizzled woman with an unsmiling face who grunted when Cindy introduced her and returned immediately to the cuff to which she was sewing a strip of beaver fur.

"How do you know that one?" Cindy jerked her head in the direction from which they had come.

"I met her in Unalaska last year."

Cindy's expression didn't change. "She sits on the board of her corporation."

"And you sit on your tribal council, I believe." Cindy stared at her, eyes fierce, and Kate said in a moderate voice, "Cindy, you both want the same things. You just go about getting them in different ways."

"We do not want the same things," Cindy said. "She is for ANCSA and the regional corporations. All she cares about is making money and paying yearly dividends to the shareholders. I say we should scrap ANCSA and go back to the old ways. I say we should make the state give us control over our own courts and our own schools and our own fish and our own game." She paused, and for a moment Kate thought she might spit in disgust. "The only thing ANCSA did for us was turn us into gussuks."

Gussuk was a Native Alaskan term for white people, roughly equivalent to honky or nigger. Kate was saddened but unsurprised by the vitriol she heard in the old woman's voice, by the divisions it indicated existed within the Alaska Native community. Through her mind flashed Ekaterina's face when she was telling Kate of the internal strife within their own regional corporation. She wondered how much Cindy's view of ANCSA had been colored by the time she spent working in the Prudhoe Bay oil field.

Many of the divisions between Alaska Natives came from differences in lifestyle; rural versus urban, northeastern versus south-central. A tribal council existed on a local level, usually as the steering committee of the local Native association, usually centered on a town or village. A Native corporation existed on a regional level and acted as the umbrella organization for the various Native communities within its geographical area. ANCSA, or the Alaska Native Claims Settlement Act of 1971, had provided for the formation of twelve regional corporations by geographical area and a thirteenth to represent those Natives living outside Alaska, to distribute nearly $1 billion and select and distribute forty-four million acres of Alaskan land among the Native peoples. During the last thirty-odd years, some of the regional corporations had flourished beneath the guidance of strong and fiscally talented boards. Some of them had not. Consequently, some of the shareholders of some regional corporations were happy with the status quo. And some were not.

Ekaterina, Kate realized now with a shock of recognition, must have to deal with conflict like this every working day, over issues like Iqaluk and a thousand others of which Kate had no knowledge. She was embarrassed not to have appreciated this before, and a little ashamed to feel relieved to be isolated from it, away off on her homestead. Not ashamed enough to run for either vacant board seat, however. The very thought was enough to stiffen her spine. At thirty-three, she had some idea of what she was and was not capable of. When she loved, she loved. When she hated, she hated forever. The rest of the garbage she could and did ignore. Like Cindy Sovalik, diplomacy was not one of her weaknesses.

A crowd was forming in front of Cindy's kuspuks and Kate let herself be elbowed to one side, until one of the elbowers recognized her. "Kate! Kate Shugak!" half a dozen people exclaimed, and the rest was madness. After thirty minutes of greeting distant cousins' newborn babies, several old classmates from the University of Alaska, Fairbanks, regional officers of CIRI, Aleut, Ahtna and Sealaska and village elders from Metlakatla to Toksook Bay, she became aware of Ekaterina working her way slowly around the room. Aha. Rescue.

Only it wasn't, because when Ekaterina finally did arrive she brought a retinue, and proceeded to introduce Kate to each and every one of them, very much in the air of an elder statesman introducing a promising young protégé. She accepted commiseration on the deaths of Sarah Kompkoff and Enakenty Barnes with dignified grace and no trace of emotion. Kate began to gaze yearningly toward the door. Unfortunately it was all the way across the room, there were about 346 people between her and it, and, at a deep, rock-bottom, atavistic level, she simply could not bring herself to snub her grandmother in public.

So she stood there, shaking hands until her fingers went numb, smiling until her cheeks hurt, nodding her head like the little doggie in the window. She hadn't seen this many people in one place since college. There was a reason she lived by herself on a homestead in the middle of the Park, and that reason wasn't that she liked crowds. Her heart was beating uncomfortably fast high up in her throat, and she longed for a breath of fresh air, even Anchorage fresh air.

The one good thing about her present predicament was that she got all the gossip. The biggest buzz, after the deaths of Sarah and Enakenty, was about Harvey Meganack's new house. Thirty-six hundred square feet, someone said, although someone else put it at forty-eight hundred, with a four-car garage and bathroom faucets plated in fourteen-karat gold, which last Kate found difficult to believe, even of Harvey.

On the other hand, gold-plated bathroom faucets would match the watch he'd been wearing at Mama Nicco's Monday night.

Rumor, that nosy and relentless bitch, also had it Billy Mike was running for public office, state senator for the Park district. Enakenty's Hawaii trip was generally envied, although the news of him not going alone didn't seem to have reached the general population as yet. It probably would by nightfall. Martha should have come this morning and gotten it over with. The leader of the Native sobriety movement had tears in his eyes as he spoke simple words of praise for Sarah Kompkoff, and Kate had had just about all she could take when Axenia materialized. "Hello—oh." She smiled, a real one this time. "Hi, Axenia."

Axenia didn't smile back, and the next thing Kate knew Axenia was standing between Ekaterina and herself, smiling and shaking and nodding with the best of the them. With true and sincere relief, Kate allowed herself to be nudged into the background. Ekaterina saw what was happening, and gave Axenia a steady, unsmiling look.

Axenia's color was high. She avoided Ekaterina's gaze and concentrated on exchanging family gossip with Diana Quijance and her two daughters, gossip she was certainly more up on than Kate was.

And then suddenly Lew Mathisen was standing before Kate and had her inescapably by the hand. "Kate, how nice to see you, ha HAH!"

It wasn't, but by then the smile and the handshake were on automatic.

"Kate, it's great to see you again, what's it been, three, four years, ha HAH?"

"More like thirty-six hours," she said, struggling unsuccessfully to free her hand. "We met at dinner Monday night."

"Of course, of course, ha HAH!" He leaned closer, the overpowering wave of Old Spice nearly pulling Kate under, and his voice dropped. "Just heard about Enakenty. Say, that's an awful thing. How is Martha? She taking the news about the girlfriend all right, I hope? I'm sure it was just one of those flings, didn't mean a damn thing. Us guys, you know how we are, ha HAH!"

Kate was afraid she did. She pulled her hand free and barely restrained the impulse to wipe it down the side of her jeans. She reached around Axenia and gripped her grandmother's elbow. ''Emaa, I've got to go, I'm meeting Jack for lunch.''

''Lunch?'' Lew said, all teeth and enthusiasm. ''Sure, hey, my treat. Where do you want to eat? Ha HAH!''

FIVE

BY ONE O'CLOCK THE LUNCHTIME CROWD WAS THINNING out at the Downtown Deli and Kate found Jack in a front booth. ''We've got a continuance until Monday,'' he greeted her, ''isn't that great?''

''What happened?''

''The judge is settling two other cases.'' He looked like one who has received a last-minute reprieve from the guillotine, which changed when he became aware of Kate's expression. ''You look whipped. Better feed you up a little, get that blood sugar up.'' He waved down a waiter and they ordered, Kate a Reuben with potato salad, Jack the deli special with a green salad.

''I feel whipped,'' she said, rolling her head, stretching her shoulders. ''I can't do this anymore. Not that I ever could. It's too much like work.''

''Work?'' Jack said, raising a skeptical eyebrow. ''What is, standing around talking all day? That's pretty much all the convention is, isn't it?''

''Work I said and work I meant. It's a performance, Jack. It's all a performance. Half the time I don't know what's real and what isn't. I don't know how emaa can tell, either.''

''It's all real to her, she's a born politician, she sees everything in shades of gray.'' He captured her hand and smiled across the butcher block table at her. ''Whereas you,

Katie, you're just a cop at heart, you see things in black and white."

She acknowledged the truth of his words by not instantly attacking them. "It would help considerably," she said, "if I knew who the hell I was supposed to be."

He threaded their fingers together. "What do you mean?"

"I'm not sure, that's the problem." She struggled to explain, the exercise as much for her own benefit as his. "Emaa sees me as the heir apparent, no matter what she says to the contrary. Axenia sees me as competition, I'm not sure for what, see above. Because I'm emaa's granddaughter Harvey Meganack sees me as the enemy, a tree-hugger and a posy-sniffer and a charter member of Greenpeace. Lew Mathisen sees me as a vote, a commodity, something to be bought and consumed. And," she added tightly, "everyone else sees me as Ekaterina Moonin Shugak's granddaughter, when all I am, all I want to be is just plain old Kate Shugak." Her head dropped against the high back of the booth and her eyes closed.

Jack looked at the still brown face across from his, at the closed, narrow Asian eyes, at the shadows lying beneath the fans of dark lashes, at the still, stern line of the wide mouth, at the shining black hair bound severely back in a French braid, and his heart, generally a more dependable organ, turned over in his chest. "You're just a cop at heart, Kate," he repeated. "You exist to serve and protect. Your problem is you want to serve and protect everybody, and you can't, and you know it. It's one of the reasons you lasted only five years in the department."

It was the second time in a week her psyche had been put under a magnifying glass by someone who knew her too well. She would have been offended if she'd had the strength. She would have pulled her hand free if his hadn't felt so warm and comforting in her own.

"You know what your problem is, Kate?"

She smiled without opening her eyes. "No, but I'm sure you'll tell me."

"Your problem is—" He stopped again. Some quality in his silence made her open her eyes and look at him. He met her gaze, took a deep breath and said simply, "Your problem is you don't need me."

"No," she said at once.

He let the breath out slowly. "It bugs me," he admitted.

"Yes," she agreed.

He surprised them both with a short, sharp bark of laughter. The sandwiches arrived and for a while there was silence at their table.

"You know that party emaa invited us to tonight?" Kate said, licking her fingers. Jack nodded. "I think I need to go."

"You what!" A piece of provolone went down the wrong pipe and Jack gagged and coughed and wheezed and gasped for breath. His face turned red and tears came to his eyes. He made so much noise that the guy at the next table looked as if he were about to offer to perform the Heimlich maneuver.

"Jack?" Kate eyed him cautiously. "You okay?"

He caught his breath. "You want to what?" he choked out.

"Well, I don't want to go, exactly, but I think I need to. There are some people I want to see that I haven't run into yet at the convention." What she really wanted, she thought, was to see who they brought to the party.

"*You* want to go to a *party*," Jack said, apparently having become hard of hearing in the last five minutes.

"Yeah," she said, brows coming together.

"A *party*," Jack repeated. He liked things clear. "With dress-up clothes, and music, and dancing."

She was starting to feel defensive and she didn't know why. Belligerence was always a good fall-back position. "So?"

He actually put his sandwich down unfinished, a sure sign she had his complete and undivided attention. "This party is at the Captain Cook."

"Yes."

"Am I to understand you want me to be your date?"

"You've got your own invitation from emaa," she snapped. "We can go separately if you want but we'll save on gas if we go together, yes. Well?'' she said, when he didn't say anything. ''You coming or not?'' He looked at her, and only then did she see the expression of unholy glee in his eyes. ''What?'' she said, suddenly wary without knowing why. ''What's the matter?''

He held up one finger. ''Wait right there.'' There was a pay phone in the back of the restaurant and contrary to orders Kate deserted the remains of her Reuben and tailed him to it, a good thing since he didn't have change and had to borrow it from her. ''Don't move,'' he told her, deposited the coins and dialed a number. ''Bill? It's Jack. How's that homicide coming, the kid they found up on Bluebell?'' He listened, his eyes going unfocused for a moment as he concentrated hard enough to forget Kate was in the room, no mean feat for Jack Morgan and one of the things she liked best about him. Kate found competence to be the single most compelling trait in a man, whether it involved lighting a fire with one match, gutting a moose without nicking the gall bladder, setting a drift net without getting it caught in the prop or conducting a murder investigation over the phone. Competence, and a deep voice, the deeper the better. A deep voice, in Kate's opinion, was good for a twenty-point rise in blood pressure any time.

''Look, Bill,'' Jack said, in a voice deeper than did ever plummet sound, ''that one dog brought home the mandible. So? So, does maybe another neighbor have a dog that might have brought home a bone? You know those people up on Hillside keep voting down police protection, they've probably all got packs of Doberman Pinschers and German Shepherds loose in their yards just in case some poor schmuck decides to go over the fence. Probably keep 'em hungry, too. The dogs, not the schmuck. We're missing the elbow down on the left arm, right? Okay, check the neighbors again, see if they've got dogs and if one of the dogs brought a bone home they maybe thought was from a bear or a moose or maybe another dog. Okay? Okay. Has the lab put the mandible together with the rest of the skeleton yet? How long before we get an I.D.?'' He listened some more. ''You sound like you've got it under control. Anything else come up? No? Good. I'm taking the rest of the day. Personal leave.'' He laughed and glanced at Kate, his eyes coming back into focus. ''You wish. See you tomorrow.''

He hung up the phone and very nearly rubbed his hands together in anticipation. The man looked ready to cackle. Maybe even crow. ''Okay.''

Kate put her fists on her hips. ''Okay, what? What the hell is going on?''

He tossed a bill at their waiter and pulled her out of the room and onto the street with such determination that Mutt had to scramble from her seat next to the *Anchorage Daily News* dispenser on the curb and run to catch up. ''If we're going to a party at the Cook, you have to dress up.''

''Dress up!'' Kate promptly dug in her heels. ''What? Why? I don't have to dress up, this is Alaska, for God's sake. You can wear jeans and a T-shirt anywhere you want anytime you want. I'm not dressing up for this party or any other party, dammit, Jack, quit dragging me down this goddam street!''

''Kate.'' He sighed and stopped. She yanked her hand free and nursed her fingers, giving him an aggrieved stare. The expression on his face was as sorrowful as hers was heated. ''How could you even think of embarrassing your grandmother that way? I'm ashamed of you. You know everybody puts on the dog when they come to town. Gives 'em a chance to strut their stuff. God knows they don't get much opportunity for it in Emmonak.''

She hadn't thought of it that way, and with a growing sense of apprehension realized that it was just within the realm of possibility that he might be right. The party at the Cook would be a proving ground, when town met bush and bush showed itself aware of fashions other than those constructed of caribou hide and trimmed in beaver and rickrack. He saw awareness dawn and tugged on her hand again. ''Wait!'' she said. ''Where are we going?''

''To buy you some dress-up clothes.'' He saw a flash of something in her eyes that in a lesser woman might have been identified as panic.

''Maybe I don't have to dress up,'' she said, getting desperate. ''Maybe I could go as a waiter or something.'' She warmed to the idea. ''Undercover. You could get me a uniform from Prop, you remember, like we did it when we went into the University cafeteria that time.''

''Kate.'' The amused indulgence in his voice made her teeth grit together. ''How many people will be there who know you? Who know what you do? Who know you came to town with Ekaterina?''

He was right. How she hated to admit it, but he was right. Her face showed it and Jack moved in for the kill. ''It's work, Kate, and you need work clothes, same as any other job. You wouldn't go on a winter hunt without your parka, would you?'' He hauled her to a stop at a red light. ''Well?''

''I guess not.''

''All right then. Let's go.''

''Where?''

''The only place in town,'' he said. The red hand changed to a walking man and he started across Fourth with her in tow. ''Nordstrom's.''

''Nordstrom's!'' Kate flashed back on Jane's closet, at the line of immaculate wool suits and pristine silk shirts hanging there with almost military precision. ''Jack! I can't go to Nordstrom's! I've never been inside Nordstrom's, not once, not ever! Besides, I can't afford to spend money like that on clothes I'll only wear one time in my life!''

''It's work,'' he repeated sternly, ''and don't whine about money, you've got plenty left from that job on the Slope last spring.''

She had more than he knew, she thought, remembering Jane's cash card in her pocket.

All too soon, Nordstrom's loomed up, brownstone-faced and imposing, on the corner of Sixth and D. To Kate, Sixth Avenue looked like the River Styx, and the glass doors of the store like Charon's boat. ''Sit,'' Jack told Mutt, and Mutt, with an expression of saintly resignation, sat down to wait next to the doors.

Nettled at this usurpation of authority over what was her dog, after all, Kate snapped, ''She can come in with us.''

"No," Jack said, holding one of the doors open. "She can't."

"Don't you want to come in?" Kate asked Mutt. "You can if you want."

Mutt lifted her muzzle in the direction of the open door, sniffed once and erupted in an enormous sneeze. Eyes wide, she looked from the building to Kate and back again. She shook herself once, all over, and sat down as far from the entrance as she could get without actually being in the street.

A woman in a fur-lined coat that swept behind her like a royal train sailed out of the store, bestowing a gracious smile upon Jack. She saw Mutt at the same time the light at the corner turned green, and crossed the street to avoid walking past her. Jack, still holding the door open, raised one eyebrow. Kate, abandoning all hope, entered therein.

On the other side of the doors it was even worse than she had imagined, a sea of gold-topped glass bottles and glittering rhinestones and patterned silk scarves and patent leather shoes, presided over by a herd of yuppies with perfectly white, perfectly straight teeth, all dressed to those teeth in glittering rhinestones and patterned silk and patent leather and scented with a cacophony of various odors from the gold-topped glass bottles.

No wonder Mutt had sneezed. Jack, with a numb, dumbstruck Kate firmly in tow, headed for the escalator.

Upstairs was worse. Upstairs there was nothing but clothes. Women's clothes, and not a decent pair of work jeans among them. Kate spied a café in the back. "Great! Let's get something to eat!"

Jack caught her, literally by her collar, and hauled her back. "We just ate," he said. He was grinning. It was a big grin, a wide grin, oh my yes, the man was certainly enjoying himself, probably hadn't enjoyed himself this much since he'd caught the now ex-FBI agent-in-charge drunk on Fourth Avenue behind the wheel of his own car, unable to explain the presence of the professional woman doing push-ups in his lap. Kate definitely bristled, and Jack was delivered from instant and total annihilation only by the approach of a sales clerk, female, lots of teeth, all on display, lots of blonde hair, ditto, lots of height, wearing a pin-striped suit over a cream silk shirt with a gold bar pin at the collar and discreet gold studs in her earlobes. "Are we finding everything all right?" She smiled kindly upon Kate.

It wasn't the "we," it wasn't even the kindly smile. Kate disliked being towered over by anyone, and in that moment she discovered that she especially disliked being towered over by blondes who looked like they would fit nicely into anything tailormade for Marilyn Monroe. Unaccountably, Jack did not appear to share in this dislike, and greeted the salesclerk with an expression that was half a drool away from outright salivation. "We were looking for some clothes for the lady," he said.

The sales clerk glanced at Kate for a nanosecond before zeroing back in on Jack. "What kind of clothes?"

He told her, in detail and at length, gazing with adoration into the big, blue eyes and hanging on every word spoken in the soft, breathy voice. With a disbelief rapidly succeeded by increasing disgust, Kate decided that if Jack had had a tail, it would have been wagging hard enough to power an electric generator. What was it with men and Marilyn Monroe? Even in retreat from the world on her homestead, just from the magazines she subscribed to Kate couldn't help being aware of the cult surrounding a woman who had, let's face it, screwed everything in pants on both sides of both oceans, only to kill herself at the age of thirty-two because, everyone seemed to agree post-mortemly, she felt used and lacked self-esteem. It was Kate's opinion that if she'd kept her fly zipped Monroe would have lived to be ninety, although it was her further opinion that Monroe would rather have been a dead legend than a live, faded ex-beauty queen any day. The only thing tragic men saw in Marilyn Monroe's untimely demise was the chance they'd missed to lay her.

By which it may be seen that Kate Shugak had no patience with the self-destructive. Neither did she have any patience with those who idolized the self-destructive, down to the beauty mark on their upper lips. Her chin, firm to begin with, became more in evidence. Jack, who hadn't survived a nine-year, on-again, off-again relationship with Kate Shugak without learning a few things, noticed the chin immediately. He broke off his conversation with his new best friend to say smoothly, "Alana, may I introduce Kate Shugak."

In lieu of Mutt, Kate bared her teeth. "Alana."

Alana smiled in a way that lifted the beauty mark on her upper lip several millimeters and Jack's temperature several more degrees, and said, just as smoothly, as if she and Jack had been rehearsing the first entrance of Ekaterina Ivana Shugak into the hallowed halls of this northern shopping Mecca for the past year, "Jack—" So it was Jack already, was it? "—Jack tells me you're looking for some evening clothes." Her eyes ran down Kate's body, and with what must have been either monumental natural restraint or excellent and intensive training did not faint at the sight of well-worn blue jeans and white T-shirt, accessorized by a Nike windbreaker and matching Nike sneakers. The scar on Kate's throat was observed, considered for a moment in context with available collar styles, and dismissed. "How tall are you, Kate?"

"Five feet one," Kate lied.

"Including the Nikes," Jack said, and she damned him with a glare.

"And what is your favorite color?" The question was accompanied by a smile of what appeared to be genuine interest.

Kate looked Alana—what kind of a name was that for a grown woman, anyway?—Kate looked Alana straight in the eye and said firmly, "Khaki."

Nordstrom's didn't hire its employees off the back of a turnip truck. The smile didn't waver. The immaculately coiffed head even gave an approving nod. "A good, solid neutral that goes with everything." The breathy but perfectly modulated voice dropped to a confidential murmur. Jack sighed a dizzy appreciation of the artistry involved, careful it wasn't loud enough for Kate to hear. "May I ask, have you had your palette done?"

Whereupon Jack Morgan had the rare and glorious experience of seeing Kate Shugak totally at sea. *"My what?"*

Jack bit his lip and stared hard at the opposite wall.

"Your palette," Alana said, irritatingly patient. "Your colors. Are you winter, summer, spring or fall? Khaki is a good color for you, yes, I can see it setting off your skin and hair, but I think a warm peach, or even a red, yes, a red might just bring out even more highlights. In fact, there's a little dress on this rack—"

"I don't wear dresses," Kate stated.

One impeccably penciled eyebrow raised ever so slightly. "Tuxedo pants it is then," Alana said without missing a beat. "This way." She wove her way through the racks and around a shopper scrutinizing the inside seam of something covered in gold sequins that Kate tried not to look at too closely.

"Here we are." Alana held the pants up for inspection. They were made of a heavy, dull black silk, with a thin strip of a lighter weight, shinier silk running down the outside seams. Kate took the hanger. The best that could be said was that they had pockets and a front fly. She held them up to her waist, and didn't even try to keep the triumph out of her voice when she observed, "I'm terribly sorry, but these seem to be about six inches too long."

"We can hem them for you," Alana said.

This time the triumph reached Kate's eyes. "I need them by seven o'clock tonight," she said gently.

Alana took the hanger from her and replied, even more gently, "We'll have them ready by five."

Jack started to laugh, caught Kate's eye and turned the laugh into a cough.

It went like that for the next hour, the longest hour of Kate's life. Alana was pleasant, knowledgeable and terrifyingly efficient. Kate loathed her. She loathed the first three tops Alana presented for her inspection, too. The first was covered with gold and black sequins. "I don't do sequins," Kate said. The second was peach and had ruffles. "*Ruffles*," Kate said, aghast. "*Ruffles*? Who do I look like, Rebecca of Sunnybrook Farm?" "You can see through it!" she said of the third top, and of the fourth she said, a little desperately, that the neckline of the beaded red jacket was too low, her bra would show. Whereupon Alana whisked them off to the lingerie department and produced a variety of skimpy brassieres that didn't look as if they would hold up a sneeze, let alone Kate's breasts. Jack, under the influence of the sight of so much silk and lace, lost his head and suggested underwear to match, since Kate's sensible, comfortable white briefs might produce a line beneath the silk of the tuxedo pants. It was immediately evident by the quickly suppressed horror in Alana's eyes that underwear lines beneath tuxedo pants were unthinkable, and a lacy pile of nylon bikini briefs appeared next to the skimpy brassieres.

Kate hated nylon briefs. The nylon felt clammy when you first put it on and then after it warmed up it felt as if there was nothing there. She hated bikini briefs, too, which had an inconvenient tendency to ride up into your crotch every time you bent over to pick reds out of a net. She did her best to explain this to both Jack and Alana, who selected bra and briefs and added them to the pile, unheeding. Kate caught Jack looking at a rack of those bra-panty-combination things she'd found behind Enakenty's bedroom door and in Jane's lingerie drawer, and snarled, "Don't even *think* about it." Jack tested the level of resistance in her expression and wisely moved on.

Shoes were next, and after five minutes Kate decided hell was a footie and the devil a shoe salesman. The devil in this case took the form of a young man named Garth with a lot of stiff brown hair, more teeth than John Kennedy, Jr., and a double-breasted, pin-striped suit so sharp you could cut yourself on it. Garth went into raptures over Kate's tiny feet and produced a pair of black spike heels carved from the carcass of some unidentified reptile, with toes that might have had enough room for the point of a pencil and an instep designed by the Marquis de Sade. "A pair of our finest heels," said Garth, beaming.

"To give you that little extra advantage in height," Alana said. She'd become remarkably adept at reading Kate's expression by that time and added, "But then, perhaps some of us are happy with our height the way it is.''

''I don't know about *us*,'' Kate said through her teeth, ''but *I* certainly am.''

Not one to give up without a fight, Alana said to Jack in the tone one used to confer with equals, ''You know, this pair would make the line of the pants.''

''The line of the pants will have to make it on its own,'' Kate said, still through her teeth. ''I have never worn high heels in my life, and I am not about to learn how tonight.''

Jack and his new best friend gave her a long, thoughtful look, exchanged a commiserative glance and compromised on a pair of black leather flats with a heel no higher than the soles of Kate's Nikes. ''The soles are too slick,'' Kate said, by then without much hope. Garth produced rubber heel and toe protectors and had them on the shoes before they went into the box.

Kate fought her way out of Nordstrom's finally and Mutt bounced to her feet with a joyous bark. Kate glared at her. ''Where the hell were you when I needed you?''

''Now the hair,'' Jack said, bags hanging from both hands, ''Alana gave me the address of her stylist.''

''What's wrong with my hair?'' Kate said, voice rising as they stepped into the street.

''Just a light trim,'' Jack said reassuringly, ''nothing major. Alana says your hairstyle is perfect for you.''

Kate stopped in the middle of Sixth Avenue. ''Jack.'' He stopped, too, eyebrows up in a mildly inquiring expression, thoughts focused on a vision of Kate future. ''Jack,'' she said, this time with more force.

He blinked at her. ''What, Kate?''

She spaced out her words, enunciating each syllable with great care. ''I Cut My Own Hair. I Just Did, Two Weeks Ago. It Doesn't Need Cutting Again This Soon.''

His brow cleared. ''Oh, we're just talking about a trim, Kate,'' he said reassuringly, ''even it up a little, maybe some conditioning, you know, to make it shinier, softer, more manageable.''

''Dammit, Jack!''

At that moment the light changed and three horns went

off, one for each lane of traffic. Jack, surprised, looked around. "For heaven's sake, Kate, what are we doing out here in the middle of the street? Come on, anybody'd think you were fresh out of the bush."

And the son-of-a-bitch had the gall to grin at her.

Twenty minutes later Kate found herself ensconced in a high chair at Winterbrooke Hair, immobilized in a plastic cape while Jack conferred with his second new best friend of the day, a trim woman with an artfully tousled mop of auburn hair and an assessing eye. They inspected Kate with the air of a pair of genetic scientists altering the latest in designer genes. Some mention was made of bangs. Kate caught Jack's eye with a glance that vowed castration. "Maybe not bangs," he said.

"An off-center part, perhaps," Jeri suggested, "to soften the effect?"

He brightened, whereupon the two of them plunged into a discussion of cosmetics. "What's wrong with Lubriderm?" Kate said, almost wailing. "It comes two bottles for twelve bucks at Costco, it lasts a year, why can't I just use that?"

They were relentless. Kate was shampooed, conditioned, trimmed and moussed within an inch of her life. When Jeri came at her with a can that hissed when she pressed down on the knob Kate panicked, snatched off her cape and stumbled out of the chair, her back to the wall. "What in the hell is that?"

"Hairspray. To fix the style."

"Hairspray my ass! Sounded like a frigging blowtorch you were fixing to light!" Kate headed for the door. "I am *out* of here."

Jeri, like Alana, was made of stern stuff. "Wait! I wanted to try this new highlighter I just got in from Paul Mitchell—"

Outside, Mutt looked her over with some alarm. "One word," Kate told her, "just one word and I'll turn you loose in front of a Fish and Game helicopter next fall." The Blazer was locked and Jack had the key. He was still inside, probably conferring with Jeri over the right way and the wrong way to pluck an eyebrow.

She took a grateful gulp of fresh air, the first in hours, or so it felt. Still no smell of snow. She'd bet her last dime there was some on the homestead, which was where she should be at this moment, not in this modern Gomorrah where the termination dust had crept barely halfway down the Chugach Mountains and no more. In the full light of day they looked half-dressed, their white robes up around their knees, and faintly embarrassed about it.

"You think you feel bad," Kate told them, "look at what they've done to me."

They didn't answer and she leaned back against the Blazer's bumper and shoved her hands in her pockets, watching the traffic and wondering how anyone could stand to drive in it every day of their lives. Winterbrooke Hair was a door off Northern Lights Boulevard, and four lanes of studded tires with no snow to grip buzzed down the pavement like angry wasps. The sound was hypnotic and she lapsed into a partial trance, staring unblinkingly at the Sears Mall and the people going in and out. A lot of them were Alaska Natives in rental cars and trucks, and she wondered if there was anyone left at the convention center for the afternoon panels. The panel on sovereignty, the one with Olga and Cindy on it, ought to prove lively, to say the least.

Sarah Kompkoff had been big on sovereignty, she remembered. "Our own laws for our own people," she had said once, just about the time the state attorney-general had gone into orbit at the thought of ceding so much as one degree of prosecutorial power, no matter how far out in the bush.

How had Lew Mathisen known that Enakenty Barnes had been in Hawaii with his girlfriend? Had Lew been in Hawaii, too? He and Harvey Meganack were acquainted, the dinner at Mama Nicco's had made that clear, but Betty hadn't been present that evening. She supposed Harvey could have told him, but it seemed awfully pat. Lew Mathisen was a lobbyist always available to the highest bidder; he was undoubtedly on some lumber or paper company's payroll, probably why he was buddying up to the one member of the Niniltna Native Association board who favored logging in Iqaluk. The North Pacific Fisherman's League could easily be another client.

The big question was if Sarah and Enakenty's deaths factored into the puzzle. Kate hoped like hell they didn't. She was greatly afraid they did.

Yes. She was going to be very interested in who brought whom to the party this evening. If new clothes and a new hairstyle was what it took to get her in the door, she would just have to suffer through it.

Which is not to say she wouldn't rather have been back on the deck of the *Avilda* in the middle of the Bering Sea in a twenty-foot swell, facing down three murderers.

"Kate!" Jack trotted down the steps. "Stop leaning up against that fender, you'll ruin your hair!"

That evening she stamped downstairs trussed up like a gift-wrapped ham. Jack was waiting at the door, his burly frame barely contained in his court suit, cleaned and pressed for the occasion. A white shirt and a brand-new bright red tie with no discernible food stains on it completed the picture. At the best of times his hair could only be described as unruly and tonight it stood up in dark curls all over his head, but he was clean-shaven and his shoes were shined. He looked comfortable. Kate was bitterly envious, so much so that she failed to notice the expression on his face when he looked up and saw her, fully assembled, so to speak, for the first time.

She couldn't miss Johnny, standing stock still between them in the middle of the hall, his mouth open. "Wow, Kate," he breathed.

The red bugle beads on the short, draped jacket glittered in the light, the tuxedo pants broke across the instep of the shoes at exactly the right length, her hair fell from the rhinestone barrette in soft, shining waves around her shoulders, no bra straps or panty lines disgraced her by their appearance, the leather of her new shoes gleamed and altogether she was a stunning sight. The scar across her neck was barely noticeable.

"Wow, Kate," Johnny said again, "you look—you look—" Words failed him. At twelve years old you haven't had a lot of time to work up a good line.

By forty-six you have, but at this point all Jack could do was hope that his tongue wasn't hanging as far out as his son's. His voice squeaked when he first tried to speak. He suppressed a blush by sheer effort of will and cleared his throat. "Where're the earrings?"

"They hurt my ears," Kate said, daring him to pursue it.

She didn't need them, he thought, it would only be gilding the lily. He cleared his throat again and didn't quite have the guts to offer his arm. "Well? Shall we?"

Mutt barked at her, a sharp, short, warning sound that startled all of them. "What?" Kate said.

In the living room doorway, Mutt lowered her head and growled. "Mutt?" Kate said. "What's the matter, girl?"

Mutt actually flattened her ears. "Mutt! It's me! It's just me! Jack! My own dog doesn't know me! Mutt, it's just me, it's Kate!" Kate held out a hand.

Mutt's lips curled back from her teeth, exposing a very large set of canines that Kate had never seen at quite that angle before. Others had, not her. She didn't move. Mutt gave her hand a wary sniff, looked at the vision standing before her, sniffed again. The lip came back down, and Mutt looked her over one last time, shining head to gleaming leather toes, gave a contemptuous and comprehensive snort, tossed her tail up in disgust and stalked into the living room to plump down in the middle of the rug with her back turned pointedly to Kate.

There was a short, charged silence.

"That does it," Kate said. Her hand went to the hidden fastening of the jacket.

Jack intercepted it just in time and Johnny scooted around them to yank open the door. As the babysitter, who had not the benefit of the before picture, watched in puzzlement, Kate was tucked securely into the Blazer and hied on her way to the Discovery Room of the Captain Cook before the first button was undone.

As has been said before, Jack Morgan was adept at reading Kate Shugak sign. His son bid fair to becoming a useful back-trailer, too.

SIX

THE CAPTAIN COOK HAD BEEN BUILT BY AN EX-BOXING champion who had come to Alaska after World War II to make his fortune in real estate. He lost the fortune and a good portion of the real estate itself in the 1964 Alaska Earthquake, and struck the right note with the citizens of the new state newly devastated by a 9.2 temblor by digging the foundations of a new hotel before the year of the quake was out. From the new hotel he went on to the governor's mansion, and from the governor's mansion to the position of Secretary of the Interior, where he lasted two years before President Nixon fired him for publicly opposing the conduct of the Vietnam War. He returned to Alaska and ran again for governor. It took him twenty years to get reelected, a great shock to the citizens of Alaska, who had voted in larger numbers to retain the decriminalization of marijuana than they had for him, a candidate who made Newt Gingrich look liberal. His second term was highlighted by a plan to build a water pipeline to California, another to ship chunks of Alaskan glacier ice to Saudi Arabia, and by an indictment for granting a state lease with very favorable terms to a building owned by his chief campaign contributor. The legislature failed to impeach, which did not come as a great shock to the citizens of Alaska, who had become inured to this kind of behavior in the thirty-five years since statehood.

Five years later the legislature even reimbursed him $302,653 for his legal fees, not much of a shock, either. He did fail of reelection, and nowadays occupied himself by running his hotel and dispensing political patronage at the behest of the present occupant of 1600 Pennsylvania Avenue. He'd always been skilled at keeping a foot in both political houses; it was good for business.

He, along with the current occupant of the governor's mansion, was very much in evidence at the Raven party. So were both U.S. senators and most of the legislature, Alaska's lone congressman of course phoning in his regrets from a duck hunt in Oregon, or maybe an elk hunt in Montana, no one was really sure. There were oil company executives and legislative aides and lobbyists from Russia, Korea and Japan rubbing shoulders with anyone who'd ever held political office in the last thirty-five years, or who'd ever been indicted for bribery, fraud and racketeering since statehood, which pretty much amounted to the same thing. The tribes were out in force; Yupik, Inupiat, Aleut, Athabaskan, Tsimshian, Haida and Tlingit, attired in their best bibs and tuckers and somewhat stiff and self-conscious in consequence.

There were two buffet tables loaded with stuffed mushrooms and boiled shrimp and raw oysters and cheese cubes and crackers and cubed cantaloupe and whole strawberries and olives and pickles and salad peppers. Two standing rib roasts were presided over by two chefs in tall white hats wielding carving knives the size of machetes. Before each buffet was a long line of people with plates. There were four bars with even longer lines in front of them. The sobriety movement was gaining momentum but there was still a long way to go. For every Native who signed the sobriety movement pledge there was another who backslid, and for every village that voted to go dry there were ten others who voted to stay wet.

Ekaterina sat in state at a table in the geographical center of the room, the focus of the longest line of all. Kate, standing in the doorway next to Jack and for the moment forgetting her silk, lace and bugle bead misery, looked across the room at her grandmother with a frown in her eyes.

"What?" Jack said.

"Nothing, probably. It's just that she usually works a room on her feet." Her grandmother looked exhausted, her face drawn and strained. Her spine was as straight as ever, though, even at this distance. She bestowed a gracious smile on the next person waiting to speak to her, appeared to listen to what he had to say with a complete and total absorption, and at the end of the audience murmured a few words that caused the man to back away from her with a proud, pleased and somewhat dazed expression on his face.

"So she's sitting down," Jack said, "she's had a busy day, and in the last month she's lost two board members, not to mention which she's about a hundred years old. You'd be tired, too. Let's pay our respects and then we can grab some grub. I'm starving. I never knew shopping was such hard work."

They walked inside.

Conversation, if it did not actually die, definitely slowed. Heads turned. Drinks paused halfway to mouths. Forks were suspended in mid-air. Hands touched shoulders, elbows nudged sides, heads nodded in their direction.

Well, in Kate's direction, Jack thought, always fair-minded. He didn't blame them. He felt a grin forming and repressed it. His ass was hanging out over the edge as it was.

Kate got three steps into the room before the first successful intercept. "Hello, Kate." The man stopped her forward motion by the simple expedient of stepping into her path and grasping her hand. She looked down at the hand, puzzled, and back up at him. He gave her a smile that reminded her of Alana, all teeth and pasteurized, processed charm. "Nice to see you again."

"Oh," she said. She vaguely remembered meeting him that morning at the convention, what the hell was his name? He worked for the state, didn't he, something in the Fish and Game. "Uh, hello."

"Mike Lonsdale," he said, "we met this morning."

"Of course, Mike Lonsdale," she said, adding insincerely, "nice to meet you again."

She moved as if to go around him. He held on to her hand so she couldn't. Surprised, she looked at him again and saw that he was considering her with an interest that was neither professional nor brotherly. There were two other men standing at his shoulder with the same expression on their faces, obviously waiting their turn. Uncomprehending and a little alarmed, she turned to Jack for guidance.

Jack, who had just discovered that dressing up your lady and taking her out on the town to show her off could have its down side, looked as if he had bitten into a fresh lemon.

It took Kate a minute to catch on. When she did, a long, slow smile, rich with mischief, spread across her face. Payback time, the smile said, as clearly as if she had shouted the words out loud. Jack's expression changed from fresh lemon to fingernail-scraped blackboard, and Kate's smile turned positively beatific. She turned that smile on Mike Lonsdale and his two friends, and as Jack watched in paralyzed disbelief, the three men gained a foot each in height, a hulk in shoulder-width and their palms covered with hair.

Kate's progress across the room slowed to a deliberate stroll. Jack was convinced there wasn't a man in the room who didn't scurry over to renew an old acquaintance, gain a new one or just plain slobber. Kate turned no one away. One idiot actually kissed her hand, another asked if she were staying in the hotel and if so what was her room number, a third invited her to dinner, lunch or breakfast, whatever she preferred, and expressed a preference for dinner himself, followed by breakfast later. She fluttered her eyelashes at the hand kisser, seemed genuinely to regret her lack of a hotel room for the benefit of the room number asker, and actually giggled at the guy who wanted her for breakfast. Jack wasn't sure he'd ever heard Kate Shugak giggle before. He stood it as long as he could before growling, "I'm going to get something to eat."

Her hand held in the sweaty clasp of an RPetCo executive who was trying earnestly to get her to promise him a dance later in the evening, Kate watched the rigid line of Jack's spine as he stalked off to the buffet with a satisfied smile on her face. The oil man requested her attention. "Huh?

What? Dance? I don't dance. Yeah, yeah, nice to meet you, see you later.'' She pulled free and threaded through the crowd to her grandmother's table.

Ekaterina looked around from a polite flourish of arms with a state senator and saw Kate. Her eyes widened. Her jaw might even have dropped. ''Katya?'' She fumbled at her breast for the chain which held her reading glasses and raised them to her eyes. The eyes, magnified by the reading lenses, blinked. *''Katya?''*

It was remarkable how an evening she had regarded as nothing more than a disaster in the making was turning into nothing less than joy unconfined. ''Emaa,'' Kate said with a bland smile. ''What a nice party.'' Just for the hell of it she bent over and kissed Ekaterina on the cheek.

Ekaterina reared back as if Kate had bit her. Her stunned expression indicated that she still wasn't entirely convinced of Kate's identity. ''You look—'' Ekaterina hesitated, and said doubtfully, ''—beautiful?'' It wasn't a word she'd ever used in connection with her granddaughter before.

''Why, thank you, emaa,'' Kate said, genial to the point of jocularity. ''So do you.''

And Ekaterina did, she looked elegant and gracious and dignified. Her dress was made of dull navy blue silk, buttoned up the front with ivory buttons, lace at the neck and wrists, the skirt softly gathered in graceful folds. Her hair knotted smoothly at the nape of her neck, she looked near enough like a queen to explain the reception line. Did Kate but know it, she herself looked near enough like a princess to double the line.

Ekaterina knew it, and pulled herself together. The startled look faded, to be replaced by something more appraising. The next thing Kate knew, she was standing next to her grandmother and bestowing identical gracious smiles and brief handshakes as each new and used mendicant, leech, moocher, parasite and even the occasional genuine friend and/or relative came up to pay their respects. It was the convention all over again, until she was cut neatly out of the receiving line by Mike Lonsdale, in hot competition with Porthos and Aramis. The three men did everything short of balancing a rubber ball on their noses to gain her attention. Not since the Shipwreck Bar in Dutch Harbor a year ago had she been the object of so much determined flirtation, and in the Shipwreck she had been in jeans and sneakers and able to hold her own. Silk and lace and bugle beads had the most demoralizing affect, but before she had time to identify it music sounded somewhere and Jack reappeared to grab her arm. "Let's dance."

"Are you kidding? You don't dance," she said, hanging back. "And neither do I, or have you forgotten that's the reason you fell in love with me in the first place?"

"Time we learned then," he said, halting in the middle of the dance floor to scoop her up into a comprehensive embrace. He was five foot sixteen, she was barely five feet and in their present position he was hunched over like Quasimodo while her toes barely scraped the floor. Quasimodo's idea of dancing was an inelegant shuffle that took them back two steps and forward one, with an infrequent quarter turn thrown in at random intervals just for show.

When she managed to unflatten her nose from his breastbone she gave him a smile so sweet he could feel teeth dissolving in his mouth and said in a voice equally saccharine, "The only reason I don't kick you in the balls is because we're the only ones out here and people would see." She smiled again, wider, showing all her teeth, reminding him of nothing so much as Mutt in a bad mood. "But don't worry. It'll keep."

Poor Jack was afraid that it would. The music ended and with fresh misery he realized that staking his claim to the first dance only proclaimed her availability for subsequent dances. Men, hundreds of them, thousands of them, hundreds of thousands of them, skulked at the edge of the dance floor, waiting only for him to turn Kate loose before they attacked. Even in the dim light he could see the gleam of fangs, the shine of saliva, taloned hands extending rapaciously out for his girl—

"Jesus Christ," he said.

"What?" Kate leaned her head back to look up.

His face was blank with amazement. "I'm jealous."

She grinned, and it was a wide, satisfied grin that took up her whole face. "No shit."

"I can't believe it," he said, still amazed. "I'm actually jealous of you. I don't fucking believe it."

"Me neither," she said cheerfully.

Their eyes met and they burst out laughing, so hard it brought them to a halt in the center of the dance floor. When Jack got his breath back he lifted Kate up off the floor to hold her nose to nose. "Who you going home with, woman?"

"I always dance with the one that brung me," she said, eyes crossed and solemn as a judge.

He let her down. "Good. Keep that in mind the next time that yo-yo shows up asking for your room number."

"I'll try."

"By the way," he said, as the music began again and others finally began to join them on the floor, "I don't believe I mentioned it before, but you look flat-out, drop-dead gorgeous. In fact, you look good enough to eat alive, which I intend to do as soon as I get you home."

She laughed again, and she was still laughing when somebody cut in and whisked her away. Jack, by damn, marched over to Ekaterina's table and said with a grin, "Ekaterina? Would you like to dance?" and she was so flabbergasted at his audacity that she found herself out on the floor before she knew what had happened. When Kate glimpsed them over her partner's shoulder, her grandmother was smiling up at Jack with what in the dim light of the cavernous room, looked like genuine affection. Kate didn't think her reaction to the sight would maim her dance partner for life, although for a while he did.

A deejay hired for the evening waded through a stack of CDs, everything from the Ronettes to Nirvana. The music went on nonstop and Kate barely had time to snatch a few bites of food between songs before another man shanghaied her out on the dance floor again. Somewhat to her own surprise, she discovered she was enjoying herself. Previously, all of Kate's dancing had taken place at potlatches and spirit days and other tribal celebrations. It wasn't that there weren't dances at high school; there were, but she had never joined in because she disliked being pawed and she had quickly discovered that pawing was what teenage boys were best at. The other dancing, the spirit dancing, the motion dancing, that was different. That kind of dance served a cultural and communal purpose, retelling a story, celebrating a birth, giving thanks for a good fishing season, summoning the spirits of the dead for a final farewell. It was danced without partners, or rather with many partners, as one of a group, as part of the whole. There was a reason they called it *spirit* dancing.

There were similarities between the two, she thought, looking around at the gesticulating, jiving crowd of rambunctious partiers, but there were more differences, not least of which the goal of this kind of dancing seemed to be to persuade participants into another activity, less spiritual in purpose and more horizontal in nature. Nothing wrong with that, Kate decided, and whirled from one partner to the next, laughing as she tried to keep off people's feet, her partner's and whoever else was foolish enough to wander into range.

Around ten o'clock, over the shoulder of her current partner, she saw Axenia swirl by in Lew Mathisen's embrace. Axenia was wearing black velvet cut down to here and up to there, rhinestones glittered from her ears and her hair was swept up into some elaborate superstructure that rivaled the cabins of some boats Kate had worked on. Far from shuffling, Lew and Axenia were dancing smoothly, gracefully, as if they'd taken lessons and had been practicing together. Kate wondered what else he was teaching her.

While she was watching, Lew saw someone, waved, whispered to Axenia and led her off the floor. Kate followed Lew's glance and saw a short, slender man whose three-piece attire could only be described as dapper. He had a mustache and a goatee and a full head of gray hair slicked back into a dramatic pompadour, a heavy gold chain stretched across his vest, and his patent leather wingtips were polished to an even higher gloss than Kate's. She recognized him at once. It was Edgar P. Dischner, an attorney who had ridden into town on the shoulders of the Kenai oil discoveries in the 1950s and had been involved in every shady speculation in Alaskan business and politics since. He had defended Governor Hickfield on his influence-peddling charge and had orchestrated the legislative payback of the governor's legal expenses, most of which he'd pocketed in fees. He was on retainer for a half dozen oil companies, he'd lobbied in Juneau against every oil tax proposed in the legislature and when his lobbying efforts failed he brought suit against the state in federal court, several of which suits were still pending but which pretty much everyone in the know confidently expected to be settled this side of a trial for figures not less than seven in number.

Mathisen and Axenia came up to Dischner. Everybody seemed awfully glad to see everyone else, and when two more couples joined the little group there was a tremendous amount of hand-shaking and back-slapping. One of the newcomers was Billy Mike, another Harvey Meganack, both with their wives. Betty wore a ruffled number that would have been more appropriate on a sixth-grader going to church and had applied makeup with a trowel, and Darlene, a sedate matron of some fifty-six years of age, sported tight-fitting, silver-studded black leather that was no doubt the latest in punk rock. She'd spiked her hair to match, spraying all the gray pink, and the expression on her husband's face whenever he dared look at her was worth all the pain and suffering Kate had incurred during her afternoon of forced shopping.

She wondered where Harvey had stashed the trophy blonde he'd brought to Mama Nicco's, and lo and behold the next man to show was John King, who had not mislaid his trophy brunette, or—Kate craned her neck to see—his mustard-yellow, silver-toed cowboy boots, either, which didn't match his double-breasted, raw silk suit. Tonight the trophy brunette was wearing a white dress with no back and a skirt like a tutu.

Wait a minute, Kate thought, amused and a little puzzled, when did I start noticing what other women were wearing? The answer was quick in coming. Since I walked into the room in an outfit that would look better on Tina Turner, is when. Good God, did wearing an outfit like this automatically put a woman into competition with all other women in the matter of dress? Amusement gave way to alarm. What if the effect was permanent? What if she spent the rest of her life comparing the way she was dressed to every woman who walked into the room?

"Uh, ouch?" her dance partner said, when her hand tightened on his.

"Oh," she said, loosening her grip. "Sorry."

"Don't worry." He smiled down at her and his arm pulled her in closer. "I liked it. Do it again."

Her left heel came down hard on his right toe. He winced. Space appeared again between them, and Kate took a deep breath and calmed herself with the reminder that she would be back in jeans and T-shirt by morning. Cold turkey, that was the only way to treat something like this before it got out of hand. The next step down that road was ordering from Victoria's Secret, a catalogue that came unsolicited in her mail which she had never opened but which, rolled and tied, made a great firestarter for the wood stove. She peered again over her partner's shoulder at the reunion taking place at the edge of the dance floor.

Edgar P. Dischner had noticed the ladies' attire. He bowed low over the trophy brunette's hand. She was tall enough and he was short enough that when he bent over her hand his forehead was very nearly in her cleavage. Neither of them seemed unhappy about it. John King was scowling, but that was his natural expression. Kate's partner turned them so that his shoulders blocked her view, and she shifted her weight to keep him turning so she could go up on tiptoe and look over his other shoulder, which wasn't quite what he had in mind when he'd started whispering sweet nothings in her ear halfway through "Smoke Gets in Your Eyes."

"Hey," her partner said—Will? Bill? something to do with the land department at Amerex—"who's leading here, anyway?" He smiled to show there were no hard feelings and snuggled in for the kill, only to find himself with an armful of air as she pulled free with a muttered excuse and headed toward the group at the edge of the floor. Jack waltzed by clasped in the torrid embrace of a redhead wearing a multicolored dress that fluttered in fragments from shoulder, bosom, waist and knee with every movement, kind of like the line of flags over a car dealer's lot fluttered in the breeze, only the flags were considerably more substantial. Kate caught his eye and jerked her head. With difficulty, Jack extricated himself from the redhead, who was half in the bag anyway and who teetered off on very high heels in search of someone else tall enough to lean up against. She and Kate's former dance partner were made for each other.

"What's up?" Jack said. She jerked her head, and he followed her gaze. "Well, well, well. Edger P. Dischner, as I live and breathe, and Lew Mathisen. And isn't that—"

"Harvey Meganack," Kate said with grim relish. "And Billy Mike. And John King again, who is proving to be downright ubiquitous."

"And Axenia." Jack looked down at her, one corner of his mouth quirking up. "Want to go over and say hi?"

Her smile matched his. "Why not?"

He crooked his arm. She fluttered her eyelashes and slid her hand inside. By the time the two of them reached the little group the grins and Billy's and Harvey's wives had disappeared and the handshakes and backslaps had deteriorated into a furiously whispered argument.

"You'll never get emaa to—" Axenia looked up and saw Kate and Jack bearing down on them. She elbowed Billy, who paled visibly when he saw Kate.

"Billy," she greeted him like her longest, lostest friend, "long time no see."

"Hello, Kate," he said with a weak smile. "You look great."

"Why, thank you, Billy," she beamed at him, and impartially around the circle.

"Shugak." John King was inclined to be curt, but his eyes widened a bit as he looked her over. The trophy brunette was clamped to his side, her smooth face showing no expression and her eyes as opaque and impenetrable as ever. Again, King didn't bother to introduce her.

Lew Mathisen was positively effusive. "Kate, I've never

seen you dressed up before, you look fantastic, you ought to do it more often, ha HAH!''

The brunette blinked once, like a lizard lying in the sun. Kate wondered if there was any there there.

''And this of course is Edgar Dischner. Kate Shugak, Jack Morgan.''

''We've met,'' Jack said, unsmiling. Like most of the Alaska law enforcement community, he'd been around the edges of enough Dischner cases to know the man was dirty, and to be bitterly resentful that he couldn't touch him.

Dischner was smooth and expansive, as he could well afford to be. ''Hello, Jack.'' His smile was full of calculated charm and no warmth. ''It's been a while.''

''Not long enough,'' Jack drawled.

Lew looked scandalized and plucked at Dischner's elbow. ''Edgar, we've got that meeting.''

No one ever shortened Edgar P. Dischner's name to plain old Ed, Kate noticed.

Dischner said, still looking at Jack, ''Relax, Lew. It's a party. Have a drink. Ask Kate to dance.''

''Ha HAH!''

Kate looked at Dischner from beneath her lashes. ''Ask me yourself.''

That surprised a real laugh out of Dischner, and Jack watched him lead her out with an impassive expression it cost a lot to maintain. He was afraid the bugle beads had gone straight to Kate's brain.

On the floor Dischner was short enough for her to look in the eye, which gave her neck muscles a rest, and her an excellent opportunity to observe his every expression. She smiled at him, after an evening of being pursued from one end of the very large, very crowded room to the other not unaware of the effect of that smile. ''Nice party.''

He smiled back, the expression not reaching the cold gray eyes. His arm did not tighten around her waist. ''Very nice.''

''Lots of people here.''

''Lots,'' he agreed, nodding to another couple, flashing a smile at someone else. Like Ekaterina, he was an expert at working the house. He could probably work an empty room if the spirit moved him. Over his shoulder she saw Harvey and Billy and Axenia deep in conversation with Lew Mathisen hovering around the perimeter. John King had been shanghaied by Jack's tipsy redhead and was currently holding her up two couples away. Jack was dancing with the trophy brunette, who was leaning languidly back in his arms and gazing up at him through her lashes, the large knot of dark hair pulling her head back and displaying the long-stemmed neck to distinct advantage. Jack's expression was wary but appreciative.

Turning to her own partner Kate took a chance, and said, "I understand you're something of an expert in Alaskan real estate, Mr. Dischner."

The smile was modest. "I don't know that I'd go so far as to call myself an expert, Ms. Shugak."

"No? Funny, I'd heard otherwise. They say you're one of Alaska's biggest property owners."

"Do they?" He threw in a fancy step and turned them to head off in the opposite direction, and by the grace of God she managed to keep up.

"They do," she said. "I was wondering—"

The smile again. "Yes?"

"Well, if perhaps you had heard anything of a firm called Arctic Investors."

His feet didn't miss a step but something flickered at the back of his eyes. "Arctic Investments?"

"No, Arctic Investors," Kate said. "Have you heard of them?"

"Arctic Investors," he said. A tiny line appeared between his eyebrows, to indicate how hard he was thinking. "No, I'm afraid I've never heard of it. Is it a local concern?"

"I believe so," she said, eyes wide and guileless. "It's a real estate and management firm, I think. They own various condominiums in Anchorage and the Valley and rent them out."

He raised his brows. "Were you thinking of investing?"

"Perhaps," she said. "If I could find the right property." She'd been on the Slope long enough, surrounded by enough wannabe entrepreneurs, that she could talk the talk if she had to. "I'd want a garage, of course, as well as good security. A woman alone can't be too careful these days."

Kate Shugak was not notorious for a timorous lifestyle but Dischner took this without a blink. "She certainly can't."

"But Arctic Investors doesn't ring a bell?"

"I'm afraid not."

"Pity." She smiled.

"Isn't it." He smiled back.

When the music ended Dischner bent his elegant gray head over her hand, expressed his gratitude and pleasure at their dance, his desolation at its premature ending, and looked forward with great anticipation to the next time before ushering her off the floor with all the panache of a courtier escorting a member of the royal family. It made a good impression on nearly everyone watching, the dignified, distinguished older man escorting the bright, beautiful young woman. Nearly everyone, that is, except Ekaterina, whose face was stony with a disapproval Kate could feel from fifty feet away.

"Really," Dischner said when they returned to the little group, "that has to be the top of the evening for me." He turned to Lew. "A few words before I head for the barn, Lew?"

"Of course, Edgar," Lew said. "You don't mind, do you, honey? Ha HAH!" He pressed a hasty kiss on Axenia's cheek.

They left. Axenia, a little forlorn, drifted off. Harvey and Billy hit the buffet. John King reclaimed his brunette and disappeared. Kate turned and met Ekaterina's condemning gaze with a cool, steady, unapologetic one of her own. To the surprise of them both, her grandmother's gaze was the first to fall.

The party began to break up at one o'clock, when the open bars stopped serving. Jack and Kate gave Ekaterina a ride back to her hotel, Ekaterina's attempt to take a cab thwarted by Kate's insistence that she come with them. By now Ekaterina was too tired to hide it anymore, and when they pulled into the Sheraton's driveway, Kate hopped out to open her door and escort her up to her room. Ekaterina leaned heavily on her granddaughter's arm all the way, and sat down on the edge of her bed to rub her left arm, her face weary.

"What's the matter with that arm, emaa?" Kate said. "You've been rubbing at it for days now."

Ekaterina's hand dropped. "I told you, Katya. A little rheumatism in the elbow. Don't fuss." She looked across at her granddaughter, brave in bright red jacket and black silk pants. "You do look beautiful, Katya. I was proud of you tonight."

In thirty-three years, it was the first time Ekaterina had ever admitted to being proud of Kate. Not when she had graduated from high school, not when she had graduated from college, certainly not when she had become the star of the Anchorage D.A.'s investigators' staff. Her voice huskier than usual, Kate said, "No more beautiful than you, emaa."

"Oh for heaven's sake, girl." Ekaterina looked exasperated. "Just say thank you, do you think you can do that much for me?"

"Fine," Kate said, annoyed. "Thank you." She raised her eyebrows in exaggerated inquiry, as if to say, Are you happy now?

Not quite through gritted teeth Ekaterina said, "You're welcome."

"Fine."

"Good."

They glared at each other. Ekaterina smiled first, a sudden, reluctant smile that broke the tension, and waved a hand. "Go on. Go home. I'm tired. I want my bed."

Kate hesitated with one hand on the door. "Emaa?"

"What?"

She turned her head to meet her grandmother's eyes. "This job I'm doing for you—"

The amusement on Ekaterina's face vanished. "Yes?"

"We may find out some things we don't want to know, about people close to us."

Ekaterina said nothing. Kate held her gaze for as long as she could. "Well. Goodnight, emaa."

"Goodnight, Katya."

Back at the townhouse, Jack paid off the babysitter, who thank God had her own car, and followed Kate upstairs, bent on seduction. Early in the evening he'd promised himself a long, slow removal of Kate's personally selected gift wrapping, one scrap of silk at a time, his reward for the longest evening of his life. He took the steps two by two, only to skid to a halt in the doorway, his face falling. Kate was down to her black lace skivvies already and was in the act of covering them up again with blue jeans and T-shirt. "What the hell?"

"Come on, shuck out of that suit." He didn't move, and she said impatiently, "Come on, Jack!"

"Why?" he said, trying and failing not to sound petulant. She stamped her feet into her Nikes and went to stand in front of the dresser mirror to pull off the barrette and bind her hair back in its usual braid. Disappointment gave way to foreboding. He swallowed, mouth suddenly dry, and with some trepidation said, "Where are we going?"

She rummaged through a drawer for one of his sweaters, a long-sleeved, navy blue turtleneck that hid the white of her T-shirt completely. Her voice was muffled as she pulled it over her head. "Dischner's office, where else?" Her head emerged and she pulled her braid free. She looked at him, rolling up the cuffs. "Well?" she said impatiently. "What are you standing around for? Go get the babysitter back!"

SEVEN

''KATE,'' JACK WHISPERED, ''THIS IS NUTS.''

''Like hell it is,'' she whispered back. ''Old Eddie P's been behind or involved in every crooked deal since statehood. Mathisen's the biggest influence peddler in the state. Those two alone in a room together make me nervous. Those two in a room together with Axenia, Harvey and Billy flat scare me to death.''

''Not to mention John King.''

She shook her head. ''He'd never get his hands really dirty, as RPetCo's CEO he's got way too much to lose.''

He paused, considering. ''It wouldn't be the first time a CEO overreached himself and wound up on the end of a criminal indictment.''

She shook her head again. ''King is a major pain in the ass but he's a straight shooter.''

''Dischner's probably on retainer for RPetCo.''

She snorted. ''So what? RPetCo spends half their waking hours in court with the state. It takes slime to beat slime. Keeping Dischner on retainer is only good business.''

He gave it one last shot. ''Nothing we find in there will be admissible.''

She grinned. ''Remember Morgan's Second Law.''

He sighed. ''Evidence First, Admissibility Second?'' She

nodded, still grinning, and he sighed again. "Sometimes I think you were too damn good a student."

"Besides, we're not trying to make a case here, we're just trying to find out what the hell's going on. Now quit stalling and pick that lock."

Two-thirty on a mid-October morning, even with no snow on the ground, wasn't Jack's favorite time to be hunched over the lock of a door of a Fourth Avenue office building. The bars had closed half an hour before but that didn't mean the odd drunk wouldn't lose himself on the way to the bus station and start trying other doors in search of a warm office lobby. At least Dischner's two stories of glass and brass wasn't big enough to rate a permanent security guard, although the sign on the window warned that the building was on Guardian Security System's evening patrol. He'd already by-passed the alarm system with a couple of alligator clips. At least he hoped he had. He wasn't as young as he used to be. "Kate, you don't seriously think Axenia . . ." They were at the back entrance and out of sight of the street but both jumped when a car started some blocks away.

"I don't know," Kate said, after the car had driven out of earshot. "All I know for sure at this moment is Sarah Kompkoff and Enakenty Barnes were on emaa's side on Iqaluk, and now both of them are dead. Axenia's hanging out with Lew Mathisen, and Lew Mathisen, the greasiest hand this side of Washington, D.C., is hanging out with one Edgar P. Dischner, who is on retainer with half the businesses in the state, and who contributes time and money to pro-development legislators the way some people tithe to a church. If there's something going on with Dischner and Iqaluk, I want to know what it is."

"And do what?"

"Turn it over to emaa," she replied.

Right, he thought, and almost yelped when a cold nose pressed against his backbone. He lost his balance and fell against the door. It opened and he somersaulted through, his butt and legs smacking down on the tiled floor of the lobby.

"Ouch." He sat up, rubbing his shoulder. "Mutt!" he whispered furiously. "Dammit, don't do that!"

Kate was still crouched outside, Mutt standing next to her, both looking across the threshold at him out of preternaturally grave faces. ''Oh ha ha, very funny,'' he said, ''get your asses in here before the cops decide to bust them.''

''You are a cop,'' Kate couldn't help but point out, only to emit a muffled shriek when he reached through the door and hauled her inside. Mutt bounced in behind her just before the door swung shut.

''What?'' Kate said to Jack, who hadn't moved and was staring at the door with a puzzled frown.

''That door was unlocked,'' he said.

She looked from him to the door and back again. ''What?''

He nodded. ''That's why it took me so long, I was trying to unlock an unlocked door.''

''Pretty swift, Morgan,'' she said. She pointed at a wall directory. ''Look, Dischner's offices are upstairs.''

He was still staring at the door. ''Why was it unlocked?''

''I don't know, Jack,'' she said patiently. ''Possibly because whoever was last out the door yesterday afternoon forgot to lock it? It happens. Now let's get a move on before the rent-a-cops show.''

He caught her arm. ''Wait a minute. Did you hear that?''

She froze, hardly breathing. ''Hear what?''

The only light came from an alcove containing the receptionist's desk. The three of them stood where they were, listening hard. Mutt's ears were straight up. Kate had one hand knotted in her ruff. The muscles beneath didn't move and she relaxed. ''Mutt didn't hear anything.''

''It was a bump or a thump or something.''

It sounded again, directly overhead. Already tense, Jack twitched in response, bumping into Kate, who knocked against Mutt, stepping on one of her feet. Mutt let out an involuntary yelp. ''Mutt!'' Kate said, and Mutt, hearing fogged by a bruised toe, misheard this as a command to investigate and streaked up the stairs.

''Mutt!'' Kate said.

''We're toast,'' Jack said.

From the second floor there was the sound of a solid

shoulder hitting wood, a door banging back against a wall, a loud ''Ooof!'' and a scream of pure terror.

Kate and Jack stared at each other with wide eyes.

''Oh my God! Nice doggie! Help! Oh my God!''

In the next instant Kate was up the stairs and down the hall, Jack faint but pursuing. The door to the corner office was wide open, and the light inside more than enough to adequately illuminate the scene.

Oh shit, Kate thought, halting in the doorway.

Oh shit, Jack thought, peering over her shoulder.

The man was spread-eagled flat on his back, surrounded by a drift of white papers and files. Mutt stood over him, lips drawn back from her teeth, a low, steady growl issuing forth, bared teeth inches away from his throat. She was probably embarrassed not to have heard anything downstairs the first time and was bent on regaining her reputation as the perfect sentry.

''Oh my God! Help! Nice doggie! Please don't bite me! Help!''

''What now, genius?'' Jack whispered.

''I don't know,'' Kate hissed.

''Nice doggie won't bite the nice man, will he! Oh god! Help! Somebody, anybody, please help!'' Mutt growled again and the voice faltered into a pitiful whimper.

There was something familiar about that whimper. Kate cocked her head.

''Call her off,'' Jack whispered.

''If I do he'll see us,'' she said, still trying to identify the man's voice.

Mutt's growl eased, and some of the man's courage returned. A quavering voice said pleadingly, ''Nice doggie, nice, nice doggie. You don't want to bite your Uncle Fred now, do you?''

Jack said in an urgent whisper, ''Call her off from the hallway and we'll make a run for it. Kate? Are you listening to me? We're fucked, let's get outta here!''

To Jack's astonishment and alarm Kate actually took a step into the room. ''Uncle Fred?'' she said in a carrying voice. ''Is that you?''

"Kate!" Jack's urgent whisper probably carried into the next borough. "What the hell are you doing?"

"Oh thank God, is someone there? Help me! Please help me! Nice doggie!" Mutt's growl rumbled in her throat. "Oh my God!"

"Mutt," Kate said. "Off."

The growl ceased. Mutt backed off the prone man and came to stand at Kate's elbow. The man sat up, breathing hard, his face a dull red and running with sweat. "Jesus," he said weakly. "Sweet Jesus."

Kate walked across the room and gave him a hand up. "You remember Fred Gamble, don't you, Jack? Fred Gamble, of the Federal Bureau of Investigation? One of J. Edgar's finest? As opposed to Edgar P., whose office all three—excuse me, Mutt—all four of us are in the process of breaking and entering?"

Gamble rose to his feet on legs that trembled visibly and released Kate's hand, looking from her to Jack and back again. "Morgan?" His face got even redder. "Jack Morgan, as in the fucking D.A.'s investigator's office?" He looked at Kate. "And Ms. Shugak, late of same?" His Adam's apple bobbed. He was so angry he was almost gobbling. "You sons-a-bitches! Would you mind telling me just what the fuck you think you're doing here!"

Mutt didn't like the way his voice raised, and the growl reappeared. Gamble's eyes shifted between Kate and Mutt and back again. "You keep control of that goddam wolf, Shugak, or I swear I'll have you arrested for assault!"

Kate, by way of reply, patted Mutt's head. Mutt's hard yellow stare never moved from Gamble's face and she kept her fangs on display but the growl eased up.

The agent swallowed and said, with a fair assumption of his former belligerence, "Now, like I said before, just what the hell are you doing here?"

The best defense is always a good offense, and Kate said promptly, "Just what the hell are you doing here, Gamble?"

"I've got a warrant," the Fibbie snapped.

"Oh shit," Jack said, repeating himself.

"Give me one good reason I shouldn't arrest your asses

and throw them in jail,'' Gamble said, his voice rising again.

Kate's knee nudged Mutt's shoulder. Mutt barked once, sharply. Gamble looked down to encounter the same hard, yellow, unwinking stare. He swallowed again. ''Then again, it wouldn't hurt to discuss the matter like civilized human beings.'' He pulled at his tie and unbuttoned the top button of his shirt as if the neck were suddenly too tight. He looked at Mutt again. ''Jesus!'' He grabbed for the chair behind the desk and sat down hard. ''As I've said before, Ms. Shugak, that is some fucking doorman you've got there.''

Jack shrugged and sat down across the desk. Kate took the chair next to him. Mutt gave a polite sneeze that nevertheless indicated her skepticism that everybody was friends now, and sat down next to Kate, a discomforting stare fixed on Gamble that he tried hard to ignore. Nobody said anything for as long as it took Gamble to get his breath back, which gave Kate time to look around.

The room took up an entire corner, about a quarter of the second floor of the building. Nearly every item in it was made of teak, the enormous desk, the base of the lamps, the coffee table, the clients' chairs, the frame of the couch and two walls of filing cabinets, even the frames of the uncurtained windows were teak. The floor was covered with lush white carpet. Kate couldn't imagine how Dischner kept it clean, but it matched the white leather cushions on the couch and chairs and maybe that was all that mattered.

On one wall was a Byron Birdsall triptych of Denali, which in daylight would echo the view out the north-facing windows behind the desk. On another was a Stonington watercolor of the Crow Creek Mine. On the desk were a soapstone carving of a bear and an ivory carving of a walrus. Kate was ungenerous enough to be pleased that both statues were clunky, amateurish and inferior to anything she'd seen at the convention crafts fair the day before.

The room reeked of money and one-stop shopping. There was no reflection of a life here, no personal mementoes, not even the framed diplomas usually so dear to the hearts of attorneys, as if they had to constantly remind themselves of their fitness to practice law. No, all this room said, indeed shouted in clear, ringing tones was, "If you have to ask how much I cost, you can't afford me."

After careful consideration, Kate hitched her chair closer to the desk and crossed her feet on its gleaming surface.

Jack had been doing some thinking, too. He laced his fingers across his chest and grinned at Gamble. "You don't have a warrant."

Gamble looked as startled as Kate felt. "Of course I have a warrant," he said, but he sounded uneasy.

Jack shook his head. "You guys work in pairs. Where's your partner?"

"Don't have one," Gamble said promptly. "Budgetary problems. Cutbacks. You know."

Jack shook his head again, still grinning. "Nope. Won't wash. Fibbies always go in two by two. Like the Ark."

Gamble gulped and this time the color in his face came from embarrassment.

Kate smiled at Gamble, giving it her best effort. It lost something in the translation from black silk to blue jeans but it was good enough to cause Gamble to very nearly begin to glow under the influence. Jack reflected yet again on the unwisdom of putting Kate into bugle beads. Who knew where it would end? He kept his mouth shut and watched the treatment take effect on a man who had once described Kate Shugak within Jack Morgan's hearing as being "as friendly as a double-bladed axe."

"I don't believe I had the opportunity earlier this year," Kate said warmly, leaning forward a little, "but I wanted to thank you for the reference you gave John King."

Her voice was low to begin with. The scar added a rough huskiness that when she chose invoked an atmosphere of intimacy. Gamble shifted in his chair like a snake in front of its charmer. "Yes. Well. Of course. I was happy to oblige. I heard you caught the perps."

"In the act." She somehow made it sound as if the successful completion of the case had been all his doing. He almost purred.

It was three in the morning and they were sitting in an office to which they had gained illegal access, located not six blocks from the Sixth and C police station. Jack, twiddling his thumbs, seemed to be the only one at present aware of that fact. He amused himself by adding up their respective sentences for the B&E. Kate would smile at the judge and be released O.R., Gamble would invoke executive privilege or some other federal nonsense and never have to call a lawyer, the pound hadn't been built that could hold Mutt, and he, of course, would spend the rest of his natural life behind bars. The idea didn't appeal to him.

"Yes, well," Gamble said again. Kate continued to smile at him, and he said apologetically, as if it were a matter in questionable taste he was forced to raise only under protest, "Do you think you could tell me what you're doing here?" As the words were spoken he seemed to recognize the pleading quality of them. The recognition stiffened his spine and gruffed his voice into a semblance of authority. "What I mean to say is, what are you doing here?"

Jack let Kate take it. The whole thing had been her idea from the start. "I expect for the same reasons you are, Mr. Gamble," Kate said, all concern. "I know, why don't you tell us what you're after, and we'll fill in any cracks?"

And Jack found himself suppressing a belly laugh as Gamble obediently complied. No wonder this guy had been posted to Alaska, where the breaking of federal laws usually meant somebody shooting a walrus on a wildlife refuge. A thought flashed through his mind. Or maybe the cutting down of trees in a prospective national park? He sat up to pay closer attention.

The Fibbie put his elbows on the desk and propped his hands into a steeple. He regarded them with a weighty frown. One felt it was a pose he had worked on in the mirror instead of the picture of the competent, judicious federal agent he no doubt felt he was portraying. We all have our little illusions, Kate thought. It wasn't her job to destroy his, and she schooled her face into an expectant expression.

"We're concerned over the influence Dischner and his associates are exerting over some of the Native corporations," Gamble said. The frown transferred from the steepled fingers to Kate's face. "I hope you will not take this amiss, Ms. Shugak, but there are certain—well, certain anomalies present in the dealings between the two."

Kate's nose almost twitched. "What kind of anomalies?"

He waved a hand, a gesture that included the files he'd been studying on the desk and the open file drawers they had come from. "Sole-source contracting, for one."

"Specifically?"

Gamble rubbed his nose and looked wise. "Were you aware that Mr. Dischner is a member of the board and part-owner of Pacific Northwest Paper Products? No, I can see that you weren't. Well, then, did you know that he is also a silent partner in UCo?"

Kate sat up straight in her chair, next to a no-less-startled Jack. "No, I didn't know that, either."

Satisfied with their reaction, Gamble gave an expansive wave of his hands. "I'm sure you see the potential for conflict of interest there."

"Not to mention kickbacks up the wazoo," Jack observed.

Gamble inclined his head.

Kate sat very still, lips tight and brows together, thinking fast and furiously. Pacific Northwest Paper Products was the company Ekaterina had mentioned as being interested in the Iqaluk logging project. UCo was RPetCo's major contractor at Prudhoe Bay, providing employees to do everything from wellhead cleanup to working ground crew for the charter aircraft to driving buses. UCo was the company she had ostensibly gone to work for undercover on the Slope the previous spring.

Dischner's piece of UCo was one explanation for why John King had been hanging out with Dischner at the party. But UCo also had a finger in every construction pie baked in the state of Alaska, everything from docks in Kodiak to utility corridors in Barrow to schools all over the bush. They were the lead contractor on the aborted road to Cordova, too, she remembered, aborted because of the careless and wanton destruction during initial excavation of approximately five miles of prime salmon spawning areas along the Kanuyaq River, which action had caused environmental groups to join with the Niniltna Native Association to successfully sue the state to halt construction.

In fact, nearly every questionable construction project to come down the Alaskan pike had UCo's hobnailed bootprints all over it. "Why am I not surprised?" she said out loud.

"Dischner and UCo," Jack agreed, "a match made in hell." Gamble grunted assent, and Jack added, "So, Gamble. What are you doing here, without a partner?" He raised his brows. "Or a warrant?"

Gamble colored and fidgeted. Kate smoothed out her furrowed brow and said in a gentle, reproving voice, "Jack. Think. If Agent Gamble can prove Dischner has exerted undue influence with local governments in the allocation of certain contracts, and if Agent Gamble can further prove that Dischner received remuneration in recompense thereof, it could result in federal charges against Dischner, as well as against his co-conspirators." She glanced at Gamble. "Who would have to include elected officials as well as contractors?" The answer was evident on his face.

Jack, playing along, said, "What kind of charges?"

Kate raised her brows. "Bribery?" She looked at Gamble again for confirmation and he nodded. "Extortion?" Gamble hesitated, then nodded again. "Fraud? Maybe even racketeering?" A third nod.

Kate's heart thudded once, high up in her chest. How much money were they talking about? Enough so that the threat of its loss would provoke someone to murder? She smiled again at the federal agent, putting her elbows on the arms of her chair and steepling her fingers to look at him over them. "My goodness me. Could we possibly be talking about tax evasion, too?" There was no hesitation this time, the nod was prompt, definite and vigorous. Oh God, emaa, she thought, what have we gotten ourselves into here? "Well," she said in a cheery voice, "is it time to call in the IRS?"

Jack said to Gamble, "None of what you find here tonight is going to be admissible in court. You don't have a warrant, do you?'' The Fibbie opened his mouth and Jack said, ''It would be easy enough for me to find out.''

There was a pause. Jack, Kate and Mutt waited expectantly for the answer. ''No,'' Gamble said reluctantly, ''I don't have a warrant.''

''So you're here on a fishing expedition,'' Jack said.

''Why the bear went round the mountain,'' Kate agreed, ''to see what he could see.''

''You're looking for something to pursue that will lead to a discovery of legitimate evidence,'' Jack said.

''Morgan's Second Law,'' Kate murmured, avoiding Jack's eye. ''Which legitimate evidence in turn will lead to a prosecutable case, with enough big names in it, perhaps, to merit Agent Gamble a promotion?''

''Not a promotion,'' Jack said, staring at Gamble through narrowed eyes, ''or not only. A transfer. Agent-in-charge somewhere warm.''

Gamble's mouth opened and shut, but nothing came out. His chagrin was so obvious that in spite of her worries Kate had difficulty in not laughing out loud. Jack had no such reservations. He grinned widely.

''A laudable objective,'' Kate said loyally, rushing to Gamble's rescue. ''Snow and ice and twenty below aren't for everyone, Jack.''

Gamble sent her a grateful look.

''Tell me, Gamble,'' Jack said irrepressibly, ''where do you want to be stationed? Miami, maybe?''

Gamble shuddered. ''No way. Too hot, and I don't mean the weather.''

''You want D.C.?''

''No.'' Gamble shook his head. ''Too many people scrambling for the same piece of pie.''

''Where, then?''

He mumbled an answer, and Kate said, ''I beg your pardon?''

''Omaha.''

''Omaha, Nebraska?'' This time Jack avoided Kate's eye.

In a kind of a furious mutter Gamble said, ''My wife's family is there.'' He read their silence correctly and said defiantly, ''It'll be good for the kids, they'll be close to their grandparents and all.''

''Of course they will,'' Kate said warmly. ''Omaha.'' She cast about wildly for something, anything appropriate to say. ''Don't they have great beef in Omaha?''

Gamble seized on it gratefully. ''It's one of the meat-packing capitals of the world.''

''There you are then.'' Her smile held more than a bit of steel and all of it for Jack. Heroicly, he swallowed his laughter and rubbed his hands together. ''Well, shall we get started?''

'' 'We?' '' said FBI Agent Gamble.

''There are an awful lot of files here,'' Kate said with persuasive charm. ''With three of us looking, it will take less time to go through them.''

Gamble considered her. Jack said, ''We're not trying to horn in on your case, Gamble. Kate's here on a family matter, and I'm just along for the ride.''

''What family matter?'' Gamble said, retaining just enough wit to be suspicious of any such thing, and coming far too late to the recognition that he had imparted a great deal of information without receiving any in return. J. Edgar would have cashiered him on the spot.

Jack again left this to Kate, who met Gamble's eyes with the frank, open expression of a born liar. ''Well, Mr. Gamble, it's like this.'' She leaned forward and dropped her voice, giving Gamble the impression she was imparting a secret so closely held that only he was worthy to share it. ''Raven Corporation, that is, my regional native corporation, has a great deal of construction going on at this time, and given Dischner's reputation my grandmother has become concerned that dealings with him might taint our organization.'' Kate sat back and spread her hands. ''She asked me to look into it.'' She smiled. ''So here I am.''

Gamble followed all of this closely, his mouth open in concentration. ''That's quite a story.''

Kate thought so, too, considering she'd just made it up this minute. Really, she thought, remembering the Susitna story she'd whipped up for Johnny, she was getting awfully good at this. Maybe even dangerously good at it.

Gamble hesitated.

"We'd better get a move on before the cleaning staff gets here," Kate said.

"They've already been and gone," Gamble said, making up his mind. "I had one of my people check on their schedule for me."

"What about the building alarm?" Jack said. "I thought I disabled it on the way in, but you'd fixed it already, hadn't you?"

Gamble gave a superior smile. "One of my people took care of it this afternoon."

Jack said to Kate, "I just love working with the federal government, don't you?"

The three of them rose to their feet. Behind Gamble's back, Jack mouthed, "Great beef in Omaha?"

Kate ignored him and followed Gamble into the file room next door.

Those files were extensive, covering nearly forty years of Dischner shenanigans and a multitude of sins. He sat on the boards of at least two local banks, had a controlling interest in a real estate firm, was a silent partner in the ex-governor's hotel and had percentages of oil leases from Cook Inlet to Prudhoe Bay. Gamble went from one file to another, uttering little cries of delight. Jack followed more slowly, looking for evidence less white collar in nature. He would have sacrificed a goat to Bacchus for the opportunity to charge Edgar P. Dischner, attorney-at-law and officer of the court, confidant of congressmen, senators and governors, with a felony and have the evidence to make it stick. He remembered a couple of trials with him on one side and Dischner on the other, and manufacturing evidence, suborning material witnesses and jury tampering leapt to mind as likely possibilities.

Kate, operating on the proven theory that in any office the secretary did all the work, went into the office on the other side of Dischner's and turned on the computer on the desk. She hadn't worked a computer in years, and had to ask Jack for help. The password was easy, the name of Dischner's first client for his first jury trial in an Alaskan court. It was Jack's inspiration, who had Dischner's client history memorized, and she was in without fuss. After that, it was a simple matter of calling up the directory, C-prompt DIR, and the screen scrolled rapidly upward with all the information anyone bent on felonious entry could wish for.

One of the files listed in the directory was labeled, helpfully, "Files." Kate accessed it and found the office's current case load, indexed twice, alphabetically by client name and chronologically by court date. Kate leaned over to turn on the printer.

Jack stuck his head out to look at her, his hands filled with file folders. "You're cackling like the Wicked Witch of the West."

Kate looked like the Wicked Witch when she smiled. "I'll get you yet, my pretty."

He gave an elaborate shudder and disappeared, looking not displeased himself.

Two of the largest files were Pacific Northwest Paper Products and UCo. She debated for a moment and accessed a smaller file to see how it was organized. It was basically a diary of events, and it included a code number. She looked at the number in silence for a few moments, and then got up and went into the file room and found the corresponding number on one of the many file drawers in the cabinet that was built into the wall. She had to stand on a footstool to reach the right drawer, but when she got it open the folder was right in front. Kate felicitated Dischner on his most practical and efficient secretary. She just hoped he paid her enough.

She went back to the computer and exited to the directory, starred the PNP and UCo files and waited for the printer. It hummed, and a minute later sucked up a sheet of paper from the feeder tray. She sat back with her feet up on the desk and scrolled more leisurely through the directory. She knew a moment of cold satisfaction when she found Arctic Investors, and gave the command to print it, too.

She thought again how wonderful modern technology

was. If she ever met Stephen Jobs she would kiss him on the lips.

In the meantime, not one to pass up an opportunity, she pulled a folded and much-creased envelope from her hip pocket and reached for the phone. Harry and David's 800 number, like Eddie Bauer's, answered twenty-four hours a day. Jane sent a year's supply of fruit to her mother, to Jane's boss, whose name Kate got out of the listing of federal numbers in the phone book, and to Archbishop Francis T. Hurley of the Catholic Archdiocese of Anchorage. Everybody needs brownie points, Kate thought, replacing the phone secure in the sense of a necessary job well done. Really, she was doing Jane a favor, getting her in good with family, employer and God.

She lingered for a few moments over the federal listings in the phone book, remembering that copy machine in Johnny's bedroom at Jane's house.

The next call was to the Elliott Bay Book Company in Seattle. Unfortunately, Elliott Bay lacked twenty-four-hour phone service. Kate put the phone down with sincere regret. She felt that Jane ought to have something appropriate to go along with the drawer full of underwear, say, the collected works of A. N. Roquelaure. Or maybe the Marquis de Sade. Why not both? She gave the phone a consoling pat. Next time.

The printer stopped chattering. She exited the computer, turned it off, reloaded the printer's paper tray and turned it off, too. Using the printout of file codes, she located the file drawer holding the paperwork on Arctic Investors. It held a lot of local addresses attached to numbers, mortgages and payments, repairs and maintenance, assets and expenses, profit and loss, but what it boiled down to was that the company had been formed in 1986 by Dischner and various partners, whose names were obscured by titles like Alaska Estates, Inc. Its primary assets were more than two hundred condominiums located in the Anchorage Bowl area. From the date and the listed assets, Kate deduced that the purpose of the company was to take advantage of the real estate bust that had flattened Anchorage in the mid-eighties. At that time there had been massive layoffs in the oil industry, and hundreds of people had quite literally walked away from their homes, most of them packing up their families and heading back Outside to look for work. Local banks, who had loaned bad money after good in the overpriced, ever-escalating real estate market, were left holding entire vaults full of worthless paper, and said banks folded right and left. The Federal Deposit Insurance Corporation had stepped in, consolidated half a dozen of the banks and put the properties up for sale at forty cents on the dollar. Arctic Investors had formed a cash consortium and promptly bought them, created an in-house estate management agency to act as landlord, and rented them out. They had made out like bandits on their initial investment, according to the figures in the files, especially since the vacancy rate in Anchorage had shrunk to one percent over the last two years.

She looked in the next drawer down. It was a deep drawer, nearly four feet in length, and it included the entire working files of the management agency. Right there in Dischner's office, when he himself not four hours before had denied all knowledge of any such business. Who says there's no God? Kate thought contentedly.

What she found most interesting was the rental agreement signed by Enakenty Barnes. Dated December 1 of the previous year, Alaska Landings unit A304 was currently renting for $250 a month. Two bedrooms, two bathrooms, and a heated garage for $250 a month in a town with a one percent vacancy rate seemed a little on the cheap side. She looked around the office for a newspaper and didn't find one. Never mind, Jack subscribed; she could look at it when they got home.

It didn't matter. She knew now that Dischner and Enakenty were connected, and to Enakenty's financial advantage. Poor emaa. She'd had even fewer votes on the board than she'd thought.

Neither Sarah Kompkoff nor Billy Mike's names had surfaced yet in Dischner's computer or in his files, which relieved her, but then Harvey Meganack's hadn't either, which seemed even less likely than Enakenty's $250 rent. Kate pondered that interesting fact for a few moments. Somebody had paid for Harvey's new house and Harvey's new watch, and Kate was pretty sure it wasn't Harvey, a Prince William Sound fisherman whose livelihood had been hurt like everyone else's by the devastation of the *RPetCo Anchorage* spill. Of course, just because Harvey's name wasn't in the computer didn't mean he wasn't connected to Dischner.

An unwelcome thought intruded. If that could be said about Harvey, it could be said about Billy, too. Her heart sank. It could even be said about Sarah. Before she went down for the third time in that slough of despond, she brought herself back from the ephemeral realm of speculation into the concrete kingdom of fact.

She knew from personal observation that Harvey was connected to Lew Mathisen, and Lew Mathisen was omnipresent in Dischner's files, even turning out, upon investigation, to be a major shareholder in Pacific Northwest Paper. She located the PNP file and browsed through it. On one of the PNP documents a reference to UCo was made in conjunction with his name. Kate returned the file, closed the drawer, consulted her list, said ''Excuse me'' to Gamble, head down in a file drawer himself, and walked around him to open another.

The UCo drawer, or drawers, as might be expected, were jammed with construction contracts. Kate concentrated on contracts in her neck of the woods. There were plenty to concentrate on. Sewers in Niniltna and half a dozen other villages, a dock in Cordova, a wastewater plant in Ahtna—Good God. Here was a job paving, curbing and signing Katalla's streets, which would have sounded like routine maintenance to anyone who didn't know that Katalla had only one street, and that one went from the only bar in town to the small boat harbor. A million and a half dollars for a couple of hundred feet of fill and pavement, a couple of hundred yards of cement for curbs—no sidewalks, however, or none mentioned—and two stop signs. Kate began to think she was in the wrong line of work.

Katalla. She raised her head, staring off into the distance with a frown. Something tickled at the back of her mind, something about Katalla, something she had known once and forgotten. She searched after it but it eluded her, vanishing into the wispy fog of memory and time. Making an involuntary frustrated sound, at which neither Gamble nor Jack so much as twitched, she bent over the files again. All of the contracts were written in legalese, but after she got past the requisite amounts of whereases and whyfors and thereats, they all had two significant features in common: Each contract was for a project in a town or village in the Alaskan bush with a large Alaska Native population, and each one had been written by or under the legal oversight of the well-known law firm of Dischner, Rousch and Ford, known familiarly to the local populace as Huckster, Shyster and Finagle.

Kate had a thought and went back through the contracts one more time, looking at signature pages. Each of the contracts regarding a prospective project within the authority of the Niniltna Native Association, as was required by association bylaws, had been approved by an Association board member. This would have been fine, except for the fact that there were five board members, and only three signatures showed up on the contracts, those of Harvey Meganack and Enakenty Barnes.

And Billy Mike.

Kate closed her eyes and swore, once and thoroughly, to herself. She opened her eyes again and flipped through the contracts one more time, running a rough total in her mind. She couldn't believe the result, and ran it through again. It came out the same. She thought of Enakenty Barnes, and of motive for murder. She had motive now.

Gamble was breathing heavily down her neck so she turned over the files and moved off to open another drawer at random, not really looking at what was in it. She remembered, with an inward shudder, the gold nugget watch with the rams' heads on Harvey Meganack's wrist. She wondered again who had paid for Harvey's new house. She wondered if Pacific Northwest Paper made other wood products. She wondered if Pacific Northwest Paper made other building products. She wondered if Pacific Northwest Paper maybe contracted out for construction work, and construction work in town as well as in the bush.

Jack looked up. "What time is it, anyway?"

Kate looked at her watch. "Almost six," she said, surprised.

"About time we packed it in," Jack said, replacing the file he was holding and closing the drawer on it. "Dischner's a workaholic, he could be here any time."

Kate looked down to close her own drawer, and the name of a file caught her eye.

"Kate? Did you hear me?"

It was a thick file. She pulled it.

"Gamble, we've pushed this about as far as we should, don't you think?" Jack said. "If we don't get caught in here, it's late enough or early enough or whatever you call it to get caught outside. Come on, let's pack it in."

She flipped through the file. They looked like leases. Subsurface leases for mineral rights. She saw Dischner's name, Mathisen's name, the names of the two ex-governors, the owner of one of the local newspapers, the president of UCo, half a dozen legislators, past and present, a couple of judges. Lew Mathisen. John King.

"Kate, come on, dammit."

Something nudged her elbow. She shrugged it off and flipped a page. The territory the lease form referred to was in map coordinates, latitude and longitude. They looked familiar. Something nudged her again and she looked down to see Mutt standing next to her. "What, you need to go outside?"

Then the other three heard what Mutt had heard, the sound of the door shutting downstairs.

Kate stuffed the file back in the drawer and took three silent steps to the light switch. The room was plunged into darkness. Footsteps rang off the parquet floor. A stair creaked. Jack's whisper breathed into her ear made her jump. "There's a back stairway." One hand closed over her arm, another opened the door, and they slid into the hallway, Gamble shrugging into his suit coat and bringing up the rear. In the dim light reflected from the street lamps outside Kate thought she saw the white flutter of a dropped piece of paper, but the footsteps were halfway up the main stairs and Jack was pulling her in the opposite direction. This seemed like a very good idea and she went.

There was the hiss of a hydraulic hinge as Jack cracked the door. It was a fire stairway, rough concrete and gray-painted steel lit with dim yellow emergency lights that stayed on twenty-four hours a day. Gamble was the last one through and trusted to the hinge to pull the door closed behind him. It did, slowly, too slowly. The light from the stairwell must have showed around the edges of the door, and whoever was climbing the main staircase saw it. "What the hell? Hey! Hey, who's there! Hey! Hey, you!"

All attempt at secrecy abandoned, Jack jumped every other riser, Kate right behind him. They hit the first floor and made for the door. "Morgan!" Gamble whispered. It was a panicked sound that carried clearly. "God dammit wait for me!" The toe of the Fibbie's wingtip caught on the last step and he went sprawling. "Shugak! Help me!"

Kate and Jack ran back to grab him by one arm each and hoist him to his feet. The exit was under the last flight of stairs and Mutt was already at the door, nose pressed to the crack. Jack shoved it open as the metal stairwell crashed with the sound of feet in a hurry. "Hey!"

And then they were outside and running for it. Gamble went up Fourth, Kate and Jack down Third, Mutt loping well ahead of them. They could hear the man's voice clearly. "I see you, you sons-of-bitches! I see you! I'm calling the cops! Run, you assholes! Run!"

They ran, flat out, for three and a half blocks. The Blazer was parked in front of the Carr-Gottstein building across from the state court house. Jack gave rapid but devout thanks for an absence of police cars around the state court building, unlocked the doors and they tumbled inside. The motor caught on the first try and they were gliding away from the curb, all in the same movement. Jack left the headlights off until they were safety on L and out of sight, succeeding so well that a Ford Pinto nearly ran into them at Fifth. Jack hit the brakes. The Pinto's driver flipped them the bird and roared off, trying to catch the light at Ninth.

"Never a cop around when you need one," Jack said, unclamping his hands from the steering wheel.

Kate let out a long sigh. "Thank God." Mutt nuzzled her with a soft whine and she reached around to rub her head. Her heart was still trying to climb out of her throat. "Good girl. *Good* girl."

"We should have scattered some of those files around," Jack said. "Made it look like vandals."

"I put all the files I looked at back and closed the drawers."

"So did I, but how much you want to bet Gamble left a trail a two-year-old could follow?"

"No bet."

"And he called me by name, and you, too."

"It wasn't Dischner. I didn't recognize the voice."

"Doesn't matter. He'll tell Dischner, and Dischner'll know. My prints are on file. Yours are, too."

"Still?"

"Probably."

There was a pause. "Doesn't matter," Kate said. "Dischner won't call the cops."

Jack looked at her. "Why not?"

"He won't call the cops," she repeated.

Jack's gaze didn't waver. "What was in that last file? You looked like you'd seen a ghost."

"He won't call the cops," Kate said for the third time.

The light turned green. Jack switched on his headlights and shifted sedately into first. Five minutes later, they were home.

EIGHT

IT WAS ALMOST SEVEN A.M. WHEN THEY STUMBLED IN THE door. it was too late to go to bed and they were both so wired it would have been impossible to sleep anyway. Jack made coffee and they sat at the kitchen table and read the morning paper. Kate found the want ads and looked up two-bedroom, two-bath apartments with heated garages. There were half a dozen for rent, not one of them for under $750, with a second month's rent as security deposit.

"Lovely morning, isn't it?" Jack said, putting down his coffee with a sigh of contentment. "Of course, I tend to see any morning I haven't been caught in the act of breaking and entering a beautiful morning, don't you?"

She got up to refill her mug and sat down again. "What is it Jane does, Jack? I think you told me she reviewed bids or something."

He looked mildly surprised. "Yeah. She reviews bids submitted by contractors for capital projects. Roads and government buildings, stuff like that. Why?"

Bingo, Kate thought. She shrugged. "Just curious."

He caught her hand and she let it stay there, which encouraged him to pick it up and kiss her palm, which was how Johnny found them when he walked into the room with a sleepy face and tousled hair. He looked at them and made a face. "Ick. Mushy stuff before breakfast. Jeez you guys."

Kate laughed and escaped upstairs, pursued by Jack into the bathroom. She was naked and in the act of stepping into the shower when he reached for her with an anticipatory grin. She warded him off with upraised hands. "No shower action with the kid in the house, Morgan."

"He's got his own bathroom." He kissed her.

"That's not what I meant and you know it." He kissed her again and she weakened. "The hell with it." She wrapped her legs around his waist as he stepped into the shower and pulled the curtain closed behind them.

She looked up from brushing her damp hair, saw his smug reflection in the dresser mirror and couldn't resist a smile. "I will say this, Morgan, you are better at changing the subject than anyone else I know."

Just for that he bit her once on her shoulder, before reaching around her to pull a pair of jeans out of a drawer. "Everybody's got to be good at something." He yanked on his jeans with brisk movements and went to the closet to investigate the possibility of a clean shirt. He found one, blue naturally, the chronic choice of the Y chromosome, and pulled it on. She put down the brush and went over to button it up, he leaned down to kiss her and that was how Johnny found them when he came out of his room, dressed in neon Jams and a T-shirt big enough for Godzilla. He paused in the open door. "Jeez you guys, are you still at it? DisGUSTing."

Footsteps crashed down the stairs. "Why, Shugak, I believe that is a blush."

"Up yours, Morgan," she said, but she didn't move.

"So, Kate," he said, nuzzling her ear, "why did you want to know where Jane works?"

She jerked, a reflexive movement she couldn't hide, and his gaze sharpened. "I told you," she said, pulling free and edging toward the door. "I was just curious."

Jack followed her down the stairs, reflecting on how well she lied, to everyone except him. The knowledge gave him a warm feeling around his heart.

"You look tired, Dad," Johnny said at the kitchen table. He glanced at Kate. "So do you, Kate."

"You are not wearing that to school," Jack said, looking his son and heir over with a critical eye that had just become aware of the younger generation's idea of sartorial splendor.

"Da-ad," Johnny said, dragging the word out into two syllables. "Did you forget again?"

"Forget what?"

"It's an in-service day. Only teachers go to school. I brought the notice home a week ago."

"Oh."

"So I'm going next door to Brad's, like usual on in-service days. His mom got him a new Super Nintendo for his birthday."

Jack hazarded a guess. "Mario Brothers?"

"*Da*-ad." Johnny rolled his eyes. "Mario Brothers is, like, *ancient*. Brad's got Master Blaster, with a joystick and everything."

"Oh." Jack dished up a plateful of scrambled eggs, onions and cheese into which his son and heir disappeared head down to give his best impression of a vacuum cleaner. Jack and Kate were hungry, too, and there was silence in the kitchen for all of five minutes.

"You going back to the convention this morning?" Jack said as they cleared the table.

Kate nodded. "The panel on subsistence is today."

"Oh boy. Is Ekaterina speaking?"

"She's the moderator."

"What's it like?" Johnny said, putting the plates in the dishwasher.

"What's what like?"

"The convention. Do you, like, dance and stuff?"

Kate paused, looking at him. "You've never been?" He shook his head. "You want to come?"

Johnny looked at his dad. "I thought—"

"What?"

"Well." The boy hesitated. "I'm, like, you know, white."

Kate grinned. "Hopelessly. So?"

"So I thought the AFN convention was only for Alaska Natives."

"Everyone's welcome," Kate said. "True, we mostly talk about issues that affect Alaska Natives, but nobody checks your family tree at the door. Besides, your family's been around this country a pretty long time." She thought of the time line they'd made together in the sand along the Coastal Trail. He caught the thought and they smiled at each other. "Probably one of your missionary grandmothers misbehaved with a Lakota brave back there somewhere. Propinquity is a wonderful thing. Look at me and your father."

"Pro-what?" he said.

"Never mind," Jack said, scowling at Kate. "You're pretty chipper this morning, considering."

"Considering what?" Johnny said.

"Never mind," Jack said, scowling at his son.

"So you want to come?" Kate asked Johnny.

Johnny hesitated, the allure of Master Blaster warring with a natural curiosity. He'd seen *Dances with Wolves* and *The Last of the Mohicans* and *Geronimo* and a lot of cowboy movies on TNT. He thought Hawkeye was a great fighter but he thought he ought to have found something better to fight over than some dumb girl. Wind in His Hair was cool, too. Geronimo scared him a little, John Wayne not at all, not even in *The Searchers*. "Okay," he said. "I guess."

Kate looked at Jack.

"Okay," Jack said. "I guess." Johnny tore upstairs for his jacket. "Kate."

There was a note in Jack's voice she hadn't heard before. She looked up from tying her sneakers. His eyes were troubled. "What's wrong?"

"Listen." He hesitated again.

She finished tying the second shoe and dropped it to the floor with a loud thump that expressed her displeasure. "For crying out loud, Morgan, just spit it out. Do you not want him to come with me or what?"

"It's not that I don't want him to go." He raked a hand through his hair.

"Then what?"

He met her eyes straight on. "I don't want him to be hurt."

"Hurt?" She straightened slowly, staring at him. "What are you talking about? He'll be in the convention center, everybody brings their kids and lets them run around, it—"

"I don't mean that." He struggled to find the right words. He could see Kate getting angry and that didn't help. "Johnny was born in Alaska, Kate. He was raised here, he's lived here all his life."

"So?"

"So he's white."

Kate folded her arms across her chest, Her chin came out. "So?"

"Oh hell," Jack said, knowing he was getting himself in deeper with every word and unable to stop digging the hole. "I just—I don't want you taking him down there and have people be mean to him because he's white." His lips pressed together. "I know what that's like."

"Good," she said.

"What?" Jack said, startled.

"First and foremost, Jack, you can't keep Johnny from being hurt. Being hurt is a part of life, it's one of the ways we learn." She waved a hand to forestall him. "All right, all right, sorry, didn't mean to lecture you on parenting. I said it was good that you know what it's like to be discriminated against because of the color of your skin. Not many white people do. Don't expect any sympathy from me because my cousin Martin called you a gussuk once. If I'd gone into Nordstrom's alone, Alana would have looked right through me." She waved her hand again. "All right, all right, I didn't mean to start a lecture on the racial inequalities inherent in American society, either." She took a deep breath and fixed a determined smile on her face.

"Look, Jack. Sure, Johnny can go over to Brad's and play Nintendo all day long and not be hurt except by Brad whipping his butt at Master Blaster. But like you said, he was born and raised in this state. He's as much of an Alaskan as any of us. Don't you think it's time he started learning something about its history and culture and the people that were here before his were?'' He was silent, and she added, ''Ignorance is the mother of fear and the grandmother of hate. You don't want Johnny to be a hater, Jack.''

Johnny clattered down the stairs, shrugging into a jean jacket, pink cheeks scrubbed clean, blond hair slicked back, big blue eyes full of innocent enthusiasm. Kate waited, looking at Jack.

He sighed, and said to Johnny, ''Did you call Brad, tell him you're not coming?''

The Kodiak Island Dancers were on stage as they entered the Egan Convention Center that morning. Kate stood in the back of the room, Mutt on one side and Johnny on the other, and watched Johnny watch them.

At first he was disappointed, although he tried to hide it. The costumes, leggings and tunics, were brightly colored and decorated but nobody had on war bonnets made of eagle feathers or carried tomahawks or long rifles. Most of the women were older and some frankly tubby. The men were younger, with one boy who might be his own age. A couple of older men stood in back, beating with sticks on skin drums in thin frames and chanting. The beat was monotonous and the chanting monotone and nothing like on TNT when they were fixing to scalp Randolph Scott, and the dancing looked to his eyes like simple shuffling and stamping.

The drums beat out a rhythm, the old men chanted, the dancers' feet echoed both. Johnny fidgeted and looked up at Kate quickly to see if she'd noticed. She pretended she hadn't. He shoved his hands in his pockets and prepared to wait it out, if not with enjoyment, then at least with polite acceptance. He'd been well brought up, Kate thought approvingly.

The song continued. As his ears grew accustomed to it, the chanting seemed to change, not in tempo but in tone, rising up, falling down, rising up again. Or maybe it had been doing that all along and he'd only just begun to hear it. The beating of the drums, which had seemed so monotonous, now took on the sound of a heartbeat, a deep, steady, reassuring throb that seemed to beat up through the soles of his shoes. The chanting went up above the beat, below it, swirled around it, now joyous, now mournful, sometimes a little teasing, maybe even a little mischievous. He couldn't tell where one voice ended and another began, they melded together so perfectly. The dancers moved as one, pulsing with the heartbeat of the drums.

One toe started to tap in time with the drumbeats. His head started to nod in the same rhythm.

Kate smiled to herself. ''So what did you think?'' she said when the dance ended and the dancers, back to being individuals again, smiled and bowed modestly in acceptance of the applause and left the stage.

''Huh?'' Johnny looked up at her. His head and foot stilled. ''Oh. It was okay, I guess.'' He was silent for a moment. ''I suppose only people who are dancers get to do that?''

''Everybody's a dancer, Johnny,'' she said.

''Everybody?''

''Everybody.''

''Even you?''

''Even me.'' She squeezed his shoulder. ''Even you, if you want. Someday when I'm in town I'll take you to a Spirit Days, or maybe your dad'll bring you out to the homestead when there's a potlatch. You can learn.''

''You mean with everybody watching?'' He was horrified. ''Couldn't you teach me when we're alone sometime?''

She shook her head. ''That's not the way. Dancing is for everybody, all at the same time. We make a circle. We dance. We dance together.'' She could see that he didn't understand, but he'd come far enough for one day, and a ship in full sail was bearing down on them at ten o'clock. ''Look,'' she said with forced cheerfulness, all the apprehension that the discoveries of the previous night had generated back in the blink of an eye. ''Here comes my grandmother.''

Johnny followed her gaze. ''She's old, isn't she?''

Kate looked at her grandmother and saw the gray hair,

the wrinkled skin, the slow movements of age through his eyes. Ekaterina still looked tired, too. "I guess she is."

"How old? Fifty?"

"More like eighty. Probably more."

"Wow."

Kate wanted to talk to her grandmother about what she had found in Dischner's office that morning but of course the minute Ekaterina joined them a crowd formed. "Great party last night, Ekaterina," someone said. "You sure do clean up nice, Shugak," someone else said, "I never would have believed it." This remark was directed to Kate, or she hoped so. At least she thought she did. For the next fifteen minutes Ekaterina accepted thanks on her appearance, her granddaughter's appearance, the disk jockey's play list, the rare roast beef, the caribou sausage, the open bar and most especially on the fresh fruit platters. The only complaint was that the party hadn't lasted long enough.

Ekaterina rubbed her rheumaticky elbow. "You look tired, emaa," Kate said. "You want to sit down?"

Ekaterina shook her head. "I'll be sitting down long enough when the panel starts."

A half hour later people began to assemble at the table on stage, and Kate accompanied her grandmother to the head of the room. More people came into the room and took seats in the audience. The chairman, he of "big brown mama" fame, introduced the panelists. Olga Shapsnikoff was the representative from the Aleut Corporation. Kate vaguely remembered dancing with the CIRI representative the night before. The other four were from Sealaska, Calista, Chugachmiut and the Bristol Bay Native Corporation. Ekaterina Moonin Shugak of Niniltna was introduced as the moderator and got by far the most applause.

The chairman said, "Ladies and gentlemen, elders, friends, family and guests. The issue is subsistence."

More people drifted in from the hall. The conversation and muted laughter didn't die but it definitely slowed. Kate was watching Ekaterina with a frown on her face. Her grandmother had dropped into her chair as if her legs were no longer capable of holding her up. Kate thought she saw the sheen of sweat on her forehead, but that could have been the heat from the lights illuminating the stage. As the chairman finished his introduction in preparation for turning the podium over to Ekaterina, Kate slipped around behind the stage and climbed up to crouch behind her grandmother. "Emaa? Are you all right?"

"No, I'm not," said her grandmother calmly. The other panelists looked at them. "Ladies and gentlemen, elders, forgive me," she said into the microphone. "I'm a little tired this morning." She smiled. "Too much partying last night, I guess." Laughter echoed from various parts of the room at those words coming from this dignified elder. "I'm going to let my granddaughter moderate this panel."

"What! Emaa!"

"You all know my granddaughter, I think, Kate Shugak. She fishes subsistence, she has fished commercial and she guides sports fishermen, so I'm sure you'll agree there is none better qualified to speak to this issue."

Kate's whisper was panicked. "No! Emaa! Olga can do it! Emaa!"

Ekaterina put one hand over the microphone. "I'm going to go back to the hotel for a nap. Come to the hotel for lunch, and you can tell me how the panel went. Thank you, Katya."

The next thing Kate knew she was standing at the podium, blinking in the glare of the stage lights. Ekaterina's broad back disappeared out through the double doors at the back of the room. Her grandmother couldn't be all that tired or she couldn't have moved that fast, Kate thought. The crowd waited, expectant, and she dredged up a smile. Her heart was beating uncomfortably high up in her throat. She looked down at the podium and there was a list, thank God, of the speakers and their order. "Ah, ladies and gentlemen, elders, friends, family and guests, as the chairman said, the issue is subsistence. Our first speaker is Olga Shapsnikoff, from Unalaska, representing the Aleut Corporation."

Olga stood and Kate walked around her to the moderator's seat. "Is Ekaterina all right?" Olga whispered.

"Just tired," Kate whispered back. And determined to

thrust her granddaughter into the convention spotlight, she thought, fuming. Damn emaa, and damn her determination to drag Kate into tribal affairs.

On the plus side, Kate's resentment was more than enough to march her back to the moderator's chair without falling flat on her face.

As Olga spoke, Kate's eyes became accustomed to the light. Mutt had flopped down next to the stage. Kate looked for Johnny. He grinned up at her from the front row of the Raven's seat section, next to the boy his own age who had been on stage with the Kodiak Island Dancers. They were taking turns scribbling on a pad of paper. Tic-tac-toe, it looked like, and without a Nintendo, too. Wonders never ceased.

She brought her attention back to the podium, wondering what in the hell she was going to say when it came the moderator's turn to sum up what had gone before. She saw Axenia in the crowd, in her eyes an easily read resentment at Kate's presence on the dais. Lew Mathisen had a proprietary hand on her elbow, Harvey Meganack stood nearby, and across the aisle Billy Mike and his family took up two entire rows. Dandy was the only Mike standing, at the back of the room, his arm around a young and nubile dancer in traditional dress who was giggling at whatever he was whispering in her ear. Cindy Sovalik sent Kate a regal nod from the Arctic Slope Regional section. She thought she saw Martha Barnes standing in the back, but it was so far away she couldn't be sure.

Few of the speakers were professional orators but all were Alaska Natives and as such vitally interested in the issue of preference for rural subsistence hunting and fishing, as was their audience. Olga spoke concisely for five minutes and concluded by saying flatly, "There will be no compromise on rural subsistence," and the crowd broke into spontaneous applause, long enough for her to sit down and for the CIRI man—what was his name? Kate had forgotten the list of panelists on the podium—to take her place.

The CIRI man, an Aleut from Seldovia, said, also flatly, "The federal government is doing a far better job of protecting Native subsistence than the state government is,'' and this time the applause was accompanied by yells of approval. He condemned the Isaac Walton League's efforts on behalf of urban and Outside sports fishermen to more yells of approval, and called for the Alaska legislature to pass a constitutional amendment for rural preference in hunting and fishing.

The representative of Chugachmiut, an Eyak from Cordova and a Baptist seminarian who had graduated with a distinction in oratory, said that subsistence was not a part-time occupation, it had to be lived. How were the people along the Yukon River supposed to feed their children if they couldn't fish for salmon or hunt for caribou except at the pleasure of the state? ''The governor says the state will fly in fish from other areas.'' He snorted. ''So people who have been self-sufficient for ten thousand years turn into welfare recipients.'' He looked around the room. ''What kind of sense does that make?''

''None!'' came the reply.

The Sealaska representative, a Tsimshian from Metlakatla, called subsistence the most basic ingredient of the Native community and condemned state inaction on the issue. The Calista representative, a genial Yupik from Akulurak, grinned and promised not to be as long-winded as some of the politicians who'd been there the day before. He sobered, to warn of oil company interest in sinking exploratory wells in Norton Sound, and of the threat this posed to marine life in the Bering Sea. ''We don't already have enough problems with the giant trawlers from Korea and Taiwan and Russia and Poland and, yes, the United States,'' he asked, ''all of them ripping up the bottom of the North Pacific Ocean and causing the Yukon-Kuskokwim River chum stocks to crash?''

Kate was of the opinion that mounting a couple of ten-inch cannons on the foredeck of a Coast Guard cutter and sending it out to blow the trawlers out of the water would be one place to start solving that particular problem, but she knew better than to say so here. This crowd was upset enough to take her seriously.

The man from Akulurak closed by saying, "The oil companies promise us they'll take every precaution to see that no harm comes to the environment from oil spills, but they don't want to talk about how they hired a known drunk to run the *RPetCo Anchorage* onto Bligh Reef. We can't trust the oil companies to take care of us. We have to take care of ourselves."

The representative of the Bristol Bay Native Corporation, another Yupik, this time from Manokotak, took a scholarly approach, defined the various federal, state, local, sports and commercial fishing, environmental and animal rights groups' pressures on Native subsistence, and recommended that the Secretary of the Interior, also known as Alaska's landlord, be encouraged to seek out traditional tribal knowledge in game management. She waited for the applause to die down and added, peering over the tops of her half-glasses, "They don't make microscopes big enough to find the state of Alaska's support of the subsistence lifestyle." Her tone was so measured and her words so evenly spoken that it took a moment for their import to sink in. When they did, there was a roar of approval and more applause. Again, she waited for it to die down. "When one word from a state biologist fresh from some Outside college is enough to cancel out a thousand years of traditional Native knowledge, it is time for a change." For a third time applause swelled. Without haste, the Yupik from Manokotak collected her papers together and returned to her seat.

All the panelists had spoken. It was Kate's turn. Olga nudged her to get up. She sat where she was, petrified with fear. She had nothing to report, no speech to give, and anything after the lady from Manokotak would be anticlimactic. I can't do this, emaa, she thought.

The audience was waiting for her, all of them, hundreds of them, silent, expectant, even eager. She knew a sudden, queer feeling of standing on the edge of a yawning chasm, the vacuum that had been left by Ekaterina's absence beginning to suck her over the edge.

Olga nudged her again and somehow Kate found herself at the podium, blinking at the lights. People were stirring in their seats and conversation was building again at the back of the room. She gripped the sides of the podium and stood on tiptoe to speak into the microphone. Her voice squeaked on the first try and she had to clear her throat and start again. There was a spark of malicious enjoyment in Axenia's eyes; Kate never saw it. The conversation got louder, and the only thing that kept her in place was the thought that, however Ekaterina had maneuvered her appearance here today, she couldn't let her grandmother down. She opened her mouth, and to her surprise, words came out.

"Ladies and gentlemen, elders, family, friends and guests. The issue is subsistence." She paused. Some people looked her way. A lot more were engrossed in conversation. There was laughter and whispering. The wail of a hungry baby cut off abruptly. Her grip on the fake wood of the podium was sweaty and her hands slipped.

And then it came to her. A story. She'd been told stories all her life. She would tell one now, to people who lived by stories, to people who lived on through them, to people who died and returned in stories to live again.

"I shot a moose in my front yard this year."

She let the statement lie there and gather attention.

"Not fifty feet from my front door."

A lot of men shook their heads, as if they couldn't believe the luck of some undeserving people. There were a few faint, frankly skeptical grins.

"I dropped him from my front door with a single shot from a thirty-ought-six."

The details began to add up into either a true story or a good one. More people began to listen.

"In any other fall, on any other year, I wouldn't have been able to.

"Not because I can't shoot," and she grinned at the skeptics, "because you know I can."

They grinned back.

"No." She let the grin fade. "I got to shoot that bull because for the first year in six, I drew a permit."

She let that sink in, and was gratified when the room became still except for a few rustles from the back where a couple of kids scuffled for possession of an Eskimo yo-yo. One's mother confiscated the yo-yo and they quieted.

"I got to shoot that bull because for the first year in ten, the feds declared a moose hunt would be permitted in the Park's game management unit."

There was a collective growl of acknowledgement.

Kate felt that growl somewhere way down deep inside, and whatever was there rose up in response.

"The hunt only lasted seven days.

"There were only ten permits issued.

"I got my moose."

She gripped the podium firmly and said into the microphone, "Nobody else in the Park got their moose.

"Just me.

"I got my moose.

"I got enough moose to last me the winter.

"I got enough moose to share with my family.

"I got enough moose to share with my friends.

"Nobody else in the Park got a moose.

"Hunters from Anchorage, they got their moose.

"Hunters from Anchorage with helicopters and four-wheelers, they got their moose.

"But nobody else in the Park got a moose.

"Just me."

The crowd was silent. Kate let her next words drop one at a time, into the waiting pool of silence.

"You know what?

"You know what I was thinking when I shot that moose?

"I was thinking I was shooting a moose where my dad shot his moose.

"I was thinking his dad's dad shot his moose there.

"I was thinking I would pick cranberries to go with that moose.

"I was thinking I would be picking those berries the same place my mother picked those berries."

"Yes," a woman's voice said from the audience.

"I was thinking I would be picking those berries the same place my mother's mother picked those berries.

"That moose, those berries, they will feed me, the same

way they fed my mother and father, the same way they fed my grandmother and grandfather.

"But they won't take away my hunger."

"No," the voice in the audience said. "No," echoed someone else.

"That moose, I shoot it where my father shoots his moose, I shoot it where my grandfather shoots his moose."

"Yes." "Yes." "Yes!"

"Those berries, I pick them where my mother picks them, I pick them where my grandmother picks them."

"Yes!"

"The land is my culture. The land is my history. The land is my living. It feeds me, it clothes me, it teaches me."

"Yes!"

"The moose."

"Yes!"

"The berries."

"Yes!"

"The caribou."

"Yes!"

"The salmon."

"YES!"

"The moose, the berries, the caribou, the salmon, the beaver, the marten, the otter, the wolf, these are my mother and my father, these are my brothers and my sisters. They feed me, they clothe me, they house me. The Old Woman She Keeps the Tides for me. Raven he gives me the land and the light. Agudar he guides me."

Agudar must have been guiding her then because she was speaking in tongues, without conscious thought, in the grip of an exhilaration as unexpected as it was unidentifiable. The crowd was on its feet, cheering her on, and she felt their support as a physical presence. Johnny stared at her from the front row, open-mouthed.

"I say," she said, grasping the sides of the podium with fingers numb from the force of her grip, "I say that when a thousand years of history and culture is judged illegal, then the law is wrong, not the People."

The crowd cried out its approval, and Kate had to raise

her voice to invoke the traditional end of the story.

"That's all!"

There was such a roaring in her ears when she collapsed into her chair that she was afraid for a moment that she might faint. It took a moment to realize that the sound was the beating together of hundreds of palms, the shouting of hundreds of voices.

Olga was looking at her with wonder. The older woman started to say something, realized she would go unheard over the noise, and closed her mouth. Slowly, her hands came up and began to clap. The other panel members joined in. The room echoed with it. Mutt was on her feet, gazing at Kate with wide, alarmed eyes.

Kate was frightened. She didn't want to be good at this kind of thing.

What frightened her even more was how much she had enjoyed it.

NINE

KATE DROPPED JOHNNY AT JACK'S OFFICE AND DROVE TO the Sheraton, parking in the rear with Mutt sacked out on the back seat. She'd had a long night, too.

Ekaterina was waiting in the cafe at a booth next to the window. Kate was happy to see the lines of her face had relaxed and smoothed out. Ekaterina looked almost sixty again. "How do you feel?"

Ekaterina brushed the question aside. "Fine. All I needed was a little nap. How did the panel go?"

"Fine." Kate picked up the menu. Her stomach was growling, she hoped loudly enough for Ekaterina to hear.

If Ekaterina heard it, she ignored it. "I hear you made a speech."

Kate sighed and put down the menu. "Who called?"

"Who didn't?" Ekaterina said.

Kate picked up the menu again, concentrating on the sandwiches, feeling color creep up into her cheeks. "All I did was tell a story."

"Ay, that one must have been some story."

Kate looked up sharply and surprised a twinkle in her grandmother's eye. She dropped her head before an answering smile crossed her face. "Is there a cheeseburger on this menu that costs less than ten bucks?"

''Hotel food,'' Ekaterina said, letting the subject go, much to Kate's relief.

They ordered. The waitress took away their menus and Kate had nothing left to hide behind. Now was the time for her to report to her employer on the early-morning raid on Dischner's offices. ''Dammit, emaa,'' she said, suddenly angry and exasperated, ''what the hell is going on?''

Ekaterina looked startled at the sudden attack. ''With what?''

''Emaa, don't do this to me again, please!''

Ekaterina managed to look even more mystified. ''Don't do what again?''

Kate wasn't buying it. ''Don't do to me what you did when I was trying to find out who killed Ken and that ranger. What the hell is going on? You come out to the homestead and tell me that Sarah is dead and there's a problem with the board over Iqaluk. Now Enakenty is dead, too, and I find out that you didn't tell me Lew Mathisen is involved, that Axenia probably got him involved, and you sure as hell didn't tell me Edgar Dischner is involved. So I'm asking. What the hell is going on?'' Ekaterina said nothing, and exasperated, Kate said, ''What is it? Is it Axenia? Are you afraid of what I'm going to find out about her? Emaa, talk to me!''

The waitress brought Kate's Diet 7-Up and Ekaterina's tea. Ekaterina waited until she had left again before meeting Kate's angry, anxious eyes, her own steady and unreadable. ''You're the investigator, Katya.'' She made an indefinable gesture with one hand. ''Investigate.''

Kate could have lost her temper at that point. Instead she repeated, ''Are you afraid of what I'll find out about Axenia? Is that it? If it is, I can find some way to fix it, but I have to know, now, before I dig any further into this mess, and believe me, emaa, it is a four-star, government-certified, Olympic gold medal mess.''

Ekaterina said nothing.

Kate said, getting desperate, ''They would need someone on the inside, and Axenia's an ideal candidate. Is that what happened? Did Mathisen romance her because she's a shareholder of the corporation that is contesting ownership of Iqaluk?''

Ekaterina said nothing. A cloud moved across the sun, and for a fleeting moment the change of light brought all the lines back to her skin, draining her face of the vigor that had once characterized it. ''Are you sure you're feeling all right, emaa?'' Kate said, brows coming together.

''I'm fine,'' Ekaterina said testily. ''Stop pestering me.''

''Fine,'' Kate snapped.

''Good,'' Ekaterina snapped back.

The food arrived and they ate in silence.

Kate mopped up salt with her last french fry and tried one last time. ''Whatever I find, I won't hide it, emaa. If you don't help me, I won't be able to.''

Ekaterina said nothing.

Kate left the hotel in a quiet rage and hit the first pay phone she saw, punching out the 800 number of Jane's credit union with savage precision. ''Account number?'' She gave it. ''Password?'' She smiled. It wasn't a nice smile. ''Wardwell. W-A-R-D-W-E-L-L. Yes, that's right. Yes, I need to withdraw five thousand dollars, and I would like that in a cashier's check, please. Yes, I'll be picking that up in person. Which branch?'' From Jane's statements it looked like she did most of her business at the Juneau Street branch, which made sense since Jane worked downtown and lived in Muldoon. ''The Benson branch, please.'' They wouldn't know Jane at the Benson branch. They might keep the check waiting—and the $5,000 out of her account—for days, maybe even as much as a week. ''Yes. Yes. Thank you.''

She hung up and dialed the 800 number for Starbuck's. Jane sent a Braun coffee maker and an assortment of coffees to her mother, her boss and Archbishop Francis T. Hurley. Kate hung up for the second time. It hadn't helped; she was still mad, and she drove around until she found an automatic teller and withdrew another $300 from Jane's account. She took the cash to the post office on Ingra and bought a money order and a stamped envelope. She addressed the envelope to Family Planning in Fairbanks, stuck the money order inside and dropped it into the mail chute.

She felt a little better then but no less determined. With a single-minded sense of purpose she ran Axenia to earth in her own office.

Except that she no longer worked there.

Two years before Kate, through Jack, had put Axenia to work typing, filing and answering the phone at the state district attorney's office. The pay wasn't bad and the benefits were excellent, and Kate had extracted a promise from Axenia to start taking classes at the University of Alaska, Anchorage. She didn't care what classes, she told Axenia, she didn't care if she wound up majoring in Eastern religions, she just wanted her taking a class every semester for a couple of years. Maybe she'd find a discipline she'd like to pursue to a degree, maybe not; regardless, the experience wouldn't hurt her, and it was one way to make friends. Town life could be lonely for bush refugees; Kate knew from personal experience. At that point in Axenia's life, Kate thought that rubbing elbows with the kind of people determined to get themselves an education was just what Axenia, a directionless, eighteen-year-old adolescent ruled by her hormones, needed more than anything else. Kate had been subsidizing Axenia's education at $64 a credit hour for the price of a copy of Axenia's grade slip every semester. Kate had followed her cousin's academic career with interest and some amusement, from Introduction to Criminal Justice, which she found mildly flattering, to Accounting 101, in which Axenia floored her by getting an A. When Axenia took English 111, she knew she had won. The only thing other than gun-point that would get Axenia into an English class was the fact that it was required for a degree.

"When did she quit?" Kate asked. If it had been in September, maybe Axenia was going to school full-time.

The fresh-faced girl sitting behind what had been Axenia's desk was dressed as if she'd just come off a Nordstrom shopping spree with Jack Morgan, only her purpose had been to Dress for Success instead of Dress to Kill. "I don't know," she said, helpless. The phone rang and the girl picked it up. "District Attorney's office, how may I help you?" She listened, concentration marring her nineteen-year-old brow. "Certainly, sir, I'll put you right through." She pressed a button, said, "Mr. Bickford is on line three, ma'am," listened to make sure the connection was made, and hung up with an air of subdued triumph that broadcast how new she was to the job. She caught sight of Kate again and her face puckered back into its worried frown. "Oh. Ah. Yes. Axenia. As I said, ma'am, I don't know when she quit. She wasn't here when I was hired, and I don't know where she is now."

With infinite patience, Kate inquired, "Might there be someone here who does?"

"Shugak!" she heard a voice say from the doorway. She turned to see a big-bellied man with a red face and a huge grin coming toward her.

"Brendan?" she said. She was engulfed in a comprehensive embrace from which she feared she would not emerge alive, and said, voice muffled, "Dammit, McCord, you're worse'n any bear I ever wrassled. Turn me loose."

He did so, leaving his meaty hands on her shoulders and giving her a friendly shake that rattled the teeth in her head. "Long time no see, lady. Jack told me you were in town. How you been?"

"Okay. Really," she added when she saw his expression. "Really okay."

Her jacket was open and the scar in plain view above the neck of her T-shirt. He touched it with one gentle forefinger. "Looks like it healed up bad."

She pushed his hand away. "Cut it out, grandma. How have you been? Still chasing the bad guys?"

His hand dropped. "Even catching some of them."

"All right."

"Brendan! Come on!" an impatient voice shouted from somewhere out of sight.

"I'm on my way!" he shouted back in a voice that shook the rafters. "What are you in town for?"

"The AFN convention."

His brow creased. "AFN—oh right, I saw something

about that on the news last night.'' He quirked an eyebrow. ''I didn't know you were into politics.''

''I'm not.''

''Oh.'' Something in the way she said it gave him pause. ''Well. You in town for a while?''

''A while.''

''Great! Let's do lunch before you leave.'' He grinned hugely. ''I'll buy. That way you'll have to listen to all my war stories.''

''Simon's?'' she said.

''Ouch.'' He winced. ''You always were a first-class eater, Shugak.''

''Then it's a date.''

''Bren, dammit!''

''On my way!''

Kate put a hand on his arm. ''Hold up, Bren. Where's Axenia?''

Sandy brows disappeared in astonishment beneath an untidy thatch of hair. ''Didn't you know? Axenia got herself a job with the fedrul gummint.''

''Say what?''

''Thee Fed-E-Ral Gov-Ern-Ment,'' he said, spacing the syllables out. ''Bureaucrats R Us. Those wonderful folks who brought you the nine-hundred-dollar monkey wrench.''

''You're kidding. How come?''

He shrugged. ''Don't know. She didn't say. I expect it's because they don't have to pay Social Security.'' He grinned. ''Or maybe it's because you Native types just purely hate the state.''

''Up yours, McCord.'' He blew her a kiss, and she walked out of the building in the best mood she'd been in all day.

She found Axenia answering the phone on the second floor of the Federal Building on Ninth Avenue. The door behind her read ''U.S. Forest Service.'' Kate hoped Jane's office wasn't close by.

Her cousin's face changed when she saw Kate and she hung up abruptly. ''Hello, Axenia,'' Kate said, exuding charm.

It didn't take; Axenia looked wary. "Hello, Kate."

Kate looked around at the file cabinets surrounding the reception area, at the several offices with titles like "Timber Management" and "Forestry Science Laboratory" on the doors. She strolled over to one of the cabinets and read the labels. Lease sales, lease bids, all by location. "You didn't tell me you'd transferred jobs."

"You didn't ask."

Kate turned and shoved her hands in her pockets. "When?"

"A year ago."

"Umm." Kate strolled back to the desk and perched on one corner. "You like it better here?"

Axenia shrugged.

"You get a raise, maybe?"

"A little one."

"You doing the same thing here you did over at the D.A.'s? Answering phones, a little typing, filing?"

"What's with the third degree?" It was clear from Axenia's face that she had meant the question to be lighthearted; instead it came out resentful and suspicious.

Kate looked at her, waiting.

At first glance the resemblance between the two women was obvious. A second look highlighted the differences: Kate was all muscle and bone, her chin was firmer, her eyes more direct, more controlled and far more self-assured. Next to her Axenia was younger, softer, rounder, less finished, a little clumsy. The potential was there, but it was as yet unrealized. Kate folded her arms and stared down at her cousin, examining her face for traces of what she had become, of what she might become.

Beneath that assessing gaze Axenia squirmed a little. "What do you want, Kate?"

"Why are you dating Lew Mathisen?" Kate said.

Axenia flushed. "That's none of your business."

"It isn't if dating is all that's going on," Kate agreed.

Axenia bristled. "What do you mean by that?"

"Do you tell him what's happening with the Association?" Kate said. That kind of blunt candor wouldn't have worked with an elder; with Axenia a frontal assault was Kate's only hope. "Do you give him inside information on what plans emaa and the board have for the future? Plans for construction of community buildings? Plans for fish processing plants? Plans for, say, logging Iqaluk?" Axenia's face changed but she continued to meet Kate's eyes steadily. "Lew Mathisen's a contractor, Axenia. Inside information on plans and bidding would help him out a lot." She added, "This new job of yours must be a big plus for him, too. He help you get it?"

Axenia's face turned a dull red and she surprised Kate by going on the attack herself. "What do you care? You've stayed as far away from Association business as you can your whole life. You spend your quarterly dividend checks and not once have you ever asked where the Association gets the money to pay them. Why all the concern now?"

Kate absorbed the sting without outward sign. Experience did that for you. "This isn't about me." She regarded Axenia with a cool eye. "Mathisen's Dischner's business partner."

It wasn't news to Axenia. "So?"

"So, Eddie P. isn't exactly a virgin when it comes to crooked contracts and sweetheart deals and payoffs and kickbacks."

"So?"

"So," Kate said patiently, "don't you think it's a little strange that when there's an internal conflict with the Niniltna board over logging Iqaluk, Mathisen and Dischner are looking very buddy-buddy with pro-development forces on the board, as well as in Raven?"

"You mean me?"

"I mean you." Kate held up one hand. "Axenia, I'm not judging you. You have every right to be pro-development if you want; damn near half the shareholders are, too. Hell, emaa's not exactly anti-development herself, she's the one pushing the road to Cordova and more tourist development for the Park."

Axenia snorted. "Penny-ante."

"That," Kate said, "is not you talking. That is Lew

Mathisen mouthing the words with Dischner saying them. It is also disrespectful of your grandmother, and we have spoken about your tendency in that direction before.''

Axenia mumbled something that could have been an apology. Kate said, ''You hear about Sarah Kompkoff and Enakenty Barnes?''

Axenia was taken back by the change of subject. ''Of course I heard. I'm really sorry.'' At Kate's raised eyebrow she flushed and said angrily, ''Okay, I didn't know Enakenty that well, but Sarah used to send me care packages of canned salmon all the time. She'd always come see me when she came into town on board business. I'll miss her.''

''So will emaa. And Enakenty, too. They usually voted with her.''

It took Axenia a moment. When she got it her face changed again. ''Wait a minute. You don't think—''

''I don't think anything, yet,'' Kate said.

''Kate,'' Axenia said. ''Kate, it's just—Kate, it's just plain silly to think that the two deaths were related, or that they had anything to do with association or corporation business.''

''Is it?'' Kate said, outwardly bland, inwardly begging to be convinced.

''Sarah died of botulism, for God's sake,'' Axenia said, her voice rising, ''and Enakenty fell off a balcony. He probably had a fight with his girlfriend and she pushed him over, for all we know!''

''How did you know about the girlfriend?'' Kate said.

Axenia stopped as if she'd run into a wall, her mouth half-open, staring at Kate. ''I—don't know, I thought everybody knew. It's common knowledge.'' Her eyes slid from beneath Kate's. ''Well, it was an accident anyway,'' she muttered. ''Nothing to do with Sarah. And nothing to do with the board.''

Her expression was mutinous and determinedly uncommunicative. Kate sighed inwardly. ''Look. All I'm asking is that you think about it. Don't let yourself be used. When they're done, when they've stolen everything they can, when they've grabbed all they can carry, those carpetbaggers will either squash you like a bug or worse, leave you alone and twisting slowly in the wind, trying to explain where all the money went. Dischner's done it before. He's famous for it. Hell, he prides himself on it."

"You don't know what you're talking about," Axenia said, but her voice was trembling. "You don't know these guys at all. ANCSA gave us land and the money to develop it. What's the point of having all these resources if we don't develop them?"

"There's a difference between development and exploitation, Axenia," Kate said, not ungently.

Axenia's phone pinged, and she snatched up the receiver with the air of a prisoner on death row waiting for a call from the governor. "Forest Service, may I help you? One moment, please." She pushed the hold button and said to Kate, "I've got to get back to work."

"Axenia—"

"I'll see you later at the convention, okay? Goodbye." Her cousin pushed the hold button again. "I'm sorry to keep you waiting, sir, let me see if I can locate Mr. Linden for you."

A door opened and a harassed-looking man came out with a sheaf of papers in one hand. "Axenia, when you have time, I need this retyped. It's got to go out this afternoon in the pouch."

"Axenia," another voice said, "where's that file I asked you to pull?"

Axenia smiled brightly and impartially at both men, giving an excellent impression of being alone in the room. Kate gave up and left.

As she was coming out of the elevator on the first floor she heard a shout. "Kate! Hey!" She turned to see Dan O'Brian coming across the lobby at a trot. "Kate, by God!" He smothered her in a hug, evidently forgetting that he'd seen her less than a month before when she'd run a gallon of blueberries for his breakfast pancakes up to the Step.

"Danny boy!" She returned the hug enthusiastically. "What are you doing in town?"

"Eating," he said, jerking his head at the cafe. "Can I buy you lunch?"

"I just ate," she said, "but you can buy me coffee."

"Great!"

They went into the cafe, where Kate watched Dan load a tray to the groaning point, and they took a table next to the window that looked out on a sunken patio. The trees were leafless but the grass was still green and the sun was still shining. Kate shook her head and turned back to Dan. "So what are you doing in town?"

Dan, his mouth full, waved a fork at the ceiling. He gulped and said, "Meetings with bigwigs in from D.C. Yawn." He filled his mouth again, reminding Kate of nothing so much as Johnny in intake mode. She settled back to watch him refuel.

Dan O'Brian was six feet tall with a bush of orange-red hair, laughing blue eyes and freckles that made him look more like a ten-year-old than his true age of forty-one. He'd started out in the rangering business in the Florida Everglades, discovered no affinity for alligators, and had moved forthwith to Hawaii Volcanoes National Park, where a volcano had promptly erupted, practically beneath his feet. He decided he had no affinity for lava, either. The third time he got it right, transferring to the Park the day after Jimmy Carter signed the d-2 lands bill into law, which act tripled the size of the Park and locked Dan into the job of protecting it for life.

Dan O'Brian was that rarest of rarities, a ranger who respected the rights of the people around whose homesteads and fishing sites and mining claims the Park had been created, and as such nobody hardly ever shot at him. As overseer of a team of seven, recently cut to five (just because d-2 tripled the size of the Park didn't mean the Parks Service had to assign any more rangers to it), he was responsible for twenty million acres of public land and for everything that took place on or near it, including homesteading, hunting, fishing, mining—and logging, Kate thought. And logging. "Dan," she said on a note of discovery.

Gulp. "What?" He drank down a glass of milk.

''What happens if an area in Alaska gets declared public land?''

''National or state?''

''National.''

''Park or forest?''

''What's the difference?''

''Plenty.'' He kept her waiting while he took another bite. ''A park is a park, it's protected, as is, by the U.S. government. It's all about conservation, land, water, birds, animals, marine mammals. It takes an act of Congress to change its status. Like ANWR.'' He pronounced it the common way, An-war. ''Which is a refuge, not a park, but it's still Interior. The oil companies been trying to get the Department of Interior and Congress to open the coast of the Arctic National Wildlife Refuge to drilling for years. If the *RPetCo Anchorage* hadn't run aground on Bligh Reef, and if Bush had been elected to a second term, they might have pulled it off.''

''How's a park different from a forest?''

''For one thing, a National Forest is administered by the Department of Agriculture, not by the Department of Interior.'' He waved a fork, splattering gravy over the table. ''Oh. Sorry. National Forests are put to economic use under policies dictated by Congress. They are administered by the National Forest Service, a bureau of the Department of Agriculture, which has never been famous for an abiding interest in conservation. The Forests sell lumber and grazing rights. National Forests can also be developed for hydroelectric power, for irrigation, and for mining.''

''Hands off the Park,'' Kate suggested, ''hands on the Forest?''

''Pretty much. There's a real history of land abuse in the Forest Service. They're in bed with the timber industry, for one thing, and if there's anything the timber industry likes it's short-term profits.''

''Clear-cutting,'' Kate said.

The fork waved again. ''Within limits, Kate. The timber companies contract with the Forest Service to log out certain areas, within certain limits.''

"Such as?"

"Such as, lately, buffer zones around the creeks. Sixty-six feet, on both sides. Nowadays, we know that it's not smart to log too near a creek because when you cut down the trees there the water is exposed to the sun, the sides of the creek erode, the water muddies up and the salmon can't find a decent stretch of gravel to bed down in and even if they could, the eggs wouldn't hatch in water that's too muddy or too warm."

He shrugged. "But any fish hawk would laugh like hell to hear me explain it this bad, Kate. You really want to know, you hunt yourself up a decent wildlife biologist or forest ranger. Probably a bunch of them right in this here building—" the fork pointed at the ceiling again "—you want I should round up one for you?"

"Thanks, anyway," Kate said, "I'll make do with you." He grinned. "What do you hear about Iqaluk?"

Dan snorted, mouth full of cherry pie. "Don't even get me started. They been fighting over Iqaluk for twenty years, the feds and the staties and the Natives between them. They'll probably be fighting over it for the next twenty." He snorted again, the fork holding a goodly portion of cherry pie unloading itself in the process and splattering red across the table. "They'll probably strike oil on it next, and then the oil companies'll get in the act, and then some-body'll discover gold up in the Raggeds and you'll have the United Mineworkers Association moving in." He scraped the saucer the pie used to be on and pointed at her with his fork loaded. She hoped it didn't go off again. "I'll tell you, Kate, it ain't easy being a ranger. Every time you turn around there's somebody else wanting to drill an exploration well or run a sluice box or plant goddamn potatoes in an experimental garden, and it's always an emergency, we're gonna run outta oil for gas or gold nuggets for watchbands or potato pancakes for the starving masses before the end of the year. Shit, Kate, I'm sorry to have to be the one to point this out, but there are always people starving some-where! For sweet Christ's sake, why can't people just let a beautiful thing be?" It was more prayer than curse. She didn't answer and he said, "Kate? You there? Yoo-hoo?"

She brought her attention back to him and produced a smile a little frayed around the edges as she got to her feet. "Thanks for the coffee, Dan, and for the information. I've got an errand to run and it won't wait."

"Hold it," he said, "I'm in town for another three days, can we get together? La Mex for dinner, maybe?" He winked. "Gotta have my margarita while I'm town, and you know Chilkoot Charlie's is right across the street."

"Ah—" She found it difficult to think clearly. "You know Jack's phone number?" He nodded. "Give us a call this evening, we'll work something out."

Mutt, irritated at being left in the Blazer, didn't speak to Kate all the way to mid-town, but Kate was preoccupied and didn't notice she was being snubbed, which irritated Mutt all the more.

The Z. J. Loussac Public Library was right where Kate had left it three years before. She parked in her usual spot, the first row, although there were so many cars she was at the end farthest away from the library building. She had to open the door again for Mutt, then headed for the stairs, feet beating an impatient tattoo against pavement, Mutt's toenails ticky-tacking behind her.

A man holding a clipboard accosted her with a practiced smile.

"Excuse me, ma'am, are you a registered voter?"

She barely paused. "Don't tell me, let me guess, you want to move the capital."

"Yeah."

"I'll sign your petition if you can tell me how you're going to pay for the move."

He couldn't. There was no escape, though; there was another of the pests lying in wait for her at the top of the stairs. "Excuse me, ma'am, are you a registered voter?"

"Don't tell me," Kate said, moving fast in a flanking maneuver, "let me guess, you want term limits."

"That's right, would you like to sign our petition?"

"We've already got term limits, they're called elections,"

and she scuttled past, safe through the gauntlet.

The library was one of half a dozen buildings foisted on an unsuspecting Anchorage public by a former mayor with more tax dollars at his disposal than sense, and who had kept a low profile in the community ever since, with good reason. This building, which gave the impression that it should be defended by drawbridge and portcullis, had been designed by an Outside architect who among other acts of inexcusable ignorance had hung two flights of steep stairs on the southern exterior of the building, evidently in hopes of killing library patrons as they slipped and slid their way up and down the icy stairs after the sun had melted the snow and temperatures had frozen it solid. Better than a drawbridge and a portcullis any day. Better even than a moat.

The subsequent mayor tried like hell to put the best face on a seriously bad situation, not to mention protect the municipality from legal attack by irate patrons with broken coccyges, by causing the stairs to be roped off in winter. When that didn't work, he allocated a large portion of the municipal budget for Icemelt and someone to apply it. Then the floor of the Sullivan Arena, another pet project of the aforesaid mayor, started to sink, and the roof of the Performing Arts Center, yet another public edifice of the same provenance, started to leak, and the current mayor said the hell with it and blamed everything on the former mayor and his sycophant assembly. It worked well enough to get him reelected.

Kate took the still mercifully ice-and snow-free steps two at a time, saluted the statue of William H. Seward doing his Fred Astaire impression, said "Stay" to Mutt and pushed through two sets of heavy glass doors. In revenge, Mutt squatted at the base of the statue, then flounced over to look mean at the few remaining Canadian geese in the park below, just to keep them on their toes.

It had been a long time since Kate had been in Loussac and as usual she got lost trying to find the Alaska Room. A research librarian took pity on her and directed her to the third floor, down a hallway that reminded her of the walkways connecting the modules housing oil field workers at

Prudhoe Bay, and back down a different stairway. It was with no little sense of triumph that she emerged into a circular room furnished with solid wooden bookshelves stained a dark red. At matching reading tables a thin old man scowled at a newspaper and a harried college student—Kate recognized the beginning stages of a term paper—sat surrounded by a mountain of books, tapping at the keyboard of a laptop computer. A tall, fair man with a friendly smile and a comfortable belly sat behind another computer to the right of the door. "Hi, my name's Dan. Can I help you find something?"

"Hi. Yes, thanks." She paused to collect her thoughts. What did she want? "A map," she said, inspired.

His eyes twinkled. "Of what?"

"The area east of the Kanuyaq delta," she said. "Ah, Iqaluk?"

"Topographical?" he said, coming around the desk and moving to a bank of file cabinets.

"Yee-es," Kate said doubtfully.

Dan paused with one hand on a drawer pull. "What specifically are you looking for?"

Kate gave a sudden, rueful smile. "I'm not really sure."

He smiled back, unalarmed. "What scale?"

"Ah, I guess I don't know that, either," she said uncertainly.

"Big enough to see Cordova to Yakutat?"

She thought about it. "No," she said slowly, "that would be too big."

His hand dropped to another drawer. "Little enough to see sand bars in the river?"

She shook her head. "No. That would be too small."

His hand dropped to a third drawer and pulled it open, revealing a stack of maps two and three feet square. He thumbed through them, muttering to himself over keys and legends until he found what he wanted. In the end he produced three for her, spreading them out on a vacant table. "This one is topographical, this one political, this one meteorological, so you can see for yourself how much it rains down there."

Kate pawed through them. "Which one shows the national parks and forests and wildlife refuges and like that?"

He turned on his heel and went back to the cabinets, returning almost immediately with a fourth map. "That do for you?"

"Perfect," Kate said, sliding into a chair. "Which one shows what minerals are found where?"

He trotted back to the cabinets, reappearing with a fifth map, which he lay down on top of the other four. "Anything else?" he inquired hospitably.

She patted her jacket pockets. "Yeah, actually. I don't have a pen." He produced one. "Or any paper, either, for that matter. I'm sorry, I didn't know I was coming here, I wasn't prepared." Before the words were all the way out of her mouth he had walked to the copy machine standing in back of his desk and yanked a handful of paper out of the eight-and-a-half-by-eleven tray.

"Anything else?"

She eyed the sheaf of paper. "You think you could send out for pizza?"

"No anchovies, extra cheese?" he said promptly, and they both laughed. The old man with the newspaper harrumphed and glared. Dan returned to his desk to help the next person through the door and Kate bent over the two maps highlighting mineral deposits and national parks and preserves.

Fifteen minutes later she looked up. Dan was there instantly. "What? Need something else?"

"I think so. Do you have anything on Katalla?"

He pulled in his chin. "Do we have anything on Katalla. Hey, Bruce." This to a slender man with glasses and dark hair just emerging from a back office. "She wants to know if we have anything on Katalla."

Dan was a bit of a flirt. Bruce was shyer and more dignified but no less charming and just as capable. "I believe we may be able to find something."

Five minutes later she was surrounded by books, texts on Alaskan history, studies and surveys of Alaska's natural resources, and relevant copies of the Alaska Geographic

Magazine, which seemed to have an issue for every separate town, mountain range, island chain and state and national park in the state. When Dan and Bruce had satisfied themselves that they weren't going to turn her away ignorant, they left her alone. Beauty and brains both, she thought with pleasure, and started opening books and consulting indexes.

There was no dearth of information on the subject. Katalla Bay was the next major coastal notch over from the Kanuyaq River delta, and had been the site of Alaska's first commercial oil development. Between 1902 and 1931 thirty-six wells had been drilled into paydirt between a thousand and two thousand feet deep. Only eighteen of the thirty-six were producers, producing, over a thirty-one-year period, all of 154,000 barrels of oil.

Prudhoe Bay it wasn't. It wasn't even Swanson River.

In 1933 the field ceased production when the topping plant the wells supplied burned down and the Chilkat Oil Company abandoned the operation.

What Kate found much more interesting was Katalla's location. North of Katalla were the Ragged Mountains, and east of the Ragged Mountains was Iqaluk, a coastal rain forest the size of Rhode Island, covered with lush stands of Western hemlock and Sitka spruce, all of it drained by the navigable Katalla River.

She looked up. Dan beat Bruce to her side by a hair. "Need something else?"

"Do you have a copy of ANCSA? The Alaska Native Claims Settlement Act?"

He pulled his chin in. "Do we have a copy of ANCSA." He looked at Bruce, Abbott to his Costello. "She wants to know if we have a copy of ANCSA."

Bruce smiled his shy smile. "I believe we may be able to find something."

Three minutes later she had a copy of ANCSA in her hands, as well as two interpretations exploring the legal ramifications thereof and a critical political analysis by a former state senator who had failed of reelection and therefore had nothing to lose by telling the truth. She located the relevant passages, took a few notes, and raised her head once more.

It was a photo finish, but Bruce beat Dan by a nose. ''Do you have anything on the differences in land use in national parks and national forests?'' Almost before the last word was out of her mouth Bruce was moving in one direction and Dan in another. Sixty seconds later she had more books piled in front of her.

It took the better part of two hours to find everything she needed. She finished taking notes, tidied her notes into a pile and folded her hands on top of the pile, staring into space for a full fifteen minutes without blinking. She came to several conclusions, shoved them all resolutely to the back of her mind, and started returning the books to the shelves, pursued up and down the aisles alternately by Dan and Bruce protesting that it wasn't necessary. ''It's okay,'' she told them, ''I'm Dewey Decimal literate, I won't put them back in the wrong place.''

They had to abandon her due to press of business. As Kate departed Bruce was looking up the 1920 Mineral Leasing Act for a purposeful *Anchorage Daily News* reporter with the word ''MISSION'' stamped on his forehead and Dan was hunting out Vitus Bering's biography for a woman leaning heavily on a cane who looked old enough to have personally witnessed the wreck of the St. Peter in the Commander Islands.

The building might have been designed by a mental midget, but the staff inside was first class all the way.

The sun was getting low in the sky when she went through the doors. Worried that she would be late picking up Jack and Johnny she said, ''Come on'' to Mutt and hurried into a trot, the crisp, clear air biting into her cheeks, Mutt's toenails again tickety-tacking on the pavement behind her. She looked to the south as she went, toward Turnagain Arm—where another explorer, Captain Cook, had been turned away again in his search for a northwest passage—and looked in vain for signs of snow.

There were none. The chill air filtered through her clothes and made her shiver. It would have to warm up to snow. She tucked her chin into her windbreaker and went down the stairs behind a man with a maroon leather portfolio in his hand and a preoccupied look on his face, who told both petitioners to fuck off without any real heat and climbed into an old Ford beater that didn't match the portfolio and drove off. She was followed by a harried woman with a mountain of books and not enough hands left over for four energetic children, who never even saw the petitioners over the books, and walked to the longest station wagon Kate had ever seen. She got the doors open and the books in and started corralling the children, who as soon as she put them in one door would spill out another. It looked like a Keystone Kops movie, or the clown car at the circus, and Kate was sorry when Mom got all the kids into their safety seats and drove off. Smiling, she called to Mutt, who was sniffing interestedly around the sculpture in the library park that had always reminded Kate of a stainless steel Dutch girl cap. They got in the Blazer and drove out of the parking lot to turn left on Thirty-Sixth and right on A. The lights were right at Benson and Northern Lights and Fireweed and she was already making good time as she came down the hill toward Chester Creek before it climbed back up to Ninth Avenue. The street sign said the speed limit was thirty-five, and she glanced down at the speedometer and saw that she was going fifty, with traffic passing her on both sides. The last thing she wanted was an appearance in court before a judge who might remember her all too well from the old life, and she braked.

The front right tire fell off.

Kate had just enough time to see it bounce into the next lane of traffic before the Blazer dropped to one knee and began to scream with the pain of metal on pavement. She took her foot off the brake, too late. The Blazer swerved to the left, rolled over on its right side and from there to the roof. There was a thud and a startled yelp as Mutt's body hit the inside of the roof, and more thumps as everything Jack had tossed in the back of the Blazer over the last ten years hit the roof, too. The Blazer stopped rolling but kept sliding. The howl of metal in agony deafened Kate to all else until the Blazer slammed into the sidewalk and fence on the left of the road, the seatbelt harness jarring the breath out of her. The windshield bulged and shattered, spraying the interior with glass. Safety glass, Kate noticed with gratitude in some detached part of her mind.

She hung upside down in the seatbelt, her hands gripping the steering wheel at ten and two, feeling cool air on her face through the broken windshield. Her breath came back to her in a great whoosh of an inhale, and she gulped air in great lungfuls. Slowly she became aware of screeching brakes and slamming doors and rapid footsteps. "Ma'am?" a voice said. "Ma'am, are you all right?"

In slow motion, as if she were moving beneath the pressure of ten fathoms of water, she turned her head and looked through the driver's side window, by a miracle still intact. An anxious face peered in at her. He was young and black and dreadlocked, and he was bent over the better to look at her so that his hair hung below his eyes like the strands of a plump black jellyfish. It bobbed gently with the movements of his head, like tentacles stirred by the movement of the sea. Kate admired the effect with a kind of dreamy detachment.

"Ma'am?" he said again, even more anxiously this time. "Are you okay? My name is Martin, what's yours? Ma'am?" He rattled the door. It was stuck. His face disappeared and she heard his voice say, "She's in shock. I can't get the door open, let's try to get her out through the window. Anybody got a blanket? And somebody better call the cops!"

Jack got there the same time the blue-and-white did and had to wait his turn, pacing back and forth on the periphery like an angry bear. Once she had assured herself that but for some bumps and bruises Mutt was all right, Kate answered all the questions they put to her and submitted to the mild indignity of a breathalyzer test. The back of her neck was sore from where she had fallen on it when she released the seat belt to crawl through the broken windshield, but other than that she was fine. Better than fine, she thought from the seat of the police car, looking through the open door at the driver of the second blue-and-white as he directed traffic around the wreck. She said suddenly, interrupting the police officer questioning her in midsentence, "Did the loose tire hit anybody? Did any other cars crash? Was anybody hurt?"

"No," he said patiently, and she wondered if she'd already asked that question. "Now if we could get back to the accident, Ms. Shugak—"

"I told you," she said, suddenly weary. "The tire fell off."

He looked skeptical but not offensively so. "Ma'am, tires don't just fall off."

I couldn't agree more, she thought. Mutt sat on the pavement next to the blue-and-white, her shoulder pressed hard against Kate's knee.

Jack stopped pacing and came forward to stand next to Kate. "Craig, for crissake. Let me take her home. We'll come down to the station tomorrow for the report."

The police officer, whose eyes were too old for his fresh young face, sighed and closed his notebook. "Okay, Jack. She staying with you?" Jack nodded, and the cop waved them away and went to direct the wrecker. Jack led Kate and Mutt to an anonymous beige four-door sedan and held the door. "Loaner from the department," he said tersely. Mutt hopped in the back and Kate, whose knees were beginning to shake, subsided gratefully into the passenger seat. She leaned her head back and closed her eyes. Jack walked around and got in. The door slammed. There was a moment of silence that was not in the least sympathetic. "What happened?" Jack said.

Without opening her eyes she said, "Someone loosened the lug nuts on the wheel. Couldn't have been anything else." She roused herself enough to add, "Better have the wrecker check the other tires."

Without another word he got out and went to talk to the wrecker driver. The driver, a laconic, gangly teenager in jeans with the knees ripped out and safety pins around the rim of one ear, walked around the Blazer with Jack and the cop who had taken Kate's statement. After a moment, he went back to the wreck and returned with a lug wrench, and Jack and the cop held the tires while he tightened the nuts on the three remaining tires. Subtle, insidious little tremors began to chase each other up and down Kate's spine. Sensing something was wrong, Mutt thrust an anxious muzzle over the back of the seat and pressed a cold nose to Kate's cheek. "It's all right, girl," Kate said, with an effort raising one hand to stroke Mutt's head. "It's all right. We're okay now."

Jack climbed back in the sedan, jaw champing at an invisible bit. "The nuts on the left front tire were loose, too."

"Always good to make sure," Kate murmured a little giddily. "The laborer is worthy of his hire."

"I don't consider this to be as amusing as you obviously do," Jack snapped. "Where'd you go today?"

She blinked through the windshield, watching without much interest as the punk rock wrecker attached the line of the come-along to the up side of the Blazer. "Where did I go today?" she said absently. "Out. What did I do? Nothing." She almost giggled, almost, but not quite.

"Knock it off, Kate." Jack's voice was hard and yanked her out of her abstraction. Still leaning against the headrest, she turned to look at him. His eyes were narrow and his mouth thin-lipped, and the visible evidence of his anger sobered her. "Sorry," she said, and a wave of fatigue swamped her, half-sinking her where she sat. "Sorry, Jack."

"Where did you go today?" he repeated.

She gathered up what few wits she had left, retrieved her memories of the day from wherever they had been scattered, and recounted her activities.

"Library?" he said. "What were you doing at the library?"

"Looking something up," she said, remembering, and unable or unwilling to elaborate, maybe a little of both. She sighed and closed her eyes.

Jack was relentless. "Where'd you park?"

"At the end of the first row."

He swore beneath his breath. "Why the end? Why didn't you park closer to the building where there's more traffic and somebody might think twice about tampering with the car?"

A faint trace of annoyance began to stir in her breast. She spoke slowly and clearly. "Because I have to park in the first row, and it was the only space in the first row that was open."

"Why," he said with awful sarcasm, "do you *have* to park in the first row?"

The annoyance became less faint. She opened her eyes. "Because it was always where I parked when I lived in town and came to the library. I have to park in the same place or I lose the car."

Jack's brows snapped together. "You 'lose the car'? What the hell are you talking about?"

"Just that," Kate snapped, defensive and angry because of it, "I lose the car. The parking lots are too big and there are too many cars and they all look alike. I always park in the same spot in the same parking lot. At Carr's, I park in the last row before the exit lane. In the Fifth Avenue parking garage, I always park on the fourth floor on the south side. At the library I always park in the first row in front of the stairs. That way I can always find the car when I come out."

Her jaw set, she dared him to laugh at her, but the truth was he'd never felt less like laughing in his life. His hand caught hers and he yanked her across the bench seat and into his arms. He lowered his head to hers, his cheek against her hair, "Thank God it wasn't worse. Thank God you're all right. Jesus, Kate, I—thank God you're all right."

"Thank God Johnny wasn't with me this afternoon," she said into his shirt, her voice somber, and was sorry when his heart skipped a beat. She sat up. "Let's go get him and head for the barn. It's been one hell of a day."

And it wasn't over yet. When they got home that evening, the townhouse had been broken into and completely trashed. They stood in the living room and looked at the VCR tossed across the room, at the broken television screen, at the CDs scattered all over the floor, many of the plastic cases splintered beneath a heavy boot. A cry of anguish from upstairs confirmed that Johnny's Game Boy had not been spared.

Outside there was the sudden revving of an engine, a

squeal of four tires burning rubber and the sound of a backfire, only backfires didn't hit picture windows and leave little round holes in the Thermopane. Mutt barked sharply. Jack hit the floor, bringing Kate down with him, yelling, ''Johnny, get down!'' There was an answering crash from upstairs.

There was just the one shot, followed by the sound of the engine roaring off down the street. There was another squeal of tires, and then nothing.

Kate's cheek was creased by a broken CD case when Jack plucked her up off the floor and held her out at arm's length. ''Kate?'' He looked her up and down, ran his hands down her arms and legs and torso. ''Are you all right?'' Mutt stood at his side, ears flattened, teeth bared, ready to spring at any available target.

''I'm fine,'' she said, calling Mutt to her side and trying to calm her down with a soothing hand. ''Johnny—''

''Dad?'' a voice quavered from the stairs. ''What was that?''

Jack was at the door in two strides. ''Are you all right?'' Mutt barked once, a sharp, inquiring bark. Jack picked his son up bodily off the floor and performed the same once-over he had with Kate.

''Yes.'' Johnny squirmed in his father's hasty, worried hands. ''I said I was okay, Dad, let me down.'' Mutt pulled free of Kate at the same time Jack turned Johnny loose and trotted across the room to make her own examination of the boy, evidently not trusting Jack to be thorough enough in his. Johnny wiggled and squirmed some more to put himself out of the reach of her cold, inquiring nose. ''Cut it out, Mutt, jeez! I'm okay!'' Mutt looked doubtful but at a signal from Kate desisted. ''What was that, Dad? It sounded like somebody shooting.''

''Stay where you are.'' Jack kicked a ripped sofa cushion out of the way and stormed into the street. A few of the neighbors were looking out of their windows. One came to the door. The street itself was deserted, not so much as a set of taillights gleaming redly in the distance.

He knocked on doors, asked questions. Three of the

neighbors had caught a glimpse of the car. One was sure it had been a two-door blue Toyota Corolla, another was positive it had been a brown Ford pickup with a supercab, a third said it looked like a red Chevy Suburban to him. Jack thanked him for his help, refrained from pointing out that the guy living next door to him had a red Chevy Suburban parked in his driveway, and went back to his own house, where Kate was putting the living room back together and Johnny was mopping up milk from the kitchen floor.

"You gonna call the cops?" his son said.

There was something in his voice, an almost imperceptible quaver, that gave Jack pause. "Why?"

Johnny kept his head down and scrubbed at the floor as if his life depended on it. "Hey," Jack said. He reached out a hand to ruffle Johnny's hair, usually a sure way to provoke a reaction, but Johnny only gave a half-hearted shake and scrubbed harder.

"Johnny." Jack's voice brooked no evasion. "What's wrong, kid. Talk to me."

The sponge slowed, stopped. Johnny got to his feet and went to the sink to run water over it, wringing it dry between his hands, wringing it out to the last drop, and wringing it out again. He kept his back to his father when he spoke. "Who do you think did this?"

Jack stared at the stiff set of the thin, childish shoulders. It took him a minute to work it out, and when he did awareness was quickly succeeded by anger, anger that his son would have cause to suspect attack by someone he knew. He kept his voice even. "Someone who's mad at me and Kate about a case we're working on."

The shoulders relaxed slightly. "Are you sure?"

"Yes, Johnny," Jack said, the words steady and certain. "I am sure. Your mother had nothing whatsoever to do with this."

There was a short, tense silence. Jack looked up to see Kate in the doorway, face shuttered. Johnny turned. "So you gonna call the cops?" he demanded hopefully. Jack nodded. "Can I dial 911?" Jack nodded. "Cool!" Johnny said, and hit the phone.

"No descriptions," Jack said, answering the question in Kate's eye. "Nobody saw nothing, and nobody heard it, either. What's it look like upstairs?"

"Not as bad," she said. "It's torn up, but nobody ripped the sinks out of the walls or took a knife to the beds like they did to the couch. Probably ran out of time, kids coming home from school, neighbors coming home from work, like that."

He nodded. "Probably. Let's clean up as best we can." Johnny handed him the phone and he spoke into it for a few minutes before hanging up. He produced a grin for Johnny, not his best effort. "I'll spring for hamburgers and fries at Lucky Wishbone after."

Johnny brightened. Like his father, an appeal to his stomach never failed.

Kate followed Jack upstairs. The linen closet, tucked into a corner of the second bathroom, had been spared. Jack got out fresh linens and they began making Johnny's bed.

"Whoever that was in Dischner's office this morning made us," Jack said. "This, and the wreck, they were messages, telling us he knows."

"He shot at a house with a kid in it," she said. She shook out the top sheet with a sharp snap. It floated down and she began to smooth it over the surface of the bed, hands brisk and sure.

She might have been talking about the weather for all the feeling in her voice, but Jack had known Kate a long time. He paused in the act of tucking in a corner. "Kate."

She met his eyes from across the bed. If his were hot, hers were cold, as cold and as opaque as glacier ice. "He shot at a house with you in it."

He had never heard her voice so flat, so completely devoid of emotion. He'd seen her annoyed and been amused, he'd seen her angry and been wary, he'd seen her enraged and gotten out of the way. This was new. This frightened him in a way he hadn't known he could be frightened, probably because for the first time in a long time Jack Morgan had absolutely no idea of what Kate Shugak would do next.

"Kate."

She tucked in her side of the sheet with military precision and reached for the blanket with no reply.

He tried again that night. ''Kate.''

She was lying very still beneath the covers, limbs confined strictly to her side of the bed, staring at the ceiling. ''What?''

''You're not going to do anything—'' He hesitated.

''Anything what?'' she said, and again, her voice was without inflection. She could have been discussing the weather.

''You're not going to do anything foolish,'' he said, his voice firm. He felt like he was talking to Johnny.

''Foolish?'' she said. ''Foolish? Somebody loosens the lug nuts on the Blazer's tire so I'll have an accident, somebody breaks into your house and trashes it, somebody drives by and shoots at your house with Johnny inside. Maybe somebody even kills Sarah Kompkoff and Enakenty Barnes.'' Her voice remained flat and calm. ''Why on earth would you think I'd do something foolish? Uh-uh. Not me. Not Mrs. Shugak's little girl. I'm smarter than that.''

There was a long silence, broken by a muffled curse. Jack rolled over, his back to her, taking most of the covers with him.

Kate watched the ceiling and waited for dawn.

TEN

THE NEXT MORNING SHE PRETENDED TO BE ASLEEP WHILE Jack got up and showered and went downstairs. When the smell of coffee reached her and she knew he was engrossed in the morning paper she reached for the phone and called Brendan McCord. His voice sounded sleepy. "Kate?" He yawned. "What time is it?"

"Six," she said, keeping her voice low.

"Six A.M.! You're an hour ahead of my alarm clock! What's the matter with you!"

"I'm sorry, Bren, but it's urgent."

There was the sound of an enormous yawn and stretch. "Well, all right," he grumbled, "but we go Dutch at Simon's."

In spite of everything she had to smile. "I should have known you'd figure out a way to save money on this."

"It's a dirty job but somebody's got to do it," he agreed. "What's up?"

"Do you know Dischner's home address?"

A pause. "Dischner as in Edgar P. Dischner, capo, fat cat and kingmaker?"

"Yes."

Another pause. "I might."

"Would you give it to me?"

A third pause, the longest. "I could," he said finally.

"You know, Kate, Jack has everything you ever wanted to know about Eddie P. but were afraid to ask." She let a moment go by, before saying distinctly, "I'm afraid to ask."

"Oh." Kate could hear the gears grinding between Bren's ears. "Oh-kay. Thirty-six-oh-eight Commerce Lane."

"How do I get there?" He told her. It was in south Anchorage, off Rabbit Loop. She repeated the directions, memorizing them. "Bren, is Dischner married?"

"Not lately. Not that I know of."

"Doe he have any kids? Any living with him, that is?"

"Neither."

"How about servants?"

"Only as in civil. His house isn't that big. He might have a weekly. I don't see him doing windows."

"Any pets?" Kate said. Bren gave a bray of laughter. "Close neighbors?"

She heard the rustle of sheets and pillows as Bren settled himself in for a nice, cozy dishing. "Did I ever tell you about the time the City of Anchorage bulldozed and surfaced a road up off Rabbit Loop that dead-ended on a seventy-five-acre tract? A tract of land acquired from the original homesteader by one of our more illustrious public figures, and which land just happens to back up against the Chugach State Park? Dischner's nearest neighbor is Gentle Ben."

"Thanks, Brendan. I owe you one."

"For what? I don't remember talking about this. I don't even remember talking to you this morning. I just remember you offering to buy me dinner at Simon's." With an evil chuckle he hung up.

Conversation over the Eggos that morning was monosyllabic. When Kate asked to borrow the loaner, Jack refused. "I have to take the kid to school."

"What?" Johnny said. "What's wrong with the bus?"

Kate called a cab and took Mutt out to the airport, where she found a cash machine and got another $300 on Jane's card and rented a Ford Escort with four on the floor and a bad clutch. Mutt sat in the passenger seat, cramped by the small space and curling her lip at the smells of it. Every now and then she put a paw on the dashboard to keep upright. Every now and then she would glance at Kate, panting slightly. She usually knew what Kate was feeling before Kate did, and this morning was no exception. Mutt's rangy, muscular body was taut and tense, ready to explode in any direction, taking no prisoners.

Mutt didn't like getting shot at, either.

They took International to Minnesota, followed Minnesota around to O'Malley and the New Seward and the New Seward out to Rabbit Creek. Commerce Lane took a long time to get to but was easy to find; it was at the very end of the road at what seemed to be the very top of McHugh Peak. Through the trees the rising sun turned Turnagain Arm into a sheet of pale silver. Kate thought she saw wisps of clouds congregating uparm, as if they were getting together to assess the possibility of the season's first snow. Kate was a creature of her environment and on any other morning the prospect would have eased the knot of tension coiled in her gut. This morning, the sound of metal against pavement still screaming in her ears, the sight of the knifed couch, even the memory of that map in the library, maybe especially the memory of that map in the library, these were what she saw and heard and remembered. If it snowed, it snowed. There would be time to appreciate it afterward.

The gears ground together as she shifted down to take another hairpin turn. Mutt lost her balance and fell on her shifting arm, which didn't help. At least the surface was good. It was better than good; the pavement looked brand-new. Kate remembered Brendan's story, and wondered how much Dischner had contributed to the mayor's reelection campaign this year. Or was this a state road? Didn't matter much; the governor was in Dischner's other pocket. The anger that had begun to burn at the sight of Enakenty on that stretcher licked up again, hot and hard and mean, refined to a white heat by the incidents of the last twenty-four hours. It was odd, but she'd almost forgotten Enakenty in last night's rush of fear and rage. This morning she welcomed the memory, deliberately calling up Enakenty's lifeless face in front of her, deliberately reliving the lunch with Martha. The car surged forward.

The road ended suddenly in a clearing and she had to slam on the brakes. The house in the clearing was new and, as Bren had said, nowhere near as large or ornate as she would have expected a man like Dischner to build. It annoyed her a little; life was so much easier when the bad guys were thoroughly bad, including their taste. This was a house she could live in, at least from the outside. A two-story frame house painted white, it had two enormous picture windows on the first floor and a row of smaller ones on the second, so many that almost all of the entire western wall was made of glass that looked out over Turnagain Arm. Dischner had built for the view. Kate didn't blame him.

There had been no attempt to put in a lawn, and trees clustered next to the eaves of the steeply pitched roof. Kate pulled around the circular driveway and parked with the nose of the Escort pointing toward the road. Kate's First Law was Always Provide for a Clean Getaway, a rule she had learned the hard way. She got out, signaled to Mutt and walked to the front door, which opened as she stepped onto the front porch.

"Why, Ms. Shugak, what a nice surprise—"

Kate looked at him without expression and said two words. "Mutt. *Take.*"

Target acquired, Mutt gathered her haunches beneath her and launched herself forward, a hurtling gray projectile weighing one hundred and forty pounds that hit Dischner squarely in the chest and knocked him flat on his back on the hardwood floor of his foyer. She landed lightly with her front paws on either side of his head, back paws solidly against his belly. Her mouth was open and her teeth were bared and a low, steady growl issued from deep in her throat with what sounded to Kate like a lot more enthusiasm than she had shown the night she nailed Gamble, but then she'd always been a quick study.

Mutt was half Husky and half Arctic gray wolf. Viewed from beneath, the Husky half was not predominant. Unlike Gamble, Dischner neither moved nor spoke. It was entirely possible he didn't blink or breathe, either, thereby showing more sense in his dealings with Kate Shugak than he had done thus far.

Kate stepped through the door over Dischner's sprawled legs. The living room was comfortably furnished with overstuffed furniture and built-in bookshelves. An intricately patterned area rug, Persian at a guess, lay before a snapping log fire in a stone fireplace. She strolled toward it and held out her hands. "There's just nothing more comforting than a warm fire on a cold morning, is there, Ed?"

An inarticulate gargle and Mutt's continuing menacing growl were her only replies. The picture window confirmed her outside estimate of the view. "My goodness, how lovely. Why, you can see practically all the way to Kalgin Island from here. And look at Susitna, and Denali, and Foraker, just as high and wide and handsome as anything I've ever seen, even in the Park."

Dischner made an abortive effort to move. Mutt barked once, sharply, right in his face, and restarted the growl. A log popped and broke in the fireplace. Kate stooped to put another log on. She gave some thought to raking a few coals out onto the rug, and decided against it only because she didn't know how fast Persian rugs burned. She wouldn't want to have to vacate the premises before the job was complete.

Dischner made a noise. Kate looked around and said, "I beg your pardon, Ed, I'm afraid I was miles away. Did you say something?"

He had. It was a struggle to get the words out. "Call it off."

Kate replaced the poker and rose to her feet, dusting her hands. "It's a she, not an it."

This time the words came out freely. "Call her off!"

Kate wandered back more or less in his direction, pausing to read a few of the titles in the bookcase on one wall. She admired the collection of plaques adorning another wall that attested to his extensive good works in both territory and state of Alaska, and the esteem in which he was held by communities from Anchorage to Juneau. She ran an appreciative finger down a soapstone musk ox, a much better piece of work than either he had on display in his office.

Dischner gave a convulsive twitch and this time Mutt snapped at him, big white teeth nipping at the skin of his throat. They left a drop of blood behind. He screamed.

Kate walked over to look at him over Mutt's shoulder. She heaved a mournful sigh. "Eddie, Eddie, Eddie. Whatever are we going to do with you?" She clicked her tongue, testimony to how hard she was working at solving this obviously insoluble problem. Her head cocked to one side as she considered. "You know, I can't help but think it might be a good thing just to turn Mutt loose on you right here and now." There was an inarticulate whimper, and she squatted down on her haunches next to him, elbows on her knees, hands clasped loosely, and said in a confidential tone, "Did you know that one adult wolf can eat twenty pounds of meat in one helping?" Eddie P's squeal was high and panicked. Kate's head gave a sorrowful shake. "Living way up here, all alone like you do, it wouldn't come as a surprise to most people that you'd been attacked on your own doorstep by a wild animal." She looked down into his terrified eyes and added softly, "And it sure would save a whole lot of people a whole lot of grief, now, wouldn't it."

An acrid smell told her he'd lost control of his bladder. She leaned foward to say in a voice barely audible above Mutt's growl, "Tell you what, Ed. I'll call off my dog, if you'll call off yours."

The words burst out of him. "Yes, yes, yes, anything, just get it off me." There wasn't much left of the dapper man in the three-piece suit and the silk rep tie. His usually elegant mane of hair was plastered to his head and his face was running with sweat.

The sight pleased Kate deeply, and she said in an almost affable tone, "If you've got a quarrel to pick with me, Ed, you send your goons after *me*. You don't send them to shoot up a suburban home with a child inside. People could get hurt, people who have nothing to do with what's going on between you and me. That's a no-no. You understand what I'm saying? It's just not done. It is beyond the bounds of decent behavior.'' She reflected for a moment, and added, ''Well, at least it's beyond the bounds of most decent people. I understand you put yourself outside those bounds on occasion.'' She raised her brows in polite inquiry.

Dischner choked out something unintelligible that Kate did not bother to translate.

''And no more loosening the lug nuts on a car I'm driving, especially when I'm driving it in traffic.'' She wagged a reproving finger. ''I could have killed somebody. Shame on you, Ed.''

The words burst out with a force that sprayed Mutt with saliva. ''All right, anything, anything, just get it off me!''

Mutt didn't like being sprayed with saliva and barked again. A new smell informed Kate that Eddie P. had lost control of his sphincter muscle. ''Now, Ed,'' Kate said, ''let's not be hasty. I wouldn't want you to make any promises under duress, because as I'm sure you as a legal practitioner are aware, promises made under duress are not binding. Are you sincere about this? Can I trust you to keep your word?''

''Yes,'' he sobbed.

She patted his shoulder. ''Good. Very good, Ed. That was the right answer. I'm proud of you. Mutt. Off.''

As if she'd thrown a switch the growl ceased and Mutt backed off, yellow eyes fixed on Dischner. He didn't move.

''Sit,'' Kate said.

Mutt sat, eyes watchful, not straying from the target. Dischner couldn't see her from his prone position. ''Can I sit up?'' he said humbly.

Eddie P's present submissive demeanor only confirmed two of Kate's long-held and, if the truth be known, frequently-tested beliefs: One, that one-inch fangs were a great leveler, and two, that people who had to lease out their fighting were always lacking in personal backbone. It was time for more carrot. ''Certainly you can sit up, Ed,'' Kate said cordially, and even gave him a hand. ''That's far enough, though,'' she cautioned, motioning him to remain on the floor. '' We aren't quite finished.''

One shaky hand raised to smooth his hair back, and Kate was almost amused that his first thought was of his appearance. Mutt, no less intimidating on defense than she was on offense, shifted her gaze from his face to his hand. Dischner's face lost what little color it had regained, and the hand froze before returning very slowly and very carefully to his lap. His voice was dull and defeated. "What do you want?"

"Well now, Ed. We've settled the personal business. Haven't we?" Kate waited until he gave a mumbled answer that might have been yes. "Good," she said, giving his shoulder an approving pat. "I was sure we had. What I'd like to discuss now is this little professional problem we have."

He looked bewildered. "Professional problem?"

"Yes, I think we could call it a professional problem." Kate pursed her lips. "Ed, I couldn't help but feel that there was something going on between you and Lew and Harvey Meganack and Enakenty Barnes and maybe even Billy Mike." She paused. "Something to do with Iqaluk, perhaps?" He started and dropped his eyes. She signaled to Mutt, who gave a sharp, warning bark. Dischner started again. Kate reached across his chest to give Mutt's head a soothing pat. "That's okay, girl, calm down, Ed's no danger to us."

But he was starting to regain some spirit and his eyes narrowed at the slur. Kate let her hand rest on Mutt's head, so that Dischner had Kate on his right, Mutt on his left and Kate's arm barring his way. "Ed," Kate said, dropping her voice to a low, confidential tone, "you know Mutt is only half Husky." Dischner looked at her. "Sometimes—" she sighed regretfully, "sometimes, the wolf half just takes over. Wolves, now—" She shook her head. "An appetite with attitude, that's what I call them. Did I mention she hasn't had breakfast yet today? Remiss of me." She smiled. "But then, Mutt always works better on an empty stomach. Don't you, girl?" She patted Mutt again. Dischner swallowed hard.

"Now about Iqaluk, Ed. I spent some time at the library

yesterday afternoon. You knew that, of course. However, you might not know what I was doing there.''

She waited, and he croaked, ''What?''

''I was looking at maps, Ed. Maps of Iqaluk, and the Ragged Mountains. The area east of the Kanuyaq River delta.'' She snapped her fingers. ''Oh, and Katalla, of course.''

Again, the tiny jerk of reaction gave him away, and she smiled. ''Yes, I thought you might be interested. It took me a while to put it together, but once I saw those claim forms in your files I knew I had the key to the whole problem.'' Her smile thinned at his reaction. ''Yes, that was me in your office night before last. But you knew that, too, didn't you.''

It wasn't a question, and, wisely, he didn't answer it. ''I know what's going on here, Ed. I will not permit it to continue. You are free to muck around in state and local politics as much as you like,'' she said, feeling extremely generous, ''in fact, there are some who would say that you and the legislature deserve each other. I myself have always thought a small nuclear device detonated beneath the Capitol when all the real Juneauites are in Douglas on a sleepover would solve the legislative problem just fine, but I've never been able to get my hands on enough plutonium to do the job properly.''

His eyes shot again to her face, clearly too near believing her, and she almost laughed. ''But I digress. Ed.'' She put a hand on his shoulder. He flinched beneath it. ''You keep away from Iqaluk. You keep away from Niniltna. Whatever connection you have with Harvey Meganack and Billy Mike, sever it. Today. If you floated the loan to remodel Harvey's house, sell the paper to NBA. If you've promised Billy you'll finance his run for state representative, renege. Any construction bids UCo has under consideration with the Association, contact the board formally and withdraw them. Any projects currently under construction, I will give you until close of business on December 31st, this year, to either complete or subcontract. UCo is fired, Ed. Consider this your sixty-day notice.''

She was gutting a large piece of his financial substructure, and he mustered up enough nerve to produce a travesty of a sneer and say, "And if I don't?"

Her smile was without humor, no more than a stretching of her mouth into a thin line. From his left, Mutt duplicated the expression, with more teeth showing. Kate patted his shoulder again. "I don't think we have to worry about that. Do we?"

In all his sixty years, Edgar P. Dischner had never before felt physical fear. The kind of board-and courtroom piracy in which he usually engaged involved a three-piece suit, an easy chair, a telephone and a stockpile of political IOUs. Over the last forty years he'd been threatened with felonious prosecution, political evisceration and social ostracism, depending on how far the state government was into the current administration, but none of those things involved physical harm. He might have been able to face down the threat of a beating, but the sight of that cold, yellow gaze and all those teeth had convinced him the way even the muzzle of a gun would not have. To his shame and fury he found his head shaking violently back and forth. "No," he heard himself saying, "no, no, no, no worry, no."

Kate gave his shoulder another approving pat before rising to her feet. "We'll be going now, Ed. You really do have a beautiful home here. I'm almost envious of your view. Magnificent. It's enough to make me consider relocating to town. But you know what they say." She smiled. "Once a Park rat, always a Park rat."

She paused in the doorway. "Oh, just one other thing, Ed." He looked up dumbly. "Arctic Investors. From what I could tell from your files, a profitable concern that bought up a lot of repossessed condominiums during the Anchorage real estate crash in the mid-eighties."

"What of it?" he muttered, eyes on Mutt.

"Is John King a partner in it?"

His silence was her answer.

They were getting in the car when they heard him shout, only it was more like a wail. "Bitch! Fucking, fucking bitch!"

"Who does he think he is," Kate told Mutt, "calling you

names like that. Want to go back and teach him a lesson?''

Mutt yawned hugely and gave herself a brisk shake.

''You're right,'' Kate said, ''he's too skinny. Not really worth the effort.'' She jammed the Ford into gear and headed back down the mountain.

At Huffman Business Park she found a pay phone and dialed a number from memory. He was home. Like Dischner, he must keep banker's hours. ''Hello. It's Kate Shugak. I want to talk.''

She listened. ''You owe me.'' She listened some more. ''You owe me,'' she repeated. She listened again. ''You owe me,'' she said for the third time. This time she winced and held the receiver away from her ear. When the volume slackened she brought it back, in time to catch the street address bellowed at her.

For the second time that morning she drove up into the mountains, this time by way of O'Malley Road. When they got to where the trees thinned out and the floor space of the homes quadrupled in square feet she started looking for street numbers. She found the right one on a gray-sided, geometric monstrosity that looked so New Age it might translate into the Fourth Dimension at any moment.

Like Dischner's the view was superb, and from this angle included Mounts Redoubt and Iliamna. The hint of cloud in the southeast had become a definite, precipitative presence. Kate could feel the rise in temperature and humidity on the skin of her face. The air, so calm and still all week, was stirring itself to wakefulness, promising more to come.

Mutt peed in front of the right front tire of John King's brand-new Humvee and wandered around the side of the house, following her nose. Kate walked a flagged path to the front porch. The door was made of oak. The knocker was the head of a longhorn steer made of brass. It was heavy to lift and came down hard, and before the tremor it left in the earth died away the door was yanked open and John King stood before her, dressed as usual in a scowl and mustard-yellow cowboy boots. He growled something and yanked the door wide.

Kate took the growl as an invitation to enter and walked past him into a sunken living room furnished in brown leather and sheepskin. Varnished wooden stairs led upstairs and down. A counter with blue tile inlaid on the surface separated the living room from a kitchen with more appliances than Sears. The floor was wood polished to so high a gloss that the morning sun reflecting off it was almost blinding. More sheepskin beneath the coffee table did not alleviate the glare. The walls were festooned with the heads of a brown bear, a Dall sheep, a mountain goat, a wolverine pelt, a black bear hide and something rectangular and scaly it took Kate a moment to recognize as a rattlesnake skin. It still had its rattle. She gave it a flick of a finger, and the resulting sound made John King jump and say explosively, "Jesus!" Beneath Kate's speculative gaze, he changed color and looked away.

Through the windows the inside view was everything the outside view had promised, with the added attraction of a fireplace big enough to roast a stalled ox. Kate had always wondered what a stalled ox was. She should have looked it up while she was at Loussac; Dan and Bruce would have known right where to find it.

The couch, an overstuffed affair quite twenty feet in length, was graced by the indolent form of the trophy brunette Kate remembered from Mama Nicco's and the Raven party. Today she was dressed in a black bodysuit that looked as if it had been sprayed on. Kate wondered how she got her breasts up in that position and how she kept them there. The miracles of modern medicine, probably. The long-haired Persian in her lap stretched and yawned.

King jerked his head. "Get lost. And take that goddam cat with you."

Her smooth face as usual blank of all expression, the brunette rose to her feet without haste. The Persian leapt down lightly, jerked her tail at King and together they disappeared downstairs, both pairs of haunches moving in similar sinuous precision.

King took the brunette's place and jerked his head at the opposite chair. Ignoring his gracious invitation, Kate walked over to the window and contemplated the view. ''Nice view,'' she said to the window. ''Nicer than Ed Dischner's.'' She turned and looked at King. ''You can't see Redoubt and Iliamna from his place.''

He went from stiff to frozen. She smiled faintly. ''He didn't call? Don't worry, he will.'' Her smiled faded. ''Believe everything he tells you, King. Everything. And then some.''

She sat down across from him and linked her hands behind her head, body relaxed, eyes watchful. ''When do you make the announcement about the new discovery at Katalla?''

His head snapped up. A multitude of expressions crossed his face, shock, alarm, anger. Their gazes held for a long beat. His head dropped and he confirmed everything she suspected with one heartfelt word. *''Shit.''*

She waited, patient. He raised his head. ''How did you find out?''

She shrugged. ''It wasn't all that difficult.'' Felonious, she thought, but not difficult. ''Once I knew Dischner and a bunch of his long-time pals were fixing to file for subsurface rights on that area if and when it became public property, all I had to do was look at the company he was keeping.''

He didn't quite believe it yet. ''You know about the leases?''

She nodded. ''And then of course there was my cousin Martin.''

''Your cousin Martin?'' King said. ''Who the hell's your cousin Martin?''

''Martin Shugak. He was carpentering for one of your subcontractors at Prudhoe last spring when I went up to the Slope for you. He told me he got the job on a trade, half a dozen Slope jobs for Association shareholders in return for permission for RPetCo to do seismic testing on tribal lands.'' She sighed. ''It's a habit with you, isn't it, King? Just like with that exploration well on Tode Point. You just can't resist poking holes where you aren't supposed to, where you've got no right to. Iqaluk butts up against Association land, and Katalla butts up against Iqaluk, and there'd been oil produced at Katalla before. You got curious, and what the hell, it was out in the back of beyond. So you stepped over the line. And you found something that looked promising, promising enough that you talked about it to Dischner. Looking for financing, maybe? Maybe looking to step out on your own? Maybe because of his connections through Lew Mathisen to the board of the Niniltna Native Association? All of the above?''

She waited, watching him. He waited, watching her. ''Martin said Billy Mike did the deal with you. Is that true?'' He didn't answer and Kate said, ''You and Dischner and a bunch of your cronies decided to file on what you thought was there in anticipation of a discovery well. Only there was this one, itsy-bitsy, teeny-weeny little problem. The land had no clear title. It was still being fought over by the federal government, which wants it for a national park, and the Niniltna Native Association, which wants it to remain as is, a traditional, tribal subsistence area.

''Or some of them do. Some of them want to develop it. There was a conflict between members of the board which you and Dischner and Mathisen exploited, because you and Dischner didn't want it to be a national park, and you didn't want it to be property of a native corporation. You wanted it to become a national forest.

Because national parks are all of them closed to mining. There is no mineral leasing in national parks, at all, period, except for those mines that were extant at the time of the creation of the park. It takes an act of Congress to change the status of park land, a fact with which you are intimately acquainted because of the difficulty your whole industry has been having with opening the Arctic National Wildlife Refuge on the North Slope to oil exploration.

''But a national forest, now, that's different. National forests are put to economic use under policies dictated by Congress. They are administered by the National Forest Service, a bureau of the Department of Agriculture. The Forests sell lumber and grazing.'' Kate leaned forward. ''A friend of mine, a career ranger, told me this, and I looked it up to confirm it. National forests can also be developed for hydroelectric power, and for irrigation, and for mining.

''Dischner knew, and you did, too, that after the *RPetCo Anchorage* spill you had about as much chance as a snowball in hell of getting Niniltna permission to drill for oil in Iqaluk. But logging, now. Trees are a renewable resource. Selective cutting and streambed maintenance and all that. The Niniltna Association lawyer told our chairman that it didn't look good for the Association to gain title to the land, so you were lobbying the board to lobby Congress and Interior to have it designated a national forest instead of a national park. And once Iqaluk was designated a forest, your toe was in the door.''

King's Adam's apple bobbed in his throat.

''So, Dischner turns Mathisen loose on the board of the Niniltna Native Association. The wishes of local native associations carry a lot of weight with the new administration in Washington, and Dischner wanted to be sure that the local spokesmen, read the Niniltna board and probably the Raven board, too, saw the advantages of turning Iqaluk into a national forest. His pitch was that they could negotiate timber rights in the new forest so that all UCo's—yet another Dischner sideline, I discover—so that all UCo's construction contracts with the Niniltna Native Association would be fulfilled using local lumber from local lands. And local labor to get it out, I'll bet. A powerful incentive for some of those Prince William Sound fisherman still trying to come back from the *RPetCo Anchorage* spill.

''State ownership would have been best of all, since the legislature for the last twenty years has been the best one oil money can buy, but of course relations between the state government and Alaska Natives have never been worse, so you knew they wouldn't even think of supporting state ownership. You probably even promised them that they'd keep their subsistence rights to Iqaluk, and why not? Oil fields don't take up that much room. All you wanted was a strip of the shore.'' King's eyes flickered and Kate nodded, satisfied. "It was a good pitch. Even my grandmother went for it at first, didn't she?"

She watched him carefully. He made no outward sign, but by the very shocked stillness of his body he confirmed every word she had said, every half-assed guess she had put together from the scanty evidence available to her. Never had she felt less triumph or less satisfaction in uncovering the truth. Oh, emaa, emaa, she thought. This was what you were afraid of telling me. It wasn't Axenia, it wasn't the board, it wasn't Sarah or Enakenty, it wasn't even Iqaluk. It was you, and the deal you almost made with the devil. Were you so ashamed that you could not tell me? Were you afraid that when I found out you would lose my respect?

She took a deep, unobtrusive breath. "Then she smelled a rat." Kate shrugged. "It might have been Harvey's house, it might have been that so many contracts were sole-sourced to UCo, it might have been that ridiculous lease Arctic Investors gave Enakenty Barnes on that condo that must be worth three times that in rent. I don't know what it was. But she knew something was wrong, and then Sarah died, and it was all just too, too convenient. And she asked me to find out what was going on. And I started looking, and then Enakenty died."

King said quickly, "There's nothing to say that those deaths weren't accidents."

Kate raised one skeptical eyebrow. "The timing is very interesting, though, don't you think? The two votes guaranteed to go with my grandmother if she chose to lobby the federal government to making Iqaluk a part of the Park, instead of a national forest? That was a three-vote majority, King, even if you did get to Billy Mike. They pretty much had it sewn up. Now two of them are dead, and the remaining members of the board will have to call a special election to fill the vacant seats."

She let the silence lie between them like a dead fish. It smelled about that bad. The brunette came back upstairs and went to the refrigerator. "Get out," King barked.

Her voice was a soft Southern drawl. "But honey, I just wanted my Coca-Cola—"

''Get out!''

Something dangerously close to a pout very nearly creased the smooth face, but then the brunette remembered that all she had was her face and banished the pout back into oblivion and herself back down the stairs.

King looked at Kate. ''What are you going to do?''

''It's not what I'm going to do,'' Kate said, ''it's what you're going to do. You're backing off Iqaluk. You're shit-canning any reports on whatever prospects you think Iqaluk might have.''

''How will I justify the expense to my board?''

Kate snorted. ''Come off it, King. The oil industry has punched enough dusters in this state. You can even make a speech on how we're all of us environmentalists, and how some natural places are so untouched and pristine they ought to be left alone, and how Iqaluk is one of them. You'll probably make the news on all four networks, not to mention every thirty minutes on CNN.'' Kate got to her feet.

''For Christ's sweet sake,'' he burst out, ''there might be—''

''I don't give a damn what there might be!'' The furious grating shout halted him halfway to his feet, eyes wide. ''Any interest you had in Iqaluk is over,'' she ground out. ''Live with it, or I'll see you tried for murder in a court of law.'' She turned.

''Shugak.'' She looked over her shoulder. He was all the way up on his feet now, teetering back and forth on his mustard-yellow cowboy boots. ''What's the point?''

''What do you mean?''

''I mean what is the fucking point?'' He looked into her face as if she were a puzzle with too many pieces missing to ever see the whole design. ''We're poking holes in Cook Inlet. We're looking for a way back into Kachemak Bay. Norton Sound and Bristol Bay look promising, Amerex is still sinking dusters in Big Lake, and you know we're not giving up on Congress letting us into ANWR. So what's the fucking point? The oil industry's not getting out of Alaska anytime soon. We're going to be here for a long time to come.''

''But not in Katalla,'' she said. ''And not in Iqaluk.'' She turned to go.

''Oh, I wouldn't be too all-fired sure of that, honey,'' another voice said.

The brunette was standing at the head of the stairs, a pistol in her hands. An automatic, Kate noticed, a nine-millimeter. With her luck, it wouldn't jam. A memory flicked in her mind, Dischner bending over the trophy brunette's cleavage at the Raven party, close enough to lick. She swore to herself. ''It wasn't you, after all,'' she said to King.

''Of course it wasn't,'' the brunette said, amused.

''Wasn't what?'' King said. ''What the hell is going on here? You put that thing down before you hurt yourself, you hear?''

''You and Dischner,'' Kate said. The brunette smiled. ''Just what the hell *is* your name, anyway?''

The brunette's smile thinned and made her smoothly perfect face look nearly ugly. ''He never did bother to introduce me, did he? He never does, even if I am his lawful wife?'' The thin smile widened. ''Well, I don't reckon it matters much now.''

''Goddam you, you stupid bitch,'' John King bellowed, ''what the fuck do you think you're doing?''

The brunette shot him a glance so filled with contempt it silenced him. ''Why, what you should have, sweetie, I'm removing the last obstacle in our path to fame and fortune? Do you know how much money we're talking about?'' she said to Kate. ''We're not talking about a few lil-bitty kickbacks from a few white-trash contractors?'' She had the southern habit of ending sentences with a question mark. ''We're talking about millions of dollars, hundreds of millions? We're talking about royalties that will last us the rest of our lives?'' She looked at John King. ''And you were just going to let her walk away, let her destroy everything we've worked for all this time?'' She shook her head. ''Sometimes I swear my mama was right when she told me I never would understand men.''

''You killed Enakenty Barnes,'' Kate said.

The brunette gave a slight shrug. "He wouldn't listen to reason. He was willing to fuck me until the cows come home, but he wouldn't change his vote? I even went to Hawaii with him? I mean, did y'all ever see him in a pair of swim trunks?" She shuddered. "It was a sacrifice just to be on the beach in company with him, let me tell you, honey. Not to mention he was the original one-minute man?"

"And Sarah Kompkoff?"

The brunette shook her head. "No, that was just your everyday ordinary low gravy good luck, as my mama used to say? Eddie told me about it, and that's when I got the idea for Enakenty."

Oh no you didn't, Kate thought with absolute certainty. Eddie P. put that jewel of an idea right into your head, and you sucked it up all unknowing. That smooth, smooth prick. She thought, too, that Dischner had probably called this house during her drive to it this morning after all; he just hadn't talked to King.

John King, overcome by too much horrific information too rapidly disseminated, managed a strangled, disbelieving sound. The brunette huffed out an impatient breath. "Oh hush up, honey, do y'all think I would have slept with a colored for the fun of it? It was just business?

Bullshit. Kate could see right where this was going and it wasn't to either her or King walking out of this house alive. She looked at him. "You really marry her, King?"

He tore his gaze away from his wife and licked his lips. He nodded once.

"So," Kate said meaningfully, "if you die, she gets everything?"

He nodded again.

Kate said, even more meaningfully, trying to prod him to awareness of their mutual danger, "Including those leases in your name?"

The realization was slow in coming. His eyes jerked back to his wife, wide and alarmed. She smiled at him with an expression Kate assumed she thought was reassuring, and in that moment Kate moved, one step ahead of a long dive, for the shelter of the kitchen island.

Her toe caught on the sheepskin underneath the coffee table. It was the only thing that saved her. She pitched foward as the pistol shot cracked through the room. As it was a hot wind fanned her cheek. She recognized it instantly and fell and kept on falling, scrabbling for cover. Another shot rang out and the lamp on the coffee table exploded and rained ceramic bits down on her. "What the fuck!" John King yelled.

Kate scuttled behind the kitchen island like a crab. She peered cautiously around the corner. The pistol jerked in the brunette's hand, the sound of the shot boomed off the ceiling and Kate felt something tug at her left arm. She looked down to find it soaked in blood.

"Jesus Christ!" John King cried.

The brunette cursed and raised the pistol, holding it in both hands, elbows locked in the best approved TV-cop style, and walked slowly toward the kitchen. Kate heard the steps and yanked open a cupboard. It was filled with copper-bottomed Revereware, the same kind she'd seen in Enakenty's rendezvous. She grabbed the first thing to hand, a one-gallon stewpot, and hurled it over the top of the island in the direction of the footsteps. There was a satisfactory sound of metal smacking against flesh followed by a wild curse and a clang as the pot hit the floor. Kate grabbed a saucepan in each hand and stood up and threw them with all her strength, one after the other. The left hand was slippery with blood and that pot glanced harmlessly off one wall, although it did make the brunette flinch and the gun waver. Her right hand was dry and her aim was true; the second pot impacted the brunette squarely in the chest and forced her to stagger backward. She flung up her arms for balance and shot a round through the roof before toppling backwards down the stairs in a series of bumps and thumps and curses. Kate took the stairs two at a time behind her, her momentum increasing to the point that she overshot the corner and crashed into the opposite wall, and again sheer clumsiness saved her life because the brunette was already on her feet and waiting at the bottom of the next flight. Another shot reverberated off the ceiling and another bullet thudded into the wall behind Kate.

She looked down the barrel at Kate, and Kate could see her hand start to squeeze.

There was a crash as the sliding glass door behind her shattered and then Mutt was there, a streak of gray menace, going for the hand holding the gun. Her teeth met around the brunette's wrist. There was a crunch of bone. The brunette's scream was high and piercing. The pistol fell to the floor and Kate pounced on it.

"What the fuck!" John King said from the top of the stairs.

"Mutt," Kate said, all at once feeling very old and very tired. "Off." Mutt, having wanted to sink her teeth into something, anything, anyone, since the first shot fired in anger the night before, didn't want to let go, and Kate had to repeat herself twice before she was obeyed. The brunette curled herself into a fetal position around her wounded wrist, a steady, animalistic moan coming from her throat.

Heavy footsteps descended the stairs. Kate sat down suddenly on the bottom step and said without looking up, "Call the cops, King."

The footsteps hesitated.

Her back to him, Kate held up the pistol she still held. "Call the cops before I shoot you."

There was a slight pause, a long, slow sigh. The footsteps retreated up the stairs.

Mutt had little shards of glass embedded in her muzzle. Kate picked them out, one by one. Beyond them, the brunette lay on the floor where she was, moaning.

"It's not that I don't appreciate it," Kate told her roommate, "but you've got to stop rescuing me through glass." She eased a sliver free. "Maybe you should learn how to open doors. You think?"

Mutt blinked at her, motionless, endlessly patient. When all the glass was out Kate muscled the brunette upstairs and shoved her down on the couch next to her husband, who sat numbly with his elbows on his knees, hands dangling over his mustard-yellow, silver-toed cowboy boots. She found some rubbing alcohol in the medicine cabinet of the bathroom and swabbed Mutt's nose with a washcloth soaked in the stuff. Mutt flinched but stood it. Afterward, she unearthed a clean dishcloth to tie around her wounded arm. It was only a graze, although it stung like fire, and she winced, pulling the cloth tight.

"What about her?" King roused himself enough to say, jerking his head at his wife, who rocked back and forth next to him, holding her wrist and moaning.

"What about her?" Kate said without looking at them. While they waited for the police and the ambulance, Kate used John King's phone to call Spiegel's 800 number and order Jane a king-size brass bed.

ELEVEN

FRIDAY WAS THE NEXT TO THE LAST DAY OF THE CONVENTION, so that everyone with jobs they couldn't get out of came anyway and brought their families with them. They had just broken for lunch and the hum of conversation had taken on the shape and size of a roar. A man with a television camera surgically attached to his shoulder made a slow path through the crowd, moving from one face to another, lingering on the faces of the elders.

Kate spotted Axenia talking hard to a middle-aged man who looked like one of Grandma Kvasnikof's many grandsons from Cordova. Jerry? Terry? Cy, that was it. Axenia's back was to her as she walked up, and she heard her cousin say, "Yes. We estimate three hundred thousand board feet per year for the first five years, selective cutting, of course, and with buffer belts along the creeks to prevent erosion. And shipping is no problem, the Katalla is navigable all the way up to Iqaluk. And the lagoon at the mouth of the river will make a natural log boom. Plus, there are already bunkhouses in place from the old Katalla oilfield days. What? Well, of course, they'll have to be renovated and brought up to speed, but the cost is negligible next to starting from scratch. There is no down side to this project, and we'll be using local timber to make lumber for local construction. I—"

Kate grasped Axenia's arm firmly above the elbow and smiled at the man. "Hello, Cy. I'm terribly sorry, I need to borrow my cousin for a moment. Will you excuse us?" Her smile widened with deliberate charm and he wilted and effaced himself.

Axenia tried to pull free without attracting attention. "Let me go, Kate."

"Nope." Kate pulled her through the door and out onto the sidewalk. "Come on."

"Where are we going? Dammit, you're hurting me! Let me go!"

Kate looked up Fifth, estimated the chances of making it across the street to the Town Square Park before the traffic thundering through the light at B caught them, and jerked. To keep from falling Axenia had to go with her. They made it across with feet to spare (it helped with Mutt nipping at Axenia's heels) and Kate led the way up one of the paved paths and found a seat on the edge of the fountain, now turned off. She slammed Axenia down on it hard enough to crack her tailbone.

"Ouch!" Tears sprang to Axenia's eyes, which made her look very young and vulnerable but not young and vulnerable enough to rouse any of Kate's protective instincts. When Axenia saw the lack of effect, she sucked her tears back up into her eyeballs and demanded, "What's wrong with you? I've got people to talk to in there!"

She half rose to her feet before Kate slammed her down again. "How much did you know about Iqaluk?"

"What? Iqaluk?" Axenia's angry bewilderment seemed genuine, but then she'd had two years in Anchorage to practice, not to mention an apprenticeship with Lew Mathisen. "We're lobbying to make it a national forest so we can lease the timber rights and use it for construction projects for the association. What's wrong with that?"

"Nothing," Kate said grimly, "if that was all it was." She searched Axenia's face for signs of knowledge of the seismic tests, the exploration wells, and found only bewilderment. Honest or assumed? Would she ever know? Did she want to know the answer badly enough to ask?

"What are you talking about?" Axenia looked at Kate's face, really looked at it for the first time, and said, less certainly, "Well? What is wrong with it?" The dishcloth caught her eye. The blood stains had dried to a ruddy brown. She paled, reaching out a finger to almost touch it, drawing back when Kate flinched away. "Kate, what's that? What happened? Are you hurt?"

"Never mind," Kate said. "Is that story you just told me what you got from Lew Mathisen?" Axenia didn't answer. "When did you two start dating?"

"None of your damn business."

Kate leaned down and snarled in Axenia's face, "It is if it's adversely affecting emaa in some way, and trust me, Axenia, it *is*."

Axenia swallowed and looked away. There was a long pause. When she spoke her voice was muffled. "Almost a year ago. Last December. We met at the CIRI Christmas party."

Well after the time Billy Mike turned John King loose on tribal grounds with a seismic truck, and right around the time Axenia went to work for the federal government. Enakenty had signed his lease on December 1, Kate remembered. A lot of things, none of them good, had happened in December.

"Did Mathisen come after you, Axenia?" Another pause, then a nod. Dischner, Kate thought. She'd bet her last dime that Mathisen dating Axenia had been Dischner's idea. She couldn't quite bring herself to say so, though, and knew a fleeting regret that she hadn't turned Mutt loose on old Eddie P. He had hurt her family in so many ways, the toll mounting hourly. She said, "Lew's using you, Axenia. He's using you for your place in Niniltna and for your job with the Forest Service. He's been in hog heaven this last year, with inside information coming at him two ways through one source. At work you must have heard about Iqaluk going public almost the same time emaa did through the Association lawyer. He couldn't afford not to romance you."

"I don't believe you."

"Axenia, listen. He's a member of the board of UCo. You

know all those construction projects UCo has with Raven and Niniltna? They were approved and signed off by either Harvey Meganack or Billy Mike. One was signed off by Enakenty last December, probably the same day he moved into that condo that cost a third of what it should in rent. It was a fee, Axenia. Just like Harvey's house and his watch and Billy's campaign financing.''

Axenia's chin went up. ''He asked me to marry him.''

Kate looked at her.

''I said yes.''

Kate looked at her.

Axenia's voice rose. ''And you can't stop me!''

Kate looked at her and said in a silken voice, ''Was marriage your fee, Axenia?''

Axenia hit her, open hand against Kate's cheek, with all the strength of her arm behind it. The crack of skin on skin echoed off the sides of the Performing Arts Center.

Eyes full of tears, Axenia ran back to the convention center.

Kate sat down suddenly on the stone bench. Mutt leapt up on the bench, too, and nosed at her with a bruised and battered snout. ''It's all right, girl,'' Kate said, putting her arm around Mutt's shoulders and leaning into the solid, furry warmth. ''It's all right.''

Mutt was unconvinced, and the words sounded false to her own ears.

The clouds crowded the sky now, thick and white and full. The smokers standing around outside the Egan Center weren't even zipping their coats. Kate went inside and was immediately pounced on by Olga Shapsnikoff. ''Kate, where have you been? You missed Paul Anahonak's talk on sovereignty. I thought we were going to go out and stone somebody, preferably a state legislator.'' She grinned. ''Speaking of great public speakers, people have been asking about you ever since your speech yesterday.''

''It wasn't a speech,'' Kate said. ''All I did was tell a story.''

''We should all be able to tell such stories. Come meet some of my family.'' She paused. ''Kate? Are you all right?

You look a little pale. Except for your cheek, how come it's all red?'' She saw the napkin. ''And what's wrong with your arm, is that blood?''

''I'm fine.''

''Are you sure?'' Olga looked her over critically. ''You look like you need a cup of coffee. Come on, I'll get you one.''

Kate summoned up a smile. ''What I really need is to talk to my grandmother. Have you seen her around?''

Olga nodded. ''Yeah, I saw her with Cindy Sovalik a while ago. Or no, that was before lunch, I think.''

Kate's stomach reminded her it hadn't had breakfast yet, let alone lunch. ''Where?''

''Downstairs, at Cindy's booth.''

''Okay, I'll go take a look. See you later.''

''You had lunch?''

''Later,'' Kate called, and escaped.

Downstairs Ekaterina was nowhere to be found. Kate stood on a chair in one corner of the room and searched in vain for the square-shaped figure with the tight black bun.

''Kate.''

The voice came from below and she looked down. ''You are looking for your grandmother,'' Cindy said. She was wearing one of her kuspuks today, made of sky blue corduroy and trimmed with silver rickrack and silver fox. Her eyes flicked to Kate's cheek, the makeshift bandage on the younger woman's arm and away again.

''Yes, I am,'' Kate said, stepping down. ''Olga said she saw her down here with you. Where is she?''

''She is at the hotel.''

Kate frowned at the note in Cindy's voice. Before she could speak Cindy said, ''You have found out what is wrong.''

Kate gave her a sharp look which Cindy endured without any expression on her broad, impassive face. ''How would you know anything was wrong?'' Cindy shrugged. Kate smiled. '' 'There is danger here?' '' she suggested.

Cindy's face didn't change. ''Not that kind.''

Kate's smile faded. ''What do you mean?''

Cindy held out a hand. It was dry to the touch, the bone and sinew beneath hard and strong. A chill rippled over Kate's skin. The two women stood motionless and silent as around them conversation rose and fell, goods were traded and bought, newborn babies exclaimed over, teenagers' basketball records bragged about, family news good and bad exchanged. Kate saw no one and nothing but Cindy Sovalik.

Cindy let go of her hand and returned to her table without a backward glance.

Kate turned on her heel and walked to the escalator, threading her way through the crowd without stopping, not responding to the greetings called her way.

Kate knocked on Ekaterina's door. There was no answer. She knocked again. Still no answer.

A short, rotund woman in a maid's uniform said in a thick accent, "Is there something I help you with, ma'am?"

Kate nodded at the door. "It's my grandmother's room. She should be here, but she's not answering the door. Do you have a passkey?"

The maid looked doubtful. "Please," Kate said. "Open the door. You can stand right here while I go in."

Something in Kate's anxious face must have convinced her. The maid produced the passkey and opened the door. Kate pushed it open. "Emaa?"

There was no answer. She stepped inside. "Emaa? Are you in here?" She walked down the little hall that led past the bathroom and the closet. The drapes were closed, the thin afternoon light seeping into the room beneath the hems.

There were two queen-size beds, one littered with Ekaterina's suitcase and various items of clothes. The bedspread had been drawn back from the other, both pillows pushed to the floor, and Ekaterina's form lay still beneath the blanket.

"Emaa? Wake up." Kate walked to the window and pulled the drapes, talking feverishly. "I haven't had lunch yet, have you? What say we head for the Lucky Wishbone, get us some fried chicken. You haven't been yet, this trip, have you?"

There was no answer. Kate walked to the bed and bent over. ''Emaa?'' Ekaterina was lying on her back, still and silent.

''Emaa,'' Kate said, her voice sounding in her own ears as if it were coming from a great distance. ''Emaa?''

Ekaterina's shoulder was still and cool. Her eyes were closed, her face unsmiling, stern even in death. The winter light filled in the wrinkles that outlined mouth and eyes, glanced off the firm chin, picked out the dark eyelashes that lay like fans on her cheeks.

''Emaa,'' Kate said again. She felt her throat swell, swallowed hard against the rise of tears. She dropped to her knees and buried her face in the bedspread. ''*Emaa.*''

''*Ay del que,*'' the maid said. There was a rustle of clothing as she crossed herself.

Outside the window large flakes of snow began to fall, like wisps of cotton, soft and thick.

Saturday morning the city lay silent and still beneath a soft, thick cover of white, the hush broken only by the scrape of shovels on sidewalks, the chatter of red-cheeked children building snowmen, the occasional rumble of a grader down a side street. The hush crept even into the Egan Convention Center, where people stood in groups of four and five, speaking in low voices.

Kate walked in at noon, alone, as the King Island Dancers took to the stage. The drums sounded. It was a dance of remembrance, marking the passage of milestones, and seasons, and of loved ones. There was no applause at the end, only a deep, expectant silence. It was traditional dress day, and every other person there wore tunic and leggings, button blankets, kuspuks and mukluks.

The outgoing chairman took the podium one last time to name the incoming chairman, and the incoming chairman took his place. He thanked the outgoing chairman for his service to his community, thanked the members for the honor of being named the new chairman, and promised to work hard at resolving the problems of subsistence and sovereignty.

There was brief, polite applause. He shuffled the pages of his acceptance speech together, waiting for it to end. "As most of you know by now, the Alaska Native community has suffered an enormous loss. Ekaterina Moonin Shugak died yesterday."

There were exclamations from the few who had not known. Heads turned toward Kate, a hand touched her shoulder. Axenia stood a few feet away, her eyes swollen and blotched with tears. Lew Mathisen stood at her side, clutching her hand, his thin face self-conscious. Kate continued to stare straight ahead.

"At this point, I will cede the floor to Harvey Meganack, a fellow board member of the Niniltna Native Association, who has agreed to speak in memory of Ekaterina."

Harvey's stocky figure climbed the stairs to the stage. The new chairman stood back and let him take the podium. He cleared his throat. His voice was hoarse but controlled. He spoke of Ekaterina's life, of how her family had been forced out of their home in the Aleutians during the Japanese occupation of Attu and Kiska, of their arrival in Niniltna to stay with distant relatives, of how when the war ended they decided to make the Park their home. He spoke of her husband and his death at sea, of her five children, and how every parent's nightmare of surviving their own children had come true for Ekaterina, and of her strength in surviving their deaths. He spoke of Ekaterina's work with Elizabeth Peratrovich and the Alaska Native Sisterhood in seeking Native rights. He reminded everyone in the room that but for their efforts and the efforts of many more like them, Alaska Natives' ability to become Alaskan citizens might still hinge upon the condition that they gave up their tribal ways for a "civilized" lifestyle. He said the words simply, telling a story, not inciting to riot, and they listened to him in silence.

He spoke of Ekaterina's work in helping the Alaska Federation of Natives negotiate the crucial loans from the village of Tyonek and the Yakima Indian Nation, which together funded the final push to congressional passage of the Alaska Native Claims Settlement Act in 1971. He spoke of her tireless efforts in helping the tribes and villages adapt to that act, of her own chairmanship of an immensely successful AFN convention in the mid-eighties, of her terms as Niniltna's tribal chief, of her seat on the Raven Corporation's board of directors, of her sponsorship of the sobriety movement.

"Ekaterina's family came first in her life," Harvey said, "but we were all her family." He spread his arms, encompassing the room, the city outside, the state beyond. "From Metlakatla to Kivalina, from Anaktuvuk Pass to Attu Island, from Anchorage to Barrow, from Nutzotin to Nome. All this was her home, and all of us were her family. That we exist today is due to her, and to all the elders of her generation who fought not just for our rights, but for our very survival."

He paused for a moment, letting them grieve their loss. His tone had changed when he spoke again, had become louder, clearer, more firm. "The passing of Ekaterina Moonin Shugak marks the passing of an age. That age, the age of living in the past, is done. The new age, the age of living in the now and working toward the future, has arrived."

There was a single clap of hands, immediately silenced. The room was heavy with a puzzled kind of expectancy, as they waited for what Harvey would say next.

"It is time," he said, "it is more than time for the Native corporations to realize that they are business corporations first, and Native corporations second. I say, as I'm sure Ekaterina would have said, that it's time to put away the beads and the feathers and integrate ourselves into the twentieth century." The rams' heads on his watch flashed coldly in the stage lights.

Kate, who had been moved nearly to tears by his previous words, raised incredulous eyes. Harvey was staring straight at her, in his steady gaze both a warning and a challenge. She looked around the room. Elders sat with faces like stone. Young people looked at each other, bewildered.

She turned her head to the right and she saw Olga, plump figure stiffly erect, brows drawn together, mobile mouth still. She turned to the left and saw Cindy, the planes of her broad face fined down somehow to their essential elements, all bone and strength. In that moment both reminded her so sharply of Ekaterina that she caught her breath against the pain. Both were in traditional dress, Olga in sealskin and Cindy in caribou hide.

They looked at her, waiting. The whole room seemed to be waiting, even though Harvey was still speaking. Again Kate had the queer feeling of standing on the edge of an abyss, the vacuum left by Ekaterina's absence tugging her inexorably, unwillingly over the edge.

Olga carried a drum. A round drum on a thin frame, seal gut stretched across it and bound with caribou sinew. Without looking away from Kate, she tapped it once. The single, sharp note echoed through the great room, demanding to be heard.

Harvey looked up and frowned, searching for the interruption.

Olga tapped the drum again, and again it echoed around the room.

With the third strike it became a song.

In time with the beat, Cindy began to chant.

The chant was the chant of remembrance, the one the King Island Dancers had performed to open the day an hour before.

It was the same, and it was different.

Another voice joined Cindy's in the chanting. Another drum began beating in time with Olga's.

Against her will—or was it?—Kate felt her feet begin to move, her arms raise in the traditional movements, as if their paths were already marked out for her against the very air of the room. One of the King Island Dancers tossed something; she caught it in mid-air, a finger mask woven of dyed rye grass, like a tiny fan, ornately beaded and trimmed with feathers. She slipped it over her right forefinger. A second followed the first and she slipped it on her left forefinger.

Olga drummed.

Cindy chanted.

Kate danced.

She did not dance alone.

The outgoing chairman was the first to join her, the incoming chairman the second. Chairs disappeared from the center of the floor and a circle formed, stamping in unison to wake up the spirits, reaching for the sky to draw them in. No word was spoken; none was necessary. Axenia joined in, and Harvey. Lew stood pressed up against the wall, watching with a look both bewildered and apprehensive.

All danced, all together, all as one.

They danced the dance the missionaries had called heathen and satanic, they danced the dance their parents had been forbidden, they danced the dance their ancestors danced for a hundred and a thousand and ten thousand years, dances to mark a birth, to celebrate a wedding, to heal the sick, to mourn the dead, to thank Agudar for the good hunt, to pray to Maniilaq for guidance.

They danced the dance they would always dance, that their children would dance, that their children's children would dance, in joy and in sorrow, in entreaty and in thanksgiving, and, yes, with beads and with feathers, in button blankets and spirit masks, in kuspuks and mukluks, in jeans and Nikes.

The last note of the drum echoed across the room.

A thousand feet stamped in unison in reply. The building shook with the force of it.

The dance was done.

Kate returned the finger masks to the King Island dancer. She bowed her head to Cindy. She bowed her head to Olga. She walked from the room.

An elder of the church in Eklutna gave the benediction in a shaken voice, and the convention was over.

TWELVE

IT WAS A CLEAR NIGHT WITH NO WIND. THEY TOOK OFF from abel's strip as a full moon crested Angqaq. The light was dazzling against the snow. Jack stood the borrowed Super Cub on her left wing and banked toward Kate's homestead, maintaining an altitude of a hundred feet and throttling back to just above stall speed when they reached the creek. He pulled the zipper on his parka up to his chin and folded open the window.

Behind him Kate opened the urn. They scattered Ekaterina's ashes all the way down the creek to its confluence with the Kanuyaq River, and down the Kanuyaq River to Niniltna and downriver to Prince William Sound. The urn empty, Kate let it fall, too.

The potlatch was held in the school gymnasium and included everyone in the Park; Bobby and Dinah, Mandy and Chick, Auntie Joy, Auntie Viola, Martin, Axenia, Dan O'Brian, George Perry, rangers, homesteaders, miners, loggers, Park rats, Aleuts. There were Eyaks from Cordova, Athabaskans from the Interior, Tlingits and Haidas and Tsimshians from Southeast, Yupiks and Inupiats from the north and west, all mourning their loss together. There was blood stew and maqtaq, macaroni and cheese, seal blubber and moose steak, pilot bread and peanut butter, Eskimo ice cream and alodiks. Kate gave away her grandmother's possessions, a mass of gifts and memorabilia that included baleen and walrus tusks, harpoons and Attu baskets, dance masks and stone lamps, countless carvings of wood and bone and ivory and soapstone, and skins of bear and seal and moose and caribou and wolf and fox.

The Association banner she gave to Billy Mike, who had been elected the new chairman of the Niniltna board.

Smiling, Billy promised Kate to remember what it stood for.

Smiling, she promised to remind him when he forgot.

Ekaterina's house by the Niniltna River she gave to Martha Barnes and her children.

A fat photo album, filled with the pictures of relatives and friends with which emaa had papered her kitchen wall, she kept for herself.

''What happened with Jane? What did the judge decide?''

A pleased chuckle rumbled up from the chest beneath her cheek. ''The damndest thing. She dropped the case.''

Kate infused her voice with surprise. ''You're kidding.''

''No, really, she flat dropped it.'' He grinned against her hair. ''The judge was so pissed off at her for wasting the court's time on a case that should have been settled before it ever got in front of him that he made Jane pay all the court costs.''

''No.''

''Yes.''

''Outstanding.''

''We thought so.''

Jack sounded very smug, but Kate didn't grudge it. She could not resist asking. ''Why? Why'd she'd drop the case, I mean.''

''Officially, I know nothing.''

''Of course not.''

''But her lawyer let it drop to my lawyer that Jane bounced a check off her. Her lawyer, not mine.''

Kate turned her face to hide a smile in the front of his shirt. ''Really?''

''Really. So her lawyer fired her, and if she was bouncing

checks off her lawyer she may have been bouncing checks all over town, and if she was bouncing checks all over town she probably couldn't get another lawyer."

"So Johnny's yours?"

"Mine. The judge made her say so, in court and in writing."

"Johnny happy?"

He thought. "More relieved than anything, I think."

"Nobody likes being the bone the dogs are fighting over."

He winced at the analogy, which was too close to the truth for comfort. "I guess not."

She raised her head and kissed him. "Congratulations, Dad."

"Thank you." He returned the kiss with interest, and shifted so she could snuggle comfortably back into his embrace. "Now," he asked the air over her head, "you want to tell me how you did it?"

She went very still. "What makes you think I had anything to do with it?"

"Simple. I know you. How'd you do it?"

Kate weighed the chance of maintaining her innocence against the tone of good-humored but relentless inquiry in his voice. It didn't look good. "I broke into her house and stole her cash card, her PIN number and her account password," she said baldly. "I put about five thousand dollars' worth of stuff on her credit cards, I ordered a cashier's check for another five thousand dollars, and I took three hundred bucks cash a day out of her bank account. I figured if she was broke, she couldn't pay her lawyer, and I don't know any lawyers who work for free, do you?"

He'd suspected something of the sort but the breadth and thoroughness of the attack was a little staggering, all the same. "No," he said weakly, "I don't."

You shouldn't have asked if you weren't prepared to hear the answer, Kate thought.

He didn't ask her where she had gone the morning after the attack on his townhouse, and prudently, Kate didn't volunteer.

From time to time she still wondered about that copy machine and all those reams of paper in Jane's spare bedroom. Federal contract bids passed through Jane's hands continuously, blind bids that certain contractors would pay well to get an advance look at so as to alter their own accordingly. Reports of those kinds of shenanigans were in the papers every day. Must be a hell of a temptation to Jane. K-Y jelly didn't come cheap. And then there were all those expensive suits in the closet, and that very nice bank balance. Well, there had been.

But, Kate had decided, along with everything else, Johnny didn't need to see his mother go to jail for bribery. Not yet, anyway. When he was older, maybe. If in future Jane started harassing Jack and Johnny again, Kate would have to rethink her decision. For now, she let it lie. "Did you arrest the brunette?" she said, without much interest. "What is her name, anyway?"

"Myra. Myra Randall Wisdon Hunt Banner King. Randall was her maiden name. Wisdon was her first husband, storekeeper in Chattanooga, Tennessee. Hunt was a banker in Tulsa, Oklahoma. Banner was a wildcatter out of Lubbock, Texas. While he was out drilling dusters, she ran off with King, all the way to Alaska."

"Goodness me."

"Yeah, she'd been working her way up the food chain for a quite a while."

"Any of her husbands survive her besides King?"

"What a suspicious broad you are," he said comfortably. "Yes. They all did. The stakes were never high enough for murder before King."

"Will King testify that he heard her say she admitted to killing Enakenty?"

"So far, he says yes. We'll see what he says when we get to trial. Right now he's mad. Later on he'll see how foolish he looks, and realize how little he's going to enjoy sitting up in court and testifying to it."

"You're such a cynic."

"Trust but verify," he replied. "Morgan's Fifth Law."

"I thought it was the Sixth."

"Whatever. At any rate, we've got her cold on attempted murder on you, so she'll be spending some time as a guest of the state."

"She going to roll on Dischner?"

"Already has. The problem is we only have her word to go on, and it ain't gonna be worth much in court against Dischner."

"I don't doubt Dischner will be indicted," Kate said. "Tried is another story."

"The loose lug nuts," Jack said, "the trashed house, the drive-by, all those have the earmarks of a summa cum laude graduate of the Dischner School of Not Guilty by Reason of an Expensive Lawyer."

"No argument here."

"He has defended some low-lifes, some say even mob-connected low-lifes. At least his firm has. He must have contracted out for the job."

"No argument here, either."

"But we'll probably never know who to. He's too smart for that." Jack sighed. "He'll walk again, won't he, that son-of-a-bitch." The words were spoken with only a trace of bitterness. They might fail of indicting Eddie P. this time, but there'd be another chance before long, and Jack wasn't going anywhere. "What about the UCo contracts? Can the new board prove kickbacks?"

"They've got about ten different accountants and lawyers looking into it now. I put them on to Gamble, to see if they can scare up some racketeering charges. You might get Dischner yet."

"Maybe." Jack sounded about as convinced of that as Kate felt. "What happens with Iqaluk now?"

"It looks like it's going federal."

"Which way?"

"That," Kate said, "is in the laps of the gods. Billy Mike promised me that he and the board will lobby that it be made a national park. The Raven board says they will, too."

"You don't sound too sure."

"I'm not. King swore he'd bag the operation but the word will get out, it's inevitable, and as soon as people know there's oil there there'll be another fight between the greenies and the oil producers and the state and the Natives, just like ANWR all over again.'' The prospect was not a pleasing one. Still, Ekaterina had never shirked her duty, and Kate would not shirk hers.

My life is changing, she thought.

The prospect did not fill her with anticipation.

''Will you be in the fight?''

She pondered his question, and the memory of that podium flashed through her mind, on stage in front of a room full of a crowd of cheering people. It was quickly succeeded by a vision of Iqaluk, glacier and stream, mountain and river, lakes and shore. The air was still clear, the water still ran clean. It had to stay that way. It *had* to. ''I think I might have to be,'' she said slowly. ''Dan O'Brian said he would help. Give me pointers on dealing with the bureaucrats, like that.''

''He want Iqaluk for the Park?''

She laughed a little. ''If Dan O'Brian had his druthers the whole state would be a federal park.''

''It'll be a long fight, Kate.''

''Years,'' she agreed. ''A lifetime, even. But for now, while it's in limbo, Iqaluk is safe.''

They watched the moon emerge from behind Angqaq, bathing the mountains and valley in pale light. It was cold, and getting colder, and he shivered inside his jacket. ''About time to go in?''

''In a while.''

''You seem—'' He hesitated.

''What?''

''I don't know. Awfully calm?''

She sat up and looked at him. ''Would you feel better if I gnashed my teeth and tore my skin and ripped my hair out at the roots?''

''No, that's okay, but thanks for thinking of me.''

''It doesn't work like that, Jack.''

''I guess I don't get just how it does work,'' he said apologetically.

She was silent, trying to think how to say it. It was something she felt so deeply it was hard to explain with mere words. "I can't be sad, Jack. She's with me, right here, right now. Here—" she touched her temple "—in my head, and here—" she touched her breast "—in my heart, and here—" she touched her stomach "—in my gut. Emaa lives on inside me, and in every other person she ever touched. While we live, she lives.

"She's in every rock and tree in the Park. She's in the water we drink. She's in the air we breathe.

"She'll be in every flake of snow that falls, all the winter long.

"She'll come up the river with the first salmon in the spring.

"She'll be on board every seiner that puts out to sea in the summer.

"She'll be on the foothills with the berrypickers in the fall.

"She'll always be here, Jack. I can't be sad she's gone, when she never left in the first place."

He could not speak, could only wrap his arms around her and hold on for as long as he could, for as long as she would let him.

After a while she pulled back and smiled at him, touching his cheek in a brief caress. "Go in now, okay? I want to sit out here alone for a while."

He went, the door to the cabin shutting softly behind him. Mutt stayed with Kate, her shoulder warm and solid against Kate's knee.

From the seat on the rock by the creek, they watched the moon make its dignified progress across the sky, trailing a veil of quicksilver, star-studded light behind it that turned the mountains into monuments of marble, and the long valley into a gleaming shell of mother-of-pearl.

WHAT'S THAT YOU DO WITH THE LEAKY EYE? SAYS THE Woman Who Keeps the Tides. It is time, you said so yourself.

I know, says Calm Water's Daughter, but it is so hard on the left behinds. I can't help feeling sorry for them.

Maybe if we, says The Woman Who Keeps the Tides.

No, says Calm Water's Daughter.

What's the point of being us if we can't help? says The Woman Who Keeps the Tides.

Look at the larger picture, says Calm Water's Daughter. Are we myth or marketing? Were we born or made?

Sometimes I just don't understand you, says The Woman Who Keeps the Tides.

Hello, says a new voice.

Oh, it's you, says The Woman Who Keeps the Tides. You're late.

I'm sorry. There seemed to be some problem with my credentials.

Well, really, says The Woman Who Keeps the Tides.

They let the scaff and raff from the Mediterranean run wild all over the place. We'll just see about *that*.

How are you? says Calm Water's Daughter.

I feel a little, I don't know, dizzy?

Don't worry, says Calm Water's Daughter. That first step is the hardest one, Everybody Talks to Her.

Call me emaa, She says.

That’s all